Secret Scandal

Trinity Masters, book 7

Mari Carr and Lila Dubois

ISBN: 978-1542640442

Editor: Kelli Collins
Cover artist: Lila Dubois
Print formatting: Mari Carr

A dashing thief. A passionate scholar. And the beautiful bodyguard engaged to protect them.

Eli Wexler is a prominent art historian, a job that under normal circumstances isn't dangerous. But Eli is a member of the Trinity Masters, and when he's called to the altar he not only meets the man and woman he's to marry, but is given a mystery to solve as well.

Jasper Ferrer realizes there's trouble coming when he meets his trinity. Given Jasper's checkered past, he doubts Eli will be thrilled by their marriage. Art historians, as a rule, dislike art thieves.

Irina Gentry knows what her trinity needs from her—her new fiancées are both art experts, and she's there to protect them. It's a job she's more than qualified for, though she doubts there will be any need for her skills.

But the task the Grand Master gives them is far more dangerous than it seems. The quest for a long lost sculpture pits the new trinity against a hidden faction within the secret society, a faction who are willing to kill to keep the secrets Eli, Jasper and Irina are working to uncover.

Chapter One

When it came right down to it, there was very little difference between fear and anticipation. Eli's blood hummed with energy, and he tapped his knuckles gently against his legs. He hoped the wide arms of the black robe were loose enough to hide his small movements.

He'd received the note calling him to the altar forty-three days ago. That was a long time for anticipation to build. Mild-mannered art history professors didn't have much in the way of excitement going on in their lives—at least this kind of excitement. Academia was always high-drama, but that he was used to. For Eli these forty-three days of anticipation had been especially stressful. At thirty-seven, he'd started to wonder if he wasn't going to be called to the altar, which had made the letter's arrival all the more shocking.

No one would ever look at him and suspect that he was a member of a secret society formed when the nation was still young. A society created to ensure the stability of the fledgling union by gathering business and scientific leaders, artists, musicians, and influential socialites. Up to that point, it was no different than many other societies, but where the Trinity Masters was unique was that members had to agree to an arranged marriage. And the marriage was not to one other person, but to two, forming a trinity. The Trinity Masters believed that a marriage, like the proverbial stool, was stronger with three legs.

Now he stood in the medallion room of the society's headquarters deep under the Boston Public Library, and much to his surprise, anticipation was the dominant feeling. The floor, walls, and vaulted ceiling were constructed from huge marble blocks. Three high-backed wing chairs faced a large medallion in the center of the floor, illuminated by a pinpoint spotlight. The bronze medallion was stamped with the Trinity Masters' symbol—a triquetra—and motto. It was the same symbol stamped into the ring he wore.

He eyed the other hooded, robed figures in the ceremony room. The Grand Master stood behind the altar wearing a black robe trimmed in gold. A slight figure, the gold chain draped across her chest from shoulder to shoulder seemed too large for her. He hadn't been at the Winter Gala, where this Grand Master had made her inaugural appearance, but the fact that—for the first time in the secret society's history—the all-powerful leader was a woman had been widely discussed.

The figure seated in the chair directly to his left—one of his two spouses—wore white. A woman. On the other side of her in the third chair was another figure in a plain black robe. A man.

"You have been called to the altar to take the next step in your lifelong commitment to the Trinity Masters." The Grand Master's voice was clean and pure. Undeniably feminine, younger than he would have guessed, but laced with an undertone of authority.

"Do you remember what I said at the Winter Gala?" the Grand Master asked.

There were two murmured responses of, "Yes, Grand Master."

Eli cleared his throat. "No, Grand Master. I wasn't there."

Deep hoods shadowed the faces of his soon-to-be-ménage marriage partners as they turned to look at him. Eli resisted the urge to reach up and pull his own hood farther down over his face. He wasn't really a party person, so he'd skipped the gala. In hindsight, not a great idea.

The Grand Master paused, as if assessing his statement, before replying.

"I will repeat myself, so there is no confusion moving forward. Since assuming the role of Grand Master, I've discovered that loyalty among our members is not absolute."

They were deep under the Boston Public Library. The only access to these chambers, to the headquarters of the Trinity Masters, was via a hidden elevator. If this wasn't actually a binding ceremony, if he'd been brought here to face the wrath of the Grand Master for being disloyal, there would be no escape.

The hair on Eli's arms stood on end as his heart rate picked up. He was loyal. He'd followed all the rules...hadn't he? Beside him, the figure in white sat straighter. She placed her hands on the arms of the chair and uncrossed her legs. She was bracing herself to jump out of the chair, to fight or run.

"There were some among us who had taken it upon themselves to cull our membership," the Grand Master continued.

Cull the membership? What was she talking about?

Eli narrowed his eyes, his complete focus now on the Grand Master. Out of the corner of his eye, he noticed the other two had leaned forward in their chairs.

When the Grand Master continued speaking, her speech pattern was less formal, as if what she said now wasn't rehearsed.

"They decided they didn't want the membership to diversify, and set out to make sure any legacy members who couldn't trace their ancestry back to the Mayflower were excluded. They intercepted and destroyed invitations and records."

"What time period are we talking about?" Eli asked, ever the scholar.

Again, his soon-to-be spouses looked at him, but the Grand Master didn't seem put off by his question. She also didn't *answer* the question.

"That was just one of the things I uncovered when I became Grand Master. There are other…mysteries in our past." She paused and the weight of the stones around and above them seemed to press down, making it hard to breathe. As if the very chamber would, at the Grand Master's bidding, crush them. Then she added, "The time has come, the walrus said, to solve them."

Everyone, including Eli, let out weak laughs, tinged with relief. The mood in the room lightened considerably.

"At the gala, I announced that from now on, all new trinities would be given a task—a puzzle to work, a mystery to solve—when they are called to the altar. Instead of returning in thirty days to be formally married, you're to return only when your task is done."

Eli sat back, shocked in a way he hadn't been since he'd first been approached about joining the Trinity Masters while a sophomore at Harvard. The Grand Master was going to assign them a *quest*? And they couldn't get married until they'd completed it?

"Calixo Garcia's illegitimate son was a member of the Trinity Masters."

Eli blinked. That seemed like a non sequitur. Calixo Garcia. Why was that ringing a bell?

"I believe the Grand Master at the time helped to bring him to the United States." The Grand Master's tone was sharper, the words coming quickly, as if she'd explained all this before and wanted to rush through the repetition.

Brought him to the United States? Now he knew why that name was ringing a bell.

"Calixo..." Eli ground his teeth to stop from barking out a million follow-up questions. Calixo Garcia was the leader of the rebels during the Spanish-American War. This unknown son may have brought information or artifacts with him that would provide insight into U.S.-Cuba relations at the turn of the last century.

"Calixo's son, Pedro, was called to the altar and placed in a trinity. They had two children, one of whom died in WWII. The other son, Luis, joined the Trinity Masters, but was never called to the altar." She paused to let that sink in. "He finally married on his own, but still wore the triquetra ring, and told his children, and grandchildren, stories about a secret society he was once a member of."

There was a low whistle from the other man—Eli's soon-to-be husband. Once they joined, members were sworn to secrecy upon penalty of death, or worse. Spilling secrets, disobeying the Grand Master, or breaking any of the society's rules, meant you lost everything.

The Grand Master's voice was alarmingly dispassionate when she continued. "Secrecy is paramount to our continued existence. All members, and legacies, are taught how to keep secrets. When legacies are lost to us, when they don't learn our rules, in this case because someone actively stopped Luis from being called to the altar, behavior like this goes against our core principles and puts us all at risk."

There was a moment of silence. That wasn't exactly a threat, but they all knew the price for disloyalty to the Trinity Masters. There were stories Eli firmly believed about people being framed for crimes they didn't commit that landed them back-to-back lifetimes in prison. Scientists who lost jobs and had research discredited, leaving them alive but with their credibility and careers destroyed. And worst of all, people who simply disappeared, never to be seen or heard from again.

"Eli Wexler."

Eli sat straighter when the Grand Master used his full name.

"You asked what time period. The records are not yet complete, but we know that in the nineteen forties, a woman named Jessica Breton was responsible for preventing Luis from being called to the altar. She was part of a movement within the Trinity Masters, a group who called—and call—themselves the purists."

Eli looked down. Purists. A bland name for the kind of people who probably objected to his being a member. Eli's parents were both mixed race—his mother half-black, half-Chinese, his father some crazy mix of North African and European. Eli had grown up feeling the probing glances as people tried to pinpoint what he was—brown skin, blue eyes, traditionally European features. Tightly curled hair, a football player's build, and he spoke conversational Mandarin. Together, the pieces of him didn't quite add up for most people. People called the purists probably wouldn't think Eli was a good candidate for membership.

"Call?" The voice of the woman beside him was smooth and cool, just a bit husky. "Present tense, Grand Master?"

"Yes, present tense. This group is still around, still active. Something we only recently learned." The Grand Master held up her hand, forestalling the questions that were on the tip of Eli's tongue. From the way the Grand Master's hood was turning to each of them, she must have sensed that the others were about to jump in with questions too. "We are in the middle of a civil war."

Eli clenched his fists. Meeting his trinity, which for the past forty-three days had consumed his thoughts, no longer seemed as dire. He'd come here expecting an engagement, and was going to leave a soldier in a war he hadn't known anything about.

"I am not asking you to fight. I'm merely letting you know what's at stake. The task I have for you relates more to our past than our present. When the ceremony is complete, you will meet with my counselors for more details." She stopped, seemed to gather herself. "Now it's time to bind you in your trinity."

After everything the Grand Master had just revealed, Eli was scrambling to find his emotional footing. The anticipation that had gripped him earlier came flooding back, but now the feeling was closer to anxiety.

"When you joined the Trinity Masters, you made a vow. You pledged your lives to our cause and our way. The time has come for you to meet your partners, your lovers, your spouses."

Silence settled over them. The medallion seemed to glow with extra light, a heavy symbol of exactly what he'd given up when he joined—there would be no traditional white picket fence in his future. He wouldn't be one half of a pair, but one third of a trinity.

"When I call your name, stand and remove your robe. Eli Wexler."

Eli was slow to rise. He was a big guy, and liked to take his time with everything. He needed those stolen moments as his legs straightened, lifting him to his full height. With the kind of single-minded focus that made him a good scholar, he compartmentalized everything they'd just learned, put it away so he could focus on this moment.

His hands were steady as he undid the hook-and-eye closures of the robe. Once it was open down the front from neck to ankle, Eli threw the hood back and shrugged out of the robe.

He'd elected to leave on a pair of black boxer briefs, but wore nothing else. The ambient cold of the stone room crept across his skin, wicked up his legs from where his bare feet touched the floor.

"Irina Gentry."

The figure in white stood and threw back her hood. Eli released the breath he'd been holding. She was beautiful. It was shallow of him to care about that, but some primal part of him was pleased. Her skin was creamy pale, a lovely contrast to her dark hair and eyes. There was a sharpness to her gaze that made him think of a bird of prey—smart and dangerous. She shed her robe.

She was completely naked underneath. Eli turned his gaze back to the Grand Master. A bit ridiculous, considering that she was going to be his wife, but it felt rude to stare at her naked body. He'd seen enough to get an impression of trim, muscular limbs and pink-tipped breasts.

"Jasper Ferrer."

The last member of their trinity stood. The name was vaguely familiar to Eli, so he wondered if he'd met Jasper at one of the few events he'd bothered to attend, but when the man shed his robe, Eli didn't recognize him.

Jasper was a hair over average height for a man, but at least three inches shorter than Eli's own six feet two. He had even, regular features, brown hair, and blue eyes. He looked like the archetype of a lawyer or businessman. Or he would have, if not for the scars that marred his chest and one arm.

Jasper was wearing boxers, but his were printed with bacon.

"You now belong to one another. Stand together."

In measured steps, they came forward until they stood on the medallion.

"Hold out your right hands."

The Grand Master removed the chain from her shoulders. She brought their hands together, Eli's on the bottom, Jasper's on top, with Irina's in the middle.

The Grand Master wrapped the chain around and around their hands, binding them to one another.

"A trinity marriage isn't easy, but if you love and trust one another, you will never be alone." The Grand Master squeezed their hands, then stepped back. "I will give you a moment of privacy. Then get dressed and return to this room. I'll send one of my counselors to get you. They'll explain the task I have for you."

The Grand Master retreated into the shadows.

Eli raised his gaze from their bound hands. Irina regarded him with an intensity that spoke of intelligence. The corners of Jasper's eyes were crinkled in what could only have been amusement.

"I think a kiss would be appropriate, don't you?" Irina's voice was huskier than it had been when she'd spoken earlier.

"A good idea." Jasper's barely contained smile spread across his face. He reached out with his left hand, grabbed Eli and kissed him.

Eli didn't have time to react to the kiss before Jasper had pulled back and treated Irina to the same quick, hard kiss Eli had gotten.

Irina quirked a brow at Jasper, then lifted onto her toes, looking at Eli. She tipped her head to the side. Eli wasn't great at nonverbal cues, but even he could read this one. Cupping her neck with his left hand, Eli lowered his mouth to Irina's, kissing her carefully. He started with lips closed, then opened his mouth slightly, massaging her lips with his.

Mindful of the brevity of the first kiss, Eli pulled back. Irina licked her lips and smiled at him.

"It's nice to meet you, Eli Wexler."

"It's nice to meet you too, Irina. I, uh, forgot your last name."

"Gentry." She turned. "It's nice to meet you, Jasper Ferrer."

Jasper was no longer grinning, but he nodded. "Irina, Eli." He unwound the chain from their hands. "Shall we go get our marching orders?"

Irina dressed with the neat efficiency with which she did everything. She'd left her clothes folded in a tidy stack in the dressing room where the white robe had been waiting for her. It took only a matter of minutes for her to be back in her street clothes—silk tank top under a black blazer. Black pencil skirt with a thin, decorative black belt. Black pumps. She folded her overcoat and draped it over her arm.

Her heels were loud on the marble floor as she returned to the medallion room. It was no less atmospheric now that she was dressed, but the shadows no longer seemed to loom.

Eli was already there, dressed in slightly rumpled flat-front khakis, a polo, and a chunky knit sweater. He carried a battered brown satchel. The clothes were a complete mismatch to his physique. Dude was *big*. Well over six feet, with broad shoulders and trim hips, he looked like the kind of man who could bust down a door with a firm shove.

He smiled tentatively at her, and Irina answered the smile with one of her own. He had beautiful eyes. They were a striking bright blue in his dark-skinned face. He was handsome bordering on beautiful, yet seemed to be completely unaware of how attractive he was.

How refreshing.

Jasper was the last one out. He wore jeans, a button-down shirt, and a well-worn leather jacket. His mussed brown hair and gray-blue eyes were classically handsome. He looked stylish and cool.

Irina looked between the two men, her husbands—or at least they *would* be her husbands, once they completed this "task."

Someone cleared their throat, drawing everyone's attention.

A handsome man appeared from the shadows. He wore slacks and a dress shirt, open at the throat. "The Grand Master asked me to escort you to her office."

Both Eli and Jasper looked at her, so Irina moved first, crossing over the medallion to follow the newcomer. She hesitated as her eyes adjusted, but was able to follow the white of the man's shirt into the shadows. Hidden in a recess in the back wall was an opening—a doorway.

Irina hesitated on the threshold. There was nothing but darkness beyond.

Behind her, Eli said, "Do you want me to go first?"

Irina smiled over her shoulder. "No, thank you."

"Am I the only one who's a bit worried this is a trap?" Jasper's words were so low, Irina almost didn't hear them.

Eli's reply was just as soft. "No, you're not."

And just like that, they were a team.

Irina stepped into the darkness, Eli so close behind she could feel the heat of his body. The small passageway curved slightly, which was what hid the light from the space beyond. Irina stepped out of the darkness into a larger hallway, which was lit by evenly spaced recessed lights. They left great pools of shadow, but it was not nearly as intimidating as the darkness of the passage.

Eli and Jasper followed her out. On instinct they lined up, this newly formed trinity, shoulder to shoulder.

The man eyed them, then held out his hand. "I'm Devon Asher."

"Asher." Jasper cocked his head to the side. "From New York?"

Devon nodded. "You're Jasper Ferrer?"

"Yes. Good to meet you."

"And nice to meet you. I've met your mother. Both of them actually."

They took turns introducing themselves. Irina made a mental note to ask Jasper how he knew Devon. From the sound of it, Jasper might be a legacy. Irina wasn't sure what the implications of that were, but she would figure it out.

"I'm going to take you to the Grand Master's office," Devon said. "Very few of our members are privy to the location of it, and we expect your discretion, both about the location of the office and the people you meet there. Though it's not strictly a secret, the identities of the Grand Master's counselors aren't widely known, and the Grand Master would like it to stay that way."

"I didn't even know the Grand Master had counselors." Eli sounded rather baffled.

"We'll keep it a secret," Irina said. Only after she'd spoken did she realize she'd used "we," speaking for all of them. She looked at Jasper and Eli, but neither seemed to mind.

Devon nodded, then motioned for them to follow. Two rights and a left later, he knocked once on a heavy wood door, then pushed it open.

The Grand Master's office was a large room lit by warm, gold light from half a dozen elegant lamps. A delicate Louis the 16th desk was positioned beneath a beautiful oil painting of the original capital. Floor-to-ceiling bookcases glowed the way only old wood could. The shelves were artfully filled with not just books, but rare antiques—a small jade and lapis globe, a shiny brass astrolabe. There was a conference table surrounded by low-backed leather executive chairs off to one side. The only jarring note was a large, glossy black box set atop a waist-high bookcase. It looked like an XL desktop printer, or maybe a 3D printer.

The Grand Master sat behind her desk, still wearing the robe, the hood hiding her face.

She rose when they entered. Eli, Irina, and Jasper clustered awkwardly just inside the door.

"They will explain." The Grand Master's voice was flat, almost toneless. She nodded toward the people seated around the conference table, then slid between two bookcases and disappeared.

Irina blinked. Apparently this place was full of secret doors. That shouldn't have surprised her, but it did.

Devon cleared his throat. "I have other things to see to. I'll leave you with these three." He looked at the people seated around the table, eyes narrowed. "Behave. All of you."

A drop-dead gorgeous blonde woman rolled her eyes and waved dismissively. The brown-haired man beside her flipped Devon the bird, and the third man, whose hair stood on end like he'd been electrocuted, didn't even look up.

Irina bit back a laugh, relaxing. Devon let out a long-suffering sigh, then turned on his heel and exited through the same door they'd entered, closing it behind him.

The blonde tossed her hair and smiled brightly. "Who's ready to get their Nancy Drew on?"

Chapter Two

Jasper grinned. This was going to be fun. He loved a mystery. His entire career—which meant his entire life—was about solving mysteries. And sometimes about creating them.

He'd much rather think about a mystery that needed solving than about his trinity. Not that Irina and Eli weren't both beautiful—they were—but he wasn't exactly Mr. Relationship.

It was a well-known fact—using the term "fact" loosely—that most members of the Trinity Masters made good use of the years before they were called to the altar to indulge in sex, drugs, and rock 'n' roll. Or at least that first one. Relationships, if they existed, were always kept casual.

Jasper had tried, and failed, to have fun, casual relationships. Somehow they always ended with him getting his face slapped, his car keyed, and the girl in question sobbing on the floor, telling him that he'd ruined her life. Hell, he'd even tried dating guys—joining the Trinity Masters meant you had to be accepting of love in all forms and genders, since you never knew who you'd get paired with.

Dating men hadn't gone much better than dating women. The last time he'd tried—two years ago—the phrase, "You're a real son of a bitch, you know that?" had been used more than Jasper was comfortable with.

He'd been living in dread of being called to the altar. This "task" was a heaven-sent reprieve.

"Have a seat." The blonde gestured to the empty chairs. "Once Franco surfaces, he'll explain."

Jasper took Irina's coat, then gallantly held out a chair. He held out a second chair for Eli, who looked baffled by the gesture, but sat.

Jasper had carefully left himself the chair at the head of the table, which put him close to the bookcase he wanted to surreptitiously examine. There was a small, framed landscape painting propped on the shelf. Was that an original Thomas Cole?

Eli, who was half a head taller than everyone else seated around the table, frowned, then said, "I'd like to ask some clarifying questions."

Irina's lips twitched and she slanted a glance at Jasper. Jasper smiled slightly in response. When her lips curved, something warm and rich slid through Jasper's belly. Maybe this wouldn't be the disaster he'd always assumed—maybe he'd finally find a place to call home.

"Clarifying questions? Go for it. I'm Seb, by the way."

"He means Sebastian. Actually, he prefers Bastian." The blonde grinned.

"Ignore her. She was dropped on her head as a child."

"Sebastian, I'm shocked you would say something so cruel." The blonde fluttered her lashes.

Sebastian narrowed his eyes and said something in what Jasper thought might have been a dialect of Farsi. He was good with languages, but mostly the Romance languages. The blonde responded in kind.

Eli sighed, stood, then grabbed the squabbling pair's chairs, one chair back in each hand. He shoved the chairs away from one another, separating the two. They squawked in surprise. With an ease that was both impressive and a bit alarming, Eli then grabbed Irina's chair, and repositioned her in between the pair. Irina yelped once, holding on to the arms of the chair as she was moved.

Silence settled over the group. Watching Eli move everyone around as if he were shelving books had gotten everyone's attention, even that of the crazy-haired man at the end of the table.

Eli resumed his seat. "Now then, I'd like to ask some questions."

"You're Eli Wexler?" Crazy-hair spoke for the first time. He too was good-looking, with dark hair and skin that said Hispanic. If the looks hadn't been a clue, the fact that he had a slight accent would have solved it.

"I am." Eli's voice was steady and calm. "And you are?"

"Franco. Francisco Garcia Santiago. That's Sebastian Stewart and Juliette Adams." Franco waved at the pair, who were behaving themselves now that they'd been separated.

It was a little hard to believe that the Grand Master had counselors who squabbled like children. If Jasper was a betting man, and he was, he'd guess their behavior was a carefully calculated front. They were probably both super assassins.

"You're one of the Grand Master's counselors?" Eli asked.

"Yes. But that's not what's important right now. I'm a historian. My family runs the Cuban Heritage Foundation in Florida."

Eli closed his eyes and tipped his head to the side. When he opened them again, there was an intensity to his gaze that Jasper had yet to see.

"You're the…great-great-grandson of Calixo Garcia."

Franco blinked. "Uh, yes."

"You're the one the Grand Master was talking about."

"Wow, you were really paying attention. Actually, it was my grandfather who was a member. He used to tell stories about this secret society. We thought he was making it up—he was a character. Until the day Devon showed up wearing a ring just like my grandfather's, and they told me all the crazy stories were true." Franco held up his hand, the triquetra ring glinting in the light.

"They tried to get rid of your family because you're…"

"Because they didn't want any brown people," Franco said frankly.

Jasper watched Eli's mouth tighten. Eli had to be at least part black, based on his skin color, though his features and eye color screamed mixed race. The Grand Master had said these people, the purists, were still active. Was Eli a target?

"But that doesn't really matter." Franco waved away the massive issue of racism with a casual hand. "What matters is *this*."

Franco picked up a heavy metal box off the floor. It was about the size of two laptops stacked on top of each other. He pulled on cloth gloves and handed a second pair to Eli, who was sitting forward, watching the box eagerly.

Franco opened it and took out a large book, roughly twelve inches by fourteen, and nearly three inches thick. It had a textured leather cover.

Franco placed it on a cloth on the tabletop, then opened to the front page.

"Brace yourselves," Juliette said to Jasper and Irina.

Irina sat forward. "Why, is it dangerous?"

"No. But if Eli is anything like Franco, he is about to lose it."

The title page of the book had writing in ornate, almost medieval calligraphy.

Eli leapt to his feet, his chair toppling back. "Is that...?"

"Yes," Franco said.

"Where? How?" Eli looked like he was going to have a stroke. He pressed his hands against the side of his head, as if to hold his brain in.

"What's happening?" Jasper asked conversationally.

"History nerd freak-out," Juliette replied.

"He's a historian?" Irina asked.

"Franco? Yes."

"No, Eli."

Sebastian laughed. "I forgot you all haven't had time to say anything more than your names. I don't want to steal your man's thunder, but yes. He's actually an art historian. A very good one."

"Art historian," Jasper said faintly. *Oh fuck.*

Juliette looked at him and winced. "Yes."

Clearly the Grand Master's counselors knew about him, and what he did. So much for Jasper finding a home in this trinity. The Grand Master either hated Jasper for reasons he didn't know, or was a sadist.

"One of the missing albums?" Eli was asking.

"Yes. And we have at least nine more," Franco said.

"Ten...ten of the missing. I need to sit down," Eli said, but stayed standing, hovering over the book. "I need my glasses." Eli upended his messenger bag on the floor, plucked out an eyeglass case. He slid glasses with thick, black rims onto his nose. Jasper saw Irina smile at the sight of the big man wearing the almost comically "geeky" glasses. Jasper's own equally thick-rimmed glasses were in his bag back in the dressing room, though he only needed them for computer work.

"Are they ever going to tell us what's going on?" Irina asked.

Sebastian cleared his throat. "It's one of the—"

Eli talked over the top of him, without looking up.

"This is a record of war crimes." He turned the page, sighed. "A record of the art the Nazis stole."

Now it was Jasper's turn to jump halfway out of his chair. "It's one of the ERR albums?"

"Yes." Eli looked at him with surprise. "You know about them?"

"Yes...yes I do."

"Well, I don't. Could someone please explain?" Irina was looking increasingly frustrated.

Eli cleared his throat, then started speaking in the measured storyteller tones of a teacher.

Bet he's a professor. Not that it matters. He'll still hate you.

"These albums were created by the Einsatzstab Reichsleiter Rosenberg task force. Einsatzstab Reichsleiter Rosenberg, aka ERR. They were the Nazi unit responsible for confiscating all the 'ownerless' works of art. But they weren't ownerless, they were art owned by Jews.

"The ERR recorded every piece they stole, taking photos of them, and putting the photos into an album. *This* album, and a hundred others like it. They weren't meant to record the thefts; they were a catalogue for Hitler and his curators to shop through. They used these to choose art for the planned Führer's Art Museum in Linz, Austria. There were...thirty-eight albums originally found?" Eli looked at Franco.

"Thirty-nine."

"Thirty-nine, thank you. The Monuments Men found them in nineteen forty-five, at Neuschwanstein. The albums were used for restitution efforts, and then as evidence in the Nuremberg trials. They were the proof and the record of the Nazis' art looting.

"Everyone knew there were missing albums, that the Monuments Men hadn't found them all, but until two thousand and seven, everyone assumed the others had been destroyed in the war. But it turns out some were taken as souvenirs by American GIs."

Eli stopped and looked again at Franco, who took over.

"There are forty-three albums in the U.S. National Archive. Forty-three out of a suspected hundred. It turns out the Trinity Masters have at least ten of the missing albums. We found them only recently."

"Found them where?" Irina asked.

Juliette's, Sebastian's, and Franco's faces turned grim.

"In a storage area belonging to the purists. They had these albums, and they hid them—for a reason."

"Why?" Jasper asked.

"That's what you need to find out."

Juliette's voice had taken on a weight that made Jasper look at her sharply. She almost sounded like...

"We're giving you this album," Sebastian said. "And we want you to see if you can figure out where any of the art pieces in it are, who has them now, and why the purists bothered to hide the albums."

"If they're really purists—Aryan-Nations' style of racist—they may have been Nazi sympathizers. Maybe the Nazis gave them the albums," Irina added.

Sebastian nodded. "We know there were Nazi sympathizers within the Trinity Masters at the start of WWII. At that point, they weren't particularly discreet about their feelings. After the war, it seems like they changed their minds. Recent events have proven that isn't true. Identifying and locating even one of the pieces in this book would help."

Jasper let out a breath. "That's why *I'm* here. He does the research and identifies the pieces." Jasper pointed at Eli. "And I find it."

"What do you do?" Irina asked.

Jasper shook his head. He wasn't ready to have that conversation yet.

Irina looked around the table. "If this was stored and forgotten about, it should be relatively low danger to look into it."

"It's not dangerous," Juliette assured them.

Sebastian's jaw clenched. "Someone died trying to keep us from finding this."

Everyone fell silent.

Franco broke the tension by putting the book back in its fancy box, which Jasper now realized was an airtight archive storage box.

"We're scanning the books." Franco pointed to the odd black box that looked like a 3D printer. "We're actually scanning everything. Here's a copy."

Franco handed Eli a black three-ring binder.

Juliette stood. "I'll walk you out."

"No, I'll do it." Sebastian pushed to his feet. "There's a limo upstairs to take you to the Boston Park Plaza."

Eli tucked the binder carefully into his bag.

Jasper hung back, trailing a few steps behind Eli and Irina as they followed Sebastian through the labyrinthine hallways. Irina and Eli took the elevator up first. The elevator led to a closet in the back of the American History rare book room in the Boston Public Library, so when exiting it was better to do it solo or in pairs.

Once the doors closed, Jasper turned to Sebastian.

"Does the Grand Master actually want us to end up in a trinity, or are we just supposed to deal with the ERR album?"

"Both."

"Eli and I—"

"You'll find a way to deal with each other. Trust me."

The elevator door dinged open. Jasper stepped in. Sebastian gave him a mock salute as the doors closed.

The three-bedroom Presidential suite at the Plaza was gorgeous, with its ornate chandeliers, elegant furnishings, and high-end finishes.

Eli saw none of it. He dropped into a chair at the dining table, pulled the binder out of his bag, then fished around in the bottom for his reading glasses.

When his glasses were safely on his nose, he flipped open the binder, laying his hand flat on the first page.

"Einsatzstab Reichsleiter Rosenberg" was written in distinct calligraphic script.

The information in these pages could mean nothing—every piece of art in here might have been destroyed in the war—or it could change the art world forever. Art pieces in both private collections and museums may, as a result of this book, find their way into the hands of the rightful owners' descendants.

He was about to turn the page when slender fingers closed over his hand. "Eli."

Eli looked up. His glasses distorted his view of Irina and he ripped them off, blinking hard.

"Let's leave that for now."

"But this—"

"It's rude to ignore someone on a first date." Irina's lips quirked in a smile, taking the sting out of her words.

"First date...right."

Eli put his glasses in their case then stood, tucking his hands into his pockets. "I forgot."

"You forgot that you were finally placed in your trinity? Forgot that you'd just met the people you're going to spend the rest of your life with?"

Eli held in a groan. "It sounds really bad when you put it like that."

Irina shook her head in mock sadness. "That's because it *was* really bad. But I forgive you. Why don't you come sit and we'll order room service? There's already champagne."

There was a bar, which Jasper was behind. The champagne cork popped—a festive sound. Jasper held out a glass to each of them.

Eli accepted his glass, looking at the pale gold liquid and bubbles. Though it seemed like days had passed, they'd been in the Trinity Masters' headquarters for less than two hours. The sun was just now starting to set. Rays of light slanted into the room through the windows, adding a halo of light to the elegant furnishings.

Irina took a seat on the couch. She paused, seeming to consider something, before she set her champagne glass down. She peeled off her jacket and kicked off her shoes, relaxing back into the cushions.

Eli headed for the chair, but Jasper beat him there, so Eli sat on the couch next to Irina.

She raised her glass. "To us."

"To us," Eli repeated.

Three flutes came together, crystal ringing like chimes.

"Eli, tell us about yourself." Irina leaned back on the arm of the couch. "You're an art historian?"

Eli took a long drink, compartmentalized the part of his brain that was clamoring to go investigate the ERR album.

"I'm a professor at the University of Colorado. I wrote my doctoral thesis on the role of art in war. It's my specialty. Not just art in WWII, though that's a big part of what I research and study. Art has actually played an important role in war throughout human history. I've written several articles and chapters on the ERR albums."

"That explains why the Grand Master gave you this assignment," Irina said.

"I'm not…I'm not very exciting," Eli said hesitantly. "I'm an academic. I spend most of my time in my office. And if I'm not there, I teach class."

"I guessed you were a teacher, the way you handled Juliette and Sebastian." Jasper spoke without looking up. His elbows were braced on his knees, and he was twirling the champagne glass slowly between his fingers.

"They were worse than undergrads." Eli shook his head.

"You must be a good art historian," Irina prompted.

Eli shrugged. "Not that good. I mean, I've gotten a few Fulbright grants, some fellowships…I curated a few things for the National Gallery and spent three months studying at the Smithsonian."

Irina laughed softly. "So you're a *very* good art historian."

Eli shrugged. "I like history. I like beautiful things. I like that people can create beautiful things, and that we find meaning in them."

"I like art too," Irina said. Eli saw something flutter across her face, a strange look that he didn't understand. The moment passed and she smiled. "But I was a comm major, with a specialty in interpersonal communications."

"What do you do?" Eli asked.

"I work for Bennett Securities. I specialize in personal security work."

Eli frowned. "Does that mean…"

"I'm a bodyguard. It's a bit more technical than that, but basically I try to keep VIPs safe. It works because no one ever suspects I'm the bodyguard."

"I was actually going to ask if that means you're one of those people who looks innocent but can kill someone with a straw." Eli was joking.

"Anything is a weapon in the right hands." Irina was not joking.

"That's terrifying."

Jasper snorted out a laugh in response to Eli's comment.

"What about you, Jasper?" Irina asked. "What do you do?"

Jasper sighed and drained his glass of champagne. "I have a PhD in archaeology."

"Another historian," Irina commented.

"But," Jasper said, "I specialize in art acquisitions."

Art acquisitions.

Jasper Ferrer.

Eli set his glass down very, very carefully. "Acquisitions?"

Jasper rolled lightly to his feet and turned to face Eli. "Yes. Acquisitions."

"I've heard of you."

"Have you?"

"You're the one they call Indiana Jones."

"Indiana Jones was an archaeologist, right?" Irina tone was light, but she was no longer lounging on the couch. She was braced to move, much the way she'd braced herself on her chair in the medallion room. She was reading the tension in the room and ready to jump to her feet.

"Indiana Jones was a terrible archaeologist, but a very good grave robber," Eli growled.

Irina looked between them. "Jasper, you're...you're an art thief?"

Jasper raised his hands. "Is it theft if you do it on behalf of a museum?"

Eli sprang up, righteous outrage vibrating through him. "You son of a bitch!"

"Exactly how many pieces do you think would have survived from the Baghdad museum if I hadn't gone in?"

"That's your excuse?"

"It's not an excuse. It's fact. Do you think the Elgin Marbles would still exist if they'd been left *in situ*?"

"The excuse used by thieves throughout history. 'I saved it when I stole it.' That's bullshit."

"That's fact. If you'd rather write papers about how sad it is when things are destroyed, instead of stopping them from *being* destroyed, you're welcome to."

Eli took a half step forward. He wasn't going to hit Jasper. He hadn't hit anyone since he was a teenager and he realized that his size and strength meant that hitting someone was actually rather dangerous.

But Irina stepped into him, her body flush against his, and in the next second he was flying through the air.

He landed on his back with a *thud.*

"Everyone calm down." Irina's tone was perfectly level.

Eli sucked in some air and cursed. Rolling to his feet, he looked at Jasper. People like Jasper treated art like pieces in some grand game they played. Art was memory; art was a slice of someone's soul.

He looked at Irina, who was balanced on the balls of her feet, looking back and forth between them.

"I'm leaving," Eli growled.

No one said anything as he stalked to the table, shoved his glasses and the binder into the bag, slung the strap over his shoulder, and walked out. The door made a satisfying *clunk* when it closed behind him.

Jasper looked at the closed door.

"Jasper?" Irina asked.

"I'm going to take a walk."

"Maybe we should talk."

Jasper shook his head. "I need some space. I'm not good at relationships at the best of times, so trying to form one with someone who automatically hates me is…" Jasper gave up, not bothering to finish the sentence.

Irina sighed. "Clearly this is something we need to deal with. Why don't you and I talk it out, and then—"

A wild kind of recklessness, the feeling that had led him to do very stupid things, like lift diamond bracelets off a particularly despicable woman when he was actually there to liberate a Cézanne from her husband, gripped Jasper.

He grabbed Irina, Rhett-Butler-to-Scarlett-O'Hara style, and kissed her. She tasted like champagne and citrus. Her hands curled around the edges of his jacket. Before she could push him away, Jasper broke the kiss. He indulged himself one moment more, resting his forehead on hers. The move seemed to surprise her.

Stepping back, he said, "I'm sorry."

Grabbing his wallet from the bar, he walked out.

Chapter Three

Irina stared at the door.

"Well isn't this just fan-freaking-tastic?"

Their binding was less than three hours old and two members of her trinity had already stormed out in snits. Men were such drama queens.

"Would have been much easier to be married to two other women," she muttered. Opening doors to the bedrooms, she finally found the one where her suitcase had been deposited. She opened it and pulled out some jogging clothes.

The day had left her with far too many emotions for her to just stay here. She needed some stress relief. Luckily, she'd lived in Boston for many years, between going to college here and training at Bennett Securities headquarters, which was located in the city. She knew exactly where to go.

Wearing ankle-length jogging tights, a sports bra, and a fleece jacket, she stuck fifty dollars cash and her hotel keycard into a pocket and headed out. One quick stop in the hotel lobby and she was the proud owner of a Red Sox T-shirt, which she charged to the room and zipped inside her fleece. She jogged around Boston Common and the Faneuil Hall area until she reached a small neighborhood that was a haven for artists. The studio was still there.

Stepping inside, she was both surprised and delighted to recognize the fifty-something-year-old woman behind the counter.

"Hi, uh, Lillian."

"Iris! I'm so glad to see you."

"Do you have space for me?" She didn't bother to correct the name.

"Of course, of course."

Irina passed over the fifty. "I don't have anything with me, so I'll take whatever that will buy me."

"Colors, canvas size?"

Irina shrugged. "Doesn't matter."

Lillian looked scandalized, but bustled though the front room, which was a small gallery, into the artist workroom in the back. Paint-stained easels were crowded together. A few pottery wheels sat in the back near the sink.

There were two other painters at the easels, and one pottery wheel was spinning.

A cage-front storage unit, like the ones hardware stores kept spray paint in, held supplies. Lillian opened it and selected a small canvas, three tubes of water-based paint, and two brushes.

"Here you go. There are palettes over there you can use."

"I'll just use one brush. Can I have a tube of white, too?" Irina looked longingly at the tubes of oil paint, but didn't have the time or money to mess with oil.

"Red, yellow, blue and white." Lillian handed everything over.

"Thanks. That's all I need." Irina selected a spot, set everything on the small shelf connected to the easel, then took off the fleece and pulled on the cheap, too-large T-shirt as a smock.

Paint to palette, palette to brush, brush to canvas. There was no sketch to guide her, no model or view to reference.

Two hours later, she stepped back. She felt mellow and loose. Every bit of tension and emotion had flowed out of her, through the brush, onto the canvas.

She washed the brush and palette clean, leaving the brush on the sink, a gift to the next artist.

Removing the stained T-shirt, she threw it away, then put her fleece back on and started to walk out.

"Iris!" Lillian called. "What do you want me to do with the painting?"

Irina looked over her shoulder at the painting—three faces, each painted in a totally different style. A purple-skinned face done in the surrealist style of Picasso, a portrait of a handsome brown-haired man, and the blurred image of a woman turned in profile, rendered in dots, which had been deposited on the canvas with the blunt end of the brush, pointillism style.

"Just throw it away."

"May I join you?"

The slightly too-loud voice broke Eli from his study of the binder. Jasper was standing beside his table, a to-go cup of coffee in one hand.

Eli studied the other man for a moment, then nodded. Jasper slid into the booth across from Eli.

"How did you find me?" Eli asked.

"Chance, I'm afraid." Jasper sipped his coffee, eyeing Eli warily. "I used to come here when I was in school."

"You went to Harvard?"

"I did. Surprised?"

"Yes," Eli answered honestly.

"I have my Ph.D. from the Oriental Institute in Chicago."

"What's your specialty?"

"This is starting to feel like a job interview."

Eli was about to say sorry, but decided not to. He didn't really care if he made Jasper uncomfortable.

"Early medieval European. But I've worked on digs all over the world—China, the Middle East—"

"And that's when you stole from the Baghdad museum?"

"I stood shoulder to shoulder with desperate museum curators as they tried to decide if they should abandon the museum and flee with their families, or stay and try to protect the artifacts. After that is when I carefully packaged a few critical items, made copies of the artifact records, and then smuggled them out of the country into Turkey." Jasper's voice was cold.

"How noble. Where are they now, these artifacts? 'Safe' with a private collector?" Eli was not going to let himself be swayed by Jasper's story. The history of art was riddled with theft and destruction. People like Jasper were a bane upon this earth.

"Actually, they're in the British Museum."

Eli snorted. "How stupid do you think I am?"

Jasper raised one brow. "It's the truth."

"The British Museum wouldn't..." Eli trailed off. *Hmm.*

Jasper's other eyebrow joined the first and a faint smile played around his mouth. "Thinking it through, aren't you?"

The British Museum didn't have the best track record when it came to artifact acquisition. No major museum did. Even brand-new institutions like the Getty in California were plagued by scandals around their artifact-acquisition practices.

"The museum director would never agree to that."

Jasper shrugged. "I didn't arrange it. I just got them there—over land, in a jeep, no less. Someone from the Admiralty arranged it, which makes sense, since they're—"

"What are nice boys like you doing in a place like this?" Irina walked up to their table, bottle of water in hand. She was flushed and glowing, her hair up in a high ponytail. Without waiting to be asked, she slid in next to Eli, who scooted over, pulling the binder with him.

"You two making nice?"

"I think I'm making inroads with Harvey Dent over there," Jasper said.

"Harvey Dent?" Eli asked.

"You know, Two-Face. The Batman villain. He saw everything as black and white—good and bad, right and wrong."

"How villainous of me to think of stealing as bad. Must be my puritanical upbringing." Eli's voice was dry.

Irina laughed. "Why don't we try a slightly different subject? What made you want to become an art historian?"

"You mean because I'm black?" Eli replied.

Irina blinked. "No, I mean because art historian isn't exactly the most common profession."

"Are you black?" Jasper asked.

Eli answered Jasper's blunt question first. "My maternal grandfather was African American. My maternal grandmother was Chinese. My father had a grandmother who was from Morocco, and a grandfather who was Welsh—or maybe it was a great-grandfather." Eli frowned, trying to remember his diverse and complex family tree.

"So you're about as mixed as they come," Irina summed up.

"How very American," Jasper added.

That made Eli pause. He smiled. "Yeah, I guess I am." He took a sip of lukewarm tea. "My parents were citizens of the world. When I was growing up it felt like we celebrated every possible holiday, because there was always someone in the family, somewhere, who was that religion. The museum near where I grew up had a cultural center, and we spent a lot of time there. By the time I was in high school, the museum was like a second home. Just like going to events at the cultural center, the art pieces in the galleries were windows into different worlds. And with art, it was also a window into the past."

Irina and Jasper were both watching him with serious, thoughtful expressions. Eli shrugged uncomfortably—he always felt a bit stupid waxing philosophical outside of a classroom.

"I got into Harvard, and was majoring in economics, because that seemed practical, but my favorite classes were art history. My sophomore year I was having trouble in school. The dean of students sat me down, and we talked about what I liked. I changed my major and never looked back. The next semester, I was approached about joining the Trinity Masters."

"Sophomore year is when they asked me too," Irina added.

"It's funny that we didn't know one another," Jasper added. "Since we all attended the same school."

They talked about college—Eli was the oldest at thirty-seven, and had graduated before the other two even started. Irina was twenty-nine and Jasper thirty-five.

"Wait," Eli said, frowning at Jasper. "If you're only two years younger than I was, did we have classes together?" That would be oddly fitting.

But Jasper shook his head. "Possible, but I was a nontraditional student. I didn't start college until I was twenty-two."

Irina caught Eli's gaze and raised a brow. Something in the clipped precision of Jasper's words made it clear there was more to that story.

"Tell us about yourself," she asked Jasper. "How did you get into archaeology?"

"Mysteries. I like solving mysteries." Jasper grinned. "Archaeology is discovery. I actually have a minor in art history, which explains how we know so many of the same professors." He nodded at Eli. "I planned to study art until I realized archaeologists got to travel, dig in the dirt, and solve mysteries."

"Did your family frequent a museum too?" Irina's question was teasing, but Jasper's expression sobered.

"Most of the men in my family are in prison or dead. My mom tried, but it took everything she had just to keep a roof over our heads. Ferrer isn't actually my last name. I changed it when I turned eighteen, with the help of some people." Jasper smiled ruefully. "With the help of *these* people." He twisted his triquetra ring around his finger.

"They approached you when you turned eighteen?" Irina asked.

"Yes. The, uh, director of the FBI recruited me."

Eli straightened. "Why did the director of the FBI recruit you when you were eighteen?"

"The real question is, how did a kid from Southie end up loving art and archaeology?" As he spoke, Jasper dropped into a hard Boston accent, losing every "r" in his sentence. He turned "art" into "ahht."

"We're going to come back to that accent," Irina said with a laugh. "But I'll take the bait. How did a kid from Southie end up loving art and archaeology?"

"When I was younger, I saw a painting. Something about it…" Jasper looked down, and Eli had a strange sense of recognition—just as he'd struggled with explaining his love of art, Jasper too was struggling.

"I understand," Eli said. "When I teach undergrads, there's always one student who finds that piece while in my class. The piece that changes everything for them."

Jasper nodded. "Changes everything…that's a good way to put it. And in my case, that's true in more ways than one."

"What painting was it?" Eli asked gently.

Jasper sighed heavily. "A Rembrandt."

Eli hummed in understanding.

Irina said, "I remember being shocked the first time I saw one of his portraits. I really thought they were photos."

Jasper nodded. "It wasn't one of his portraits that changed my life, but I know what you mean. I stood in front of this painting and I understood what I was looking at. As if I were looking at a representation of my own soul."

"One of the landscapes?" Eli asked, flipping through his mental catalogue of Rembrandts.

Jasper looked at Irina. "You put him down once before. Can you do it again?"

Irina straightened slowly, her smile fading. "Not without making a scene."

"Can you hold him long enough to give me a head start?"

Irina nodded. "If I have to."

"What are you talking about?" Eli asked, utterly confused. "Why does she need to hold me?"

Jasper looked at Eli, their gazes meeting. "The painting that changed my life was a seascape."

Eli frowned. "Rembrandt only did one sea…scape…" Eli blinked hard. "You son of a bitch."

Jasper scooted a few inches toward the end of the bench. "Only an art historian would put it together so fast."

Eli reached across the table, ready to strangle the other man, but Irina caught his arm. Her fingers dug into the space between his wrist bones, causing his nerves to sing. She jerked his hand back to their side of the table, laced her fingers with his, and held their joined hands in her lap.

"Jasper, don't you dare run away. You two already pulled that. Never again. We're in this together, so we'll *deal* with everything together." Her words were silk-covered steel—this wasn't a plea, it was a proclamation.

Eli squeezed her fingers and exhaled slowly.

Jasper looked at them, then scooted back. "That's reasonable, but unrealistic, because I'm pretty sure Eli is going to strangle me as soon as you let go of him."

"I could still strangle you with this hand." Eli bared his teeth and raised his free hand.

"How about you two art nerds explain to me exactly what you're talking about."

"Art nerds?"

"Art nerds!"

Eli and Jasper both looked at Irina, who merely raised her eyebrows. "If the shoe fits. Someone explain."

Jasper cleared his throat. "The painting I saw was Rembrandt's only seascape. It's called *Christ in the Storm on the Sea of Galilee*."

"And why does that mean Eli wants to strangle you?"

"Because *Christ in the Storm on the Sea of Galilee* is one of the Gardner paintings," Eli growled.

"That sounds vaguely familiar, but you're still in art nerd territory. Keep talking."

Eli cleared his throat, as if he were about to start a lecture. "It was one of thirteen paintings stolen from the Gardner Museum here in Boston in nineteen ninety. Still missing." Eli's eye started to twitch. "Jasper, if you have it, or know where it is—"

"Wait, nineteen ninety?" Irina released Eli's hand, then grabbed his shoulder and gave him a little shake. "Eli, do the math. Jasper was just a little kid."

Eli blinked. She was right. He looked at Jasper, whose head was bowed.

Eli prided himself on being open-minded, and yet he'd jumped to a conclusion that made no logical sense.

"I'm sorry, Jasper," he said stiffly.

Jasper raised his head. Grinned. "Don't apologize. I *did* steal it."

Eli sputtered, pointed at Jasper, then at Irina, growled, and finally dropped his head into his hands.

"I think I broke him," Jasper said.

"I'm starting to suspect that you're enjoying this. Next time I'm going to let him hit you."

"That's fair."

"But," Irina continued, "I'm having trouble believing you robbed a museum while still in elementary school."

"If you're lying just to see if you can give me a stroke..." Eli mumbled.

"Nope. I'm not lying. I was part of the crew. Little kid, little fingers. Able to squeeze through tight spaces."

Eli raised his head. "The theft was carried out by two men posing as Boston PD. They tricked the museum staff into letting them in. The FBI suspected there was a larger crew."

Jasper nodded. "A crew including the ringleader's little cousin, who was tucked into the duffel bag one of the fake cops was carrying. A little kid who smuggled the rolled-up paintings out through the ventilation system."

"Rolled up...I might pass out."

Irina frowned. "They stuck you in a duffel bag, then made you get the stolen goods out of the building? You were practically a baby."

Jasper shrugged. "I was a minor. Safer for me to be caught with anything."

"Yeah, yeah, tragic childhood. What. Happened. To. The. Paintings?" Eli asked.

Jasper laughed. "I'm sure you know part of the story. My idiot cousin and his idiot friends didn't steal the right paintings."

"What?" Irina asked.

"It was a commissioned job. They were good thieves, able to talk their way into, and out of, almost anything. But they were idiots. They had a list of paintings they were supposed to grab, but just assumed one would be as good as another." Jasper shook his head. "Except for the Rembrandt. That's my fault. And I do deserve a beating for that. I loved that painting. The glow of hope in the middle of chaos. I wanted that hope. So they took it. For me. And they hung it on the wall in my mother's basement. With thumbtacks."

Eli felt faint.

"Stay with me, big guy." Irina cupped his head in her hands.

"Basement...thumbtacks..."

"I don't know much about what went sideways," Jasper continued, "but I know the buyer backed out, and then they couldn't move the paintings."

"The others. The other twelve. Where are they?" Eli asked desperately.

"I don't know. They might be with the Rembrandt."

"Where *is* the Rembrandt?" Eli whispered the question, suddenly paranoid someone else would hear them and steal it before he, Eli, managed to get his hands on it and restore it to its rightful place.

"Six months after the robbery, I walked into the FBI's Boston offices with a poster tube, and turned over the Rembrandt. I was scared because of all the publicity, and I felt bad that I was the only one who got to see it. Staring at that painting day after day made me braver, made me think about the future, about the hope. Plus, Catholic guilt."

Eli sat back and looked at Jasper. "Your family…"

"I was placed in witness protection and put in foster care out of state." Jasper's voice was flat. "My mom wouldn't go. I have two sisters, who were just little, plus my mom was caring for my grandma."

"You did the right thing, and lost everything." Irina's voice was husky with reflected heartache.

"I did. But there's a semi-happy ending. I joined the Trinity Masters, my idiot cousin and his partner died. The FBI knows who the rest of the crew was, and they're just biding their time, hoping that on their death beds, someone will confess to the theft. Hopefully the paintings are safe, but without a confession they'll never get the buyer."

Eli tried to imagine being in Jasper's position, and he wasn't sure that he would have had the courage to do what Jasper did. Eli loved art, but Jasper had suffered for it.

"I'm sorry," Eli said.

"Don't be sorry. I have other stories where I don't come out looking so good. But I'd like to point out that I've never been convicted of anything. Suspected, but never convicted."

"I have two follow-up questions." Eli cleared his throat. "One. The FBI has the Rembrandt?"

"Yes. And if your second question is why haven't they announced that, or given it back, the answer is because it's technically evidence in an ongoing investigation."

Eli blew out a breath. "Okay. I have an alternate question two. Have you ever really stolen something? I don't like it, but I get that things like taking pieces out of the National Museum of Iraq may have saved them from destruction."

"You mean have I ever walked into someone's house and taken a Cezanne off the wall, then stolen the hostess's diamond bracelet on my way out the door just for fun?" Jasper's grin was wide and wicked.

Eli bared his teeth. "Yes, that's exactly what I mean."

"Then…no. Nope. Not me."

Irina laughed. Jasper laughed.

Eli frowned at both of them. "Wait, does that mean he *did* do it? Which Cezanne?"

"What did the bracelet look like?" Irina countered, still laughing.

Eli decided to rise above it. Pointedly ignoring them, he went back to studying the binder.

Irina and Jasper went up to the counter—Irina came back with a cup of tea and a banana, and Jasper with a coffee refill, and another cup of tea for Eli. He grunted his thanks when Jasper tapped his arm and pointed at the mug.

"Hmm, that grunt sounded thoughtful," Irina said. "Anything you want to share with the class?"

Eli looked first at Irina, then at Jasper. "I think I know where this sculpture is." He took his phone from his pocket, then showed them an email he'd unearthed from his trash. It was an invitation to a fundraising gala, cosponsored by his university, with proceeds going to a scholarship program for visual arts students. It was a major event for his university, and he'd gotten what felt like hundreds of email about it.

The event was cocktails and an art show, featuring both some student pieces, and "never-before-exhibited pieces from private collections." The header image for the email had five panels, alternating images of art pieces and fresh-faced art students. The center image was a photo of a sculpture that looked similar to the grainy photo in the ERR album.

Jasper and Irina looked at each other, then leaned forward, studying Eli's phone and the copy of the ERR album page.

Jasper touched the page reverently. "A Rodin sculpture." His voice was colored by wonder, as if he'd just opened the perfect present Christmas morning.

"And if I'm right, we need to leave Boston." Eli tucked his phone into his pocket. "Tonight."

Chapter Four

"I hate these things." Eli tugged on the collar of his shirt with one hand, keeping the other on the wheel.

"Elegant parties?" Irina had reclined the passenger seat as far back as it would go. Eli had looked at her like she was crazy when she told him that sitting up would wrinkle her dress. The gold dress, made of heavy but wrinkle-prone silk, had been the best she could do on such short notice. She had an entire closet full of appropriate dresses at her condo in D.C., but there hadn't been time for her to have one shipped to her.

Twenty-four hours ago they'd been sitting in a coffee shop in Boston. Now they were in Denver, having taken the first flight out this morning. They'd used Eli's house as command central. It was a lovely Craftsman-style, single-family home with a view of the mountains. Irina had wanted to explore every inch of it—to snoop through his books and his medicine cabinet. But instead she'd grabbed Eli's car keys, made a whirlwind trip through a cute boutique for the dress, shoes, and clutch, then done a few other errands, and returned with just enough time to shower and get dressed.

By the time she was dry, she'd had less than half an hour to get out the door. No time for exploring.

"Grown-up clothes?" Jasper guessed in response to Eli's statement. His voice was crystal clear in her left ear. Before they left Boston last night, Irina had taken Jasper to the Bennett Securities' headquarters. No questions asked when Irina and Jasper told the tech department what they needed, and they'd left with a whole bag of fun gizmos.

Eli veered toward oncoming traffic when Jasper spoke. Irina yelped.

"You two okay?" Jasper asked. He'd left before they did, setting up shop in a twenty-four-hour diner two miles away from the factory-turned-hip-event space where the gala was taking place.

"Eli almost drove us off the road."

"You startled me," Eli protested. "This is weird, having this thing in my ear. It's probably giving me brain cancer."

Jasper snorted.

"I guess I'm dying young, since I spend most of my working hours wearing one of these," Irina said dryly.

There was a beat of silence, then Jasper said, "Don't joke about dying."

Irina's heart clenched. These weren't her team members on a protection detail. These were her husbands. Or they would be, and sooner than anyone expected, if Eli was right and he'd identified the sculpture correctly.

She had to keep reminding herself that they were a trinity, bound together. The task they'd been given had put their relationship on the back burner. Last night they'd all gone to their separate rooms by mutual, if silent, accord.

"I'm sorry, to both of you." Irina hoped they could tell she was sincere. "But I'm fairly certain the earbuds aren't causing brain cancer."

"We're here." Eli pulled up to a valet.

Irina flipped down the visor and checked her makeup. She'd gone for gold tones on her eyes, and bronzer used as blush to play off the dark gold dress. With her dark hair pulled back in a tight bun, the whole look had a regal Egyptian feel.

The valet offered his hand, but Eli was already circling around to her door. The valet backed off.

When Irina put her fingers in Eli's, awareness shot through her. She'd opted for low heels with ankle straps, and when she stepped out of the car, Eli towered over her. He was wearing cologne, or aftershave, and smelled amazing.

The way his eyes lingered on her décolletage made Irina think she wasn't the only one who was affected.

Irina slipped the strap of the wristlet purse onto her left arm, leaving her dominant right hand free.

"Wait," Eli said. "I have something for you. It's not anything special. When I saw your dress, well..." He frowned, blinked, tugged on his jacket, then opened the back door and pulled out a folded piece of fabric. He shook it out, holding it up for Irina to see.

It was a rectangular scarf, long enough to be used as a drape. It was black, painted with gold lotuses and Chinese dogs.

"It was a gag gift from a colleague, after I wrote a paper on the mixing of artistic styles. They thought it was funny since these are—"

"Egyptian lotuses and Chinese Fu dogs." Irina turned her back to Eli, who hesitated then laid it over her shoulders. His hands stayed there, and Irina shivered.

"Are you cold?" Eli asked.

"No, not cold."

"I can feel the sexual tension from here, you two." Jasper sounded decidedly grumpy.

Irina turned to the valet. "We have to leave early. Could you park our car right there?" Irina pointed to one of the metered street parking spots the valets had blocked off with cones. She wiggled her fingers, making sure to draw attention to the folded fifty she was using as a pointer. The valet grinned, moved the cones, jumped in the car, pulled it into the spot, and jumped out, running up to Irina.

"Keys," she said.

With a shrug, the valet gave Irina back the keys and took the fifty. Irina tucked the keys into her wristlet.

Eli looked adorably befuddled. Irina touched his cheek. That seemed to snap him out of it, and Eli turned and kissed the inside of her wrist. Irina gasped as arousal shot through her.

"What was that? What are you two doing?" Jasper demanded.

Eli grinned and winked at Irina, who bit back a smile.

"I heard that," Jasper said.

"We didn't say anything," Eli replied.

"I still heard it. From now on I want a running dialogue of what's going on. You're together, so everyone will assume you're just talking to each other."

"I think maybe you're not used to being the one in the van." Irina took Eli's arm and let him guide her to the entrance. "I made sure the valet left the car parked at the curb and got the keys back."

"He's in a van?" Eli asked.

"No, I'm eating vegan cheese fries, God help me. Good call on the car, Irina."

"'In the van' just means the person left behind," she told Eli.

The gala was being held at an old warehouse, in a once industrial section of the city. "Old warehouse" painted a picture of rusted metal and decay, but this was a lovely three-story brick building with high arched windows. The main entrance was recessed into a large archway. A small desk was set up to one side, with a cluster of evening-wear-clad people poring over sheets of paper secured to clipboards.

"Welcome." An elegant man, wearing a chic, if nontraditional suit with visible stitching, greeted them as they reached the desk. "Name, please?"

"Dr. Eli Wexler and guest."

"Dr. Wexler, welcome. We're so glad you were able to attend, at the last minute." The end of the sentence was precisely enunciated.

Eli didn't react, but Irina had to hide a smile. This guy must be the event planner, and clearly none too pleased by Eli's very last-minute RSVP.

"We accept cash or credit for the tickets. And we'll need some information from your guest."

Irina accepted the clipboard as Eli dug out his wallet. She filled out her information, using her work email address, since she was sure that she would forevermore receive invitations and solicitations from the event organizers, and Bennett Securities' spam filters were some of the best.

They were passed off to a perky, young Asian girl in a black cocktail dress and gaudy green earrings. "Right, uh, this way, Professor Wexler."

Eli frowned at her. "Did you take my class last semester?"

She smiled, opening the door for them. "Yes. I loved your class. It was, like, the best."

Eli reached over her head, held the door open, and motioned for her to precede him. "Maxine, correct?"

"Wow, you remember. Yeah, yes. But I go by Max. I'm getting a minor in Art History now. I'm totally going to take the next class you teach."

"Max. Well, thank you. That's quite a compliment."

Max led them into the building. The ceiling here was low, probably eight feet, with narrow corridors. They turned left, then right, and another right before reaching an elevator, and Irina realized that every guest would need to be escorted, otherwise there would be a lot of lost partygoers. The route was also marked out on the unfinished concrete floor with periodically placed floor decals bearing the event name.

"I volunteered to help with the party so I could look at the art. The tickets are like, crazy expensive."

"Crazy expensive is an accurate description." Eli smiled down at Max, who blushed under his regard. "I'm not a fan of parties. But I wanted to see the exhibit too."

Max looked at Irina out of the corner of her eye, a quick assessment. Then she smiled hesitantly. Irina returned her smile. It was clear Max either had a crush on Eli, or some academic hero worship. She'd assessed Irina, and rather than being jealous, had realized that the professor she idolized had a beautiful adult woman on his arm.

Eli caught Max looking at Irina. "Oh, excuse me. Irina, this is Max, one of my students."

"It's a pleasure to meet you, Max." Irina nodded, rather than offer her hand.

"Nice to meet you too." The elevator doors dinged open, and Max reached in, pressed a button, then held the door. "The party just started, so you're one of the first people here. I already pushed the button for you."

"Thank you, Max." Eli guided Irina into the elevator. The doors dinged closed.

"Let me guess," Jasper said. "Max is a gorgeous coed?"

"With a big crush on *Professor Wexler*," Irina replied.

Eli shifted. "She does not have a crush on me."

"Yes, she does. Also you're blushing."

"Take a picture," Jasper begged.

"I'm ignoring both of you." Eli faced straight ahead as the doors opened.

The second floor of the warehouse stretched before them, a massive space, open to the elegant wood beams of the roof two stories above.

A network of spotlights hung from a large rigging grid that had been suspended halfway between floor and ceiling. Freestanding walls provided hanging space for the art, each piece lit by a spotlight. Another black-clad undergrad handed them programs, then pointed out the silent auction area and bar.

Eli dropped Irina's arm and immediately started flipping through the program.

Irina cleared her throat. "I'd love something to drink."

Eli frowned at the program.

The elevator dinged. They were blocking the way, and the undergrad with the programs was starting to look alarmed. Irina cleared her throat again, tugging on Eli's arm.

"For God's sake, man, get the woman a drink!" Jasper yelled.

Eli jumped, program flapping in his hand. He started to curse, then blinked hard. "Drink. Right."

Eli started walking. Irina nudged him until they were headed in the right direction.

"Talk to me," Jasper demanded.

"We're headed to the bar, calm down," Eli grumped.

"That's not what he means." Irina didn't bother to hide her amusement. "We're on the second floor, which was clearly the machinery floor. Large open space. Five, six thousand square feet. Elevator shaft and one, maybe two closed rooms on the east end of the building. Windows in the north and south walls. I can't see the west wall. I'd assume there's a fire exit there. No visible stairs near the elevator."

"What's on the first floor?" Jasper asked.

"Just so you know, Eli is looking at me like I have two heads," Irina reported.

"I didn't think real people talked like that." There was a frown line between Eli's brows.

"People who work security do," Irina responded.

"And people who like to break into places."

Eli opened his mouth. Closed it, then said, "What do you want to drink?"

"Champagne if they have it. Prosecco if they don't."

Irina remained silent while the bartender poured her sparkling wine and Eli's vodka tonic.

When they walked away from the bar, she finished her report. "The first floor is a rabbit warren. They have hostesses guiding partygoers from the front door to the elevator. The front door is in the south wall, but not in the center. It's closer to the east end of the building."

"That explains Max," Jasper said.

"Can I ask a question?" Eli handed Irina his drink. She didn't like having both hands occupied, but she allowed it.

"Of course," Irina said.

Eli opened the program. "We're just here to find the sculpture, look at it, and figure out who owns it. Why does it matter what the layout of the building is?"

"It's just...what you do," Irina answered. It had never occurred to her *not* to assess the location.

"Always have a backup plan. Know your exits," Jasper added.

Eli shook his head. "The two of you are what I figured the majority of the Trinity Masters' members are like."

"What do you mean?" Irina laced her arm carefully through Eli's, still holding both drinks.

"More James Bond than Joseph Campbell." Eli frowned at the program. "I actually thought maybe I wasn't going to get called to the altar. Like maybe I was a pity member."

"Pity member?" Irina frowned at him. "If anything, you're what the Trinity Masters should be. A scholar."

"A towering intellect," Jasper added.

"A man above reproach," Irina teased.

"It's above suspicion," Eli said. "And it's a woman above suspicion."

Irina smiled. "You're proving my point."

"*Ave Uxor Caesar*," Jasper added.

Eli rolled his eyes, so Irina assumed whatever Jasper had said was snarky.

She nudged Eli with her shoulder, wanting to make sure to address his original statement. "I know a lot of members. There are plenty of musicians, artists, and academics. The Trinity Masters aren't just about protection and power. It's meant to be more than that. The Trinity Masters should stand for everything that makes this country great. That's you."

"Here, here," Jasper said.

Irina hoped Eli would smile, but he didn't.

"He's blushing again," Irina lied. He hadn't been blushing, but once she said it, his eyes crinkled with embarrassment.

"Picture!" Jasper demanded.

"You two are..." Eli trailed off, eyes on the program, then he stiffened. "Here it is. A Rodin. Just like the listing in the ERR album."

"You found it?" Jasper asked.

"Just a listing for a Rodin bronze. There's no photo in the program. And there's also no map."

"So now you put the program away, take your drink, and we'll stroll through the gallery until we find it." Irina wanted to be in and out before the party really got going.

"What does the program say about who owns it?" Jasper asked.

"It doesn't. Just says 'from a private collection'." Eli tucked the program into his pocket and took his drink.

"I don't like that," Jasper said.

"Agreed," Eli said.

"Why?" Now it was Irina's turn to be confused.

"Because usually private collectors love to show off. Art is like an expensive car, or a Rolex. You could have something cheaper that did the same thing, but the point is that you're showing off your wealth. Lots of times people buy art and never hang or display it in their homes. It stays in a museum or gallery with a plaque with their name on it."

"So the fact that this piece isn't identified..."

"Means the owner wants to keep it private. They may just be private people..." Eli trailed off.

"Or they may be fully aware they own stolen Nazi art."

"If they know that, then why display it at all?"

"Because without the ERR album, the chance of someone being able to claim it is slim to none."

"So they're both showing off, and not showing off?" That didn't make sense to Irina.

"Exactly," Jasper said. "Arrogance tempered by caution. A classic rich-person combination."

"Let's find it." Eli changed position, putting his hand on the small of Irina's back, and guided her toward the first display.

Jasper hummed the Indiana Jones' theme song.

Eli looked at his empty glass and seriously contemplated throwing it against a brick wall.

"You're sure?" Jasper's voice in his ear had his fingers curling around the glass until his fingernails turned white.

"Of course we're—"

Irina put a hand on his chest, cutting him off. "Eli, take a deep breath. Jasper, we've been through the whole place twice. There are only three pieces of sculpture on display. None of them are ours."

"And none of them are Rodins," Eli added.

"Well, kids, I'm starting to have a bad feeling about this," Jasper said. "But that might be because I'm paranoid."

"I'm going to head downstairs and ask the event organizer." Irina eyed Eli. "You okay staying here?"

"Of course I'm okay."

"How about we get another drink first?" Irina towed him toward the bar.

"I just don't understand," Eli said, not for the first time. His stomach was burning with acid, something the vodka tonic Irina handed him wasn't going to help with. Part of the problem was, he didn't know why he was having such a strong reaction, why his muscles were tensed to the point that his shoulders were starting to ache. They'd checked every inch twice and even asked Max, who'd showed up an hour in, relieved of her hostess duties, to help. She'd come up empty-handed too.

"Drink," Irina said.

He took a sip, realized it wasn't a vodka tonic—it was just tonic water. The quinine flavor burned his tongue, but his stomach calmed down.

Irina touched his arm. "Stay here, I'll be right back."

"Wait. There's the dean. She'll know." Eli pulled Irina though the crowd, which was now thick enough to make navigating an exercise in social nicety.

The dean of the College of Letters, Arts, and Sciences, which included art history, was just finishing up a conversation when Eli swooped in. "Aliza."

Aliza Jones was an elegant African-American woman in her early seventies. She had skin many shades darker than Eli's, and hair that had turned mostly white, making her a visually striking figure. The effect was enhanced by the white coat and brightly patterned scarf she wore. She'd personally recruited him to the art history department, and he'd had dinner with her and her wife on several occasions.

"Eli. I didn't realize you were coming."

"I just RSVP'd yesterday."

"Eli." Aliza shook her head gently. "I hope this is a sign you plan to attend university events more regularly." Aliza's attention shifted to Irina. "Please introduce me."

Eli froze. *How was he supposed to introduce Irina?* He hadn't thought this all the way through.

"Eli. You need to say something. Act normal," Jasper barked.

"This is Irina…my fiancée."

Irina offered her hand to Aliza. "It's a pleasure to meet you."

Jasper's reaction was less controlled. "Wow. That's nice. Glad we had a conversation, all three of us, about how we were going to present our relationship to the outside world. I would hate it if one of us was a dick about it and just blurted out something. Why didn't you just say 'this is my friend Irina'?"

Eli fought to ignore Jasper—who had a point, but was distracting—focusing on Irina and Aliza.

"We were introduced by mutual friends," Irina was saying. Clearly Aliza had asked how they'd met while Eli had been distracted.

"That's lovely. I didn't realize Eli was seeing anyone."

"I travel quite a lot for work, so we're keeping it casual." Irina smiled.

"But you're engaged?"

Irina continued to smile, but Eli saw the slight panic in her eyes. "Given that we live in different states, we decided that we needed to make a commitment to one another if the relationship was going to move forward."

Aliza frowned at Eli. "Are you leaving us, Eli?"

This whole conversation was a cluster-fuck. "No. I'm not." There was a brief, awkward pause that Eli felt the need to fill. "Aliza, the only reason I'm here is because there was supposed to be a Rodin on display, but it's not here."

"It's not?" Aliza frowned. "Let me find out why not." She picked up her phone and sent a quick text. "The event manager is on his way up."

Luckily, someone else said "excuse me," interrupting their talk in hopes of speaking with the dean, which saved Irina and Eli from any more questions about their engagement.

"What was that, telling her we're engaged?" Irina asked him.

"Well, it's true," Eli said defensively.

"Yes, but we need to get our stories straight, and Jasper's right, it should have been something we discussed all together."

"I'm sorry, to both of you. It seemed like the logical thing to say."

"Well, what if Irina and I were the ones everyone thought were married, and you had to publicly remain single?" Jasper demanded. "Or what if we decided to be outside-the-box thinkers and actually present ourselves as being in a relationship, all three of us? Stoning is, mostly, out of fashion. Or what if *I* wanted to be your fiancé?"

"What? Are you serious?" Eli asked.

"Are you saying you think marriage should only be between hetero couples, you gender-norming troglodyte?"

"What?" Eli's voice was loud enough to have people looking over.

Irina faked a laugh, throwing her head back to show off the line of her throat, tapping Eli on the chest with her palm. She finished the laugh and turned her face toward Eli's chest, hiding her mouth.

"Jasper, knock it off. The vein in Eli's temple is going to pop."

"Fine, but we're having this conversation later."

"Of course," Irina soothed.

Eli raised his hand and thumped himself on the forehead with the heel of his palm. It was either that or start bashing his head against the wall.

Irina bit back a smile and pulled his hand down. She rubbed his forehead and winked at him.

"Eli?" Aliza called them over. The hip-looking man from downstairs who'd taken Eli's credit card was standing with the dean.

"One of our faculty members had a question about the pieces," Aliza said.

Eli took the program out of his pocket. "There's a Rodin sculpture listed in the program, but I don't see it on display."

The event planner pursed his lips. "The owner chose not to display some of the pieces."

"But the Rodin is in the program," Eli said.

"I'm well aware of that, but they made the request this morning, and we were unable to reprint the programs in time to reflect the changes." The man was speaking through gritted teeth.

"Well, that's disappointing. Did they say why?" Aliza asked.

"No, they didn't. If you'll excuse me, I'm going to check on the bar."

"Wait." Eli caught the man's arm. "I need the owner's name."

"I'm sorry, I can't give that information out."

Eli looked at the dean. "Aliza?"

"I'm afraid I don't know who the owners are. These events are organized entirely by the event company, along with the university advancement. Someone in development may know."

"Anonymity was a condition of the exhibition agreement. If you'll excuse me." The clearly irritated and stressed man pulled away.

Aliza frowned. "Email my assistant. She can connect you with our contact in advancement. If you really want to see the piece, maybe they'll be able to arrange something." Aliza patted Eli's forearm. "And while you do that, get on my calendar. We'll have you two over for dinner." She turned to talk to someone hovering at her elbow, waiting anxiously to speak to her.

Eli and Irina made their way to a bare stretch of exterior wall. Eli set his drink on the windowsill then rubbed the bridge of his nose.

"Irina." Jasper's voice was low and intense.

"I'm looking. I don't see anything, and how could they…" Irina's tone matched his. She trailed off, frowning.

"What?" Eli asked, alarm bells beginning to ring. Clearly he was late to that party, because Irina and Jasper had gone into crisis mode, and he had no idea why.

Irina had her back against the wall and was scanning the crowd.

"I've had a bad feeling for the past hour." Eli mimicked her posture. "I thought it was just me."

"This went from slightly concerning to a potential problem, so your gut was right," Jasper said. "I'm packing up. I'm coming to you."

"Why?" Eli asked. "What am I missing?"

"This unidentified private owner pulled art on the morning of an event. They wouldn't do that without a reason." Irina stopped scanning the crowd and looked at Eli. "When you RSVP'd, did you say anything? Mention the Rodin?"

Eli shook his head. "No, I just...I said I was interested in seeing the private collection. That's it."

"If they're paranoid, really paranoid, that might be enough. Especially if you're known for not attending things like this." There was background noise coming through the headset, along with Jasper's voice.

"You broke your behavior pattern." Irina adjusted the shawl he'd given her, looping it over her elbows then knotting the ends together behind her back so she didn't have to hold on to it. "I would be concerned, from a security standpoint."

"You're kidding. I'm just some random art history professor."

"And if you owned stolen art that you were planning to display, who would you be worried about?" Jasper was breathing heavily, and it sounded like he was running.

The fact that Jasper was running took Eli's alarm up several levels. "I'd be worried about...about anyone who might question the provenance of the pieces."

"Like an art history professor who specializes in the role of art in war."

"They had an alert set up, in case any art history people showed up?" Eli started looking around. "That can't be right. I'm sure there are other people from my department here."

"That's a question we need to answer, because the other possibility is that someone knows who you are...knows what you're a member of." Irina's words were calm, and she was smiling, but her eyes were tight.

Eli closed his eyes, exhaled, then opened his eyes again. "Let's just go. We'll walk out of here. You have the car keys. We'll go back to my place."

"Agreed that we should leave, but we're not going back to your place. We'll need to go to a hotel."

Eli's stomach clenched. "Is the situation really that bad?"

"I don't know, but safety requires extraordinary precaution." Irina turned to Eli. "In case anyone is watching, let's give them a hint about why we're leaving." She smiled at him and raised one brow.

Eli blinked. "I have no idea what you're talking about."

"Kiss her, you idiot," Jasper whispered.

"Uh, yeah. I can do that."

"I hope so, you chucklehead." The Boston accent was back in Jasper's voice, despite the fact that he was whispering.

Eli grabbed Irina, jerked her against him, and kissed her. She tasted like champagne, and smelled amazing. He had to bend to reach her lips, but when she stood up on her tiptoes, clinging to his shoulders, Eli was able to straighten enough to pull her body flush against his.

Irina broke the kiss. The way she looked up at him, eyes liquid pools of desire, her lips flushed and parted, made Eli want to push her against the wall and rip that dress right down the middle.

"Time to go," she whispered.

Eli nodded, but held her against his chest for another minute, giving himself time to settle down.

When he wouldn't embarrass himself, Eli offered her his arm. They were waiting for the elevator when Max ran over.

"Professor Wexler!"

"Hi, Max."

"I know where it is!"

Eli froze, turning his full attention to the girl. She dropped her gaze to his feet and fiddled with her earrings.

"You know where the Rodin sculpture is?"

"Yeah, I mean yes. It's on the first floor. That's where all the boxes and stuff for the rest of the art are. One of the event people I asked said that there were some pieces they hadn't unpacked, including one sculpture. That must be your Rodin, right?"

Eli grinned. "That's great, Max, thank—"

Irina cut in. "Who did you ask?"

In his ear, Jasper said, "Still boxed up. Copy."

"Uh, a couple of different people?" Max looked aghast at Irina's harsh tone.

"Where are you from, Maxine?" Irina asked.

"Seattle."

"Go downstairs, order a car, and go to the airport. Get on the first flight home. Say it was a family emergency."

"What? No. Why?"

"Because you may have put yourself in danger by asking about that sculpture."

Max's eyes widened. Eli's blood ran cold. Had they put this kid in harm's way?

Irina opened her clutch, pulled out some cash, and handed it to Max. "Use this. Go."

"Who are you?" she asked.

"It's safer that you don't know. Stay in Seattle for a week. Do you know anyone else at the party?"

"My roommate..."

"Go get her. Tell her there's a family emergency and you want her to come with you to the airport. Stay by her side. Walk out with her. You go together in the car. You keep your phone in your hand, not in your pocket. You ask her to wait with you at the airport. If you can't get a flight out tonight, you stay in the airport. Do you understand?"

"Is this real? Are you serious?" Max looked at Eli.

Eli nodded. "I'm so sorry, Max. I shouldn't have told you what I was looking for. Do what she says."

"I...okay. I'll do it."

"Go find your roommate." Irina pointed into the crowd and Max stumbled away, looking both terrified and excited.

"Irina, if that kid gets hurt because of me..."

"I'm sure she's going to be fine, but I like to cover all contingencies. The real question is—" Irina stabbed the down arrow. "Jasper, where are you?"

There was no answer.

"Shit." When the elevator door dinged open, Irina dragged Eli in. "Jasper, where are you?"

Chapter Five

Somebody has something to hide.

Jasper lowered the binoculars, scanned the alley, then went back to studying the security cameras covering the back door of the warehouse where Eli and Irina were. There were two cameras. One was a larger, industrial-looking piece of equipment. It had a long, tan, cylindrical body and was aimed to cover the alley. The second was a compact black camera with a 360-degree swivel, mounted on the doorframe. The wiring for that camera straggled along the brick, seemingly taped into place.

A secondary camera setup meant private security. The black camera was temporary, brought in by whoever was handling security for the event, the art, or both.

Jasper was crouched by a window in the stairwell of the residential building directly behind the event space. It too had once been a warehouse, but had been converted into condos. They'd stripped out the warehouse infrastructure, but kept the double-story windows. The stairwell gave him access to one of these windows, which meant a perfect—if not exactly private—vantage point for a little recon.

There was an elevator in the lobby, and Jasper was betting most residents would use that instead of the stairs. Just to be safe, he was keeping his voice to a whisper, since concrete, brick, and glass weren't known to muffle sounds.

Unlike Eli and Irina, he wasn't using an in-ear receiver/transmitter. He'd gone for normal bud-style headphones, which made it look like he was on the phone. That had saved him from having to hide the fact that he was talking while he'd been sitting in the diner. Not that sitting in a diner for hours, ordering odd vegan versions of comfort food while on what probably seemed like the world's longest phone call, wasn't odd. It was. But it wasn't call-the-cops territory.

However, if anyone stumbled across him now, it would be a different story. No one crouched near a window with binoculars to make a phone call. He might as well have a blinking sign over his head that said "nefarious."

He'd turned down the volume on Eli's and Irina's feeds so he could concentrate. When he heard Eli mention "Max," he turned up the volume. There was no one to see him grin when the girl reported that the sculpture was on the first floor.

"Still boxed up. Copy," Jasper said.

Time to move.

Slinging his gym bag over his shoulder, Jasper jogged down the stairs and out the lobby door, which some kind person had stupidly propped open.

He pulled the face mask—designed to keep neck and face up to the eye warm in cold weather running—bunched around his neck up over his face. If it had been the dead of winter in Denver, someone jogging in a hood and mask would make sense. At this time of year…not so much, but an active-wear mask was a lot less conspicuous than a full ski mask.

He slid his arms through the straps of his gym bag, which could be worn backpack style. He paused, stretched a bit, jogged in place, then started down the sidewalk. When he reached the corner of the building, he turned into the alley that separated the warehouse and condos. He watched the black camera out of the corner of his eye. It swiveled to follow him.

He kept going, and when he reached the end of the alley he turned left, so he was on the west side of the warehouse. He'd circled the building in his rental car before finding the recon position in the condo, so he knew there were two fire exit doors in the west wall, one atop the other. The staircase for the second-floor door partially obscured the lower door.

Jasper stopped, propped his heel on the fourth step, and leaned over his leg, as if he was working out a cramp. There was a second large camera here, but no smaller black camera.

He changed legs and quickly ran through what he knew.

First, there was someone actively monitoring and manipulating a secondary camera on the back door. Second, there were three doors on the ground level. The first door was the main entrance, covered by event staff and party guests. The door immediately opposite that one had the camera. That left only this emergency exit door.

Either this door didn't open or was wired to an alarm. Only one way to find out.

Jasper slid up to the door, which was helpfully shadowed by the landing directly overhead. He jumped up, grabbed the landing support and did a few pull-ups, maintaining the guise of slightly-shady-dude-out-exercising for as long as possible.

He dropped down, took off his backpack, and grabbed a small magnetic plate, tucking it into his pocket, then he pulled out a suction cup and shim.

Breaking in was a big gamble, but worth it. If the alarm went off, they'd evacuate the building—they'd have to, for safety purposes, and the chaos might provide a chance for him to sneak in, though the alarm would put the security team on high alert.

If he managed to keep the alarm from going off, he'd have a chance to snoop around.

He was vaguely aware of Irina's voice coming through the headphones, but his attention was on the door. Like most fire doors, there was no external handle. It was designed to let panicky people out, not nefarious people in. However, the fact that it opened out meant it was vulnerable. There was no doorjamb guarding the vulnerable space between door and frame.

Jasper attached the small suction cup, no bigger than his palm, to the door, then slid the thin, flexible, u-shaped metal shim between door and frame. He wiggled it until he felt the tongue of the lock. Rocking the shim back and forth, he managed to position it so that the ends were sticking out. Grabbing both in one hand, he grabbed the suction cup with the other.

He pulled the metal shim. The bend of the "u" slid along the tongue of the door closure mechanism, retracting it as if the door handle had been pushed.

Leaving the shim in place so the door couldn't catch again, Jasper took the magnet from his pocket. This was the dangerous part. If this door followed a standard layout, the alarm would be controlled by a magnetic connection in the top corner of the frame. Once the door was opened, and the magnetic connection was broken, the alarm would sound. If he could slap his magnet into place before the broken connection triggered the alarm, he'd have the door open, no alarm.

If he couldn't, or if this particular door had the magnets in a different place, or used a different kind of contact system, such as a laser, the alarm was about to go off and things were about to get tricky.

"Brace yourselves," he said, sotto voce.

"Why?" Irina asked sharply, her voice a mere thread of sound through his headphones.

"Oh hell," was Eli's response.

Grinning despite his irritation at the other man—Jasper couldn't believe Eli had blurted out that Irina was his fiancée—Jasper started to whistle the tune to "The Gambler."

"Is that a clue?" Eli demanded. "Know when to fold 'em?"

"Jasper, we're on the first floor." Irina's voice was controlled but intense. "Do we leave or stay?"

Jasper yanked open the door and slammed the magnet into the top corner of the doorjamb.

He waited one second, two. Nothing happened.

"I'm in," he whispered.

"In *where?*" Irina hissed.

Jasper hooked his foot in the backpack straps, kicked it inside, then entered and let the door close behind him. The magnet was just thin enough to allow the door to close. That was what he'd hoped. It meant that if he had to exit at a run, he could leave through this door and the alarm wouldn't go off.

Irina and Eli were talking, but not to him. It sounded like Irina was being introduced to someone Eli knew. He heard Eli use the word fiancée. Jasper gritted his teeth.

The space on the other side of the door was dark, and felt closed in, as if he'd walked into a closet. He carefully extended his arms. He was in a hallway, narrow enough that he could touch both sides. Fishing through his bag, he found the night-vision monocle by feel and held it up.

There was just enough ambient light that the night-vision device worked.

"I'm going for the Rodin," he said, hoping they could hear him through the mask. He moved quickly, speed more important than stealth. He reached a T-junction, turned north. Best bet was that the art was stored near the monitored back door, which was on the east side of the north wall.

Drawing a mental map as he went, Jasper was, by his estimation, halfway to the back door when he heard voices. Light seeping from around an ill-fitted door glared white in the night vision, so he tucked the monocle into his bag.

Dropping to his belly, he was able to peer through the gap under the door.

Four feet. Two people. Black tactical pants and combat boots.

Whoa.

Security for an event like this should have been wearing suits and those ugly black shoes bouncers favored, the kind that allowed people to stand for hours. Tactical gear was completely out of character.

Jasper considered his options. He could turn around and go back. He was loath to let a truly beautiful unlawful entry go to waste. It needed some grand larceny to really round out the night.

Jasper moved and started going through his bag, thinking as he quietly sorted his gear. He needed a distraction. Irina's raised voice got his attention.

"I am pulling the fire alarm in twenty, nineteen, eighteen—"

"Hold on." Jasper adjusted the volume on the headphones so he could hear them clearly, but dropped one earphone out, tucking it into the edge of the mask, so he wasn't completely deaf to what was happening around him.

"Where are you?" Eli demanded.

"I'm in the building. On the first floor. I think I know where the Rodin is. I have two guards. They look more military than secret service."

There was a pregnant pause. "Get out." Irina's voice was sharp.

"I'm setting up a distraction, then I'm going in."

"Can you hear us?" Eli's voice rumbled with irritation and a hint of alarm. "Irina, who is a professional, said get out."

"She's a professional protector of people. I'm a professional protector of things. We're talking about art. My area. You two follow my lead." Jasper kept his voice low, but let the steel seep into his words. He did not enjoy being questioned or directed. Not in the middle of a heist.

There was a pregnant pause.

"You need a distraction?" Irina asked.

Jasper plucked at the mask as he considered. He was so used to working alone, it hadn't occurred to him to ask them to create the distraction. This was definitely the other side of the double-edged sword that was working with a "team."

"Yeah, I do. You got something?"

Eli's groan was audible. "I'm not going to like this, am I?"

"You're not going to be involved." Irina's tone was firm, brooking no argument. "I don't want to draw any more attention to you. We're going to find you somewhere to stay out of sight."

Jasper filled his pockets with what he thought he'd need while he listened to Irina. He crouched, hand on the doorknob, head down, backpack zipped and on, when she made her move.

Eli put his back against the wall. He'd thought he was nervous when he'd waited to meet his trinity, but those feelings were nothing compared to the heart-exploding level of anxiety he was currently dealing with as he listened to Irina leave.

"Excuse me, excuse me!" Her heels clicked as she ran toward the front door. Eli started to lean to the side to listen to Irina's retreating voice, before he remembered that he'd be able to hear what happened next through the earpiece.

Eli inched farther into the shadows. He was standing in a short hallway that dead-ended in a battered door. The renovation of this space into an event venue clearly hadn't included a full revamp of every nook and corner of the first floor. They'd turned away from the main route that took guests from the front door to the elevator while talking to Jasper. Irina had checked the corridors, hallways, and alcoves, before designating this as the safest place for Eli to wait.

"Ma'am, are you okay?" The speaker's voice coming though the earpiece was faint, but audible.

"No, my bracelet. It's gone." Irina's tone was worried, bordering on panicked.

"Bracelet?"

"Yes. I have to find it."

"Are you sure you were wearing it?" The man's voice sounded calm and professional, not at all concerned. Eli thought it was the same event planner they'd dealt with two other times tonight.

"Yes, I'm sure. It's a Grande Gioielli cuff. It's on loan from a jeweler in Boston."

"On loan." Now a note of alarm crept into the man's voice. "What does it look like?"

"Rose gold. White and black diamonds. It's a large piece. Please, my fiancé is looking around upstairs, but there's no way he'll find it with all the people. Can you make an announcement?"

"We'll help you look. Javier, stay here. The rest of you, come with me."

"What if someone stole it? Where's the guest list? Has anyone left? Are there security cameras?" Irina's voice rose with each question.

There was a pause, then the man Irina was speaking to said, "I'm sure it simply fell off. Give me a moment to gather everyone."

There was a moment of silence, then the sound of people talking, but they were far enough away from Irina that they weren't understandable.

"He's speaking with someone," Irina reported, sotto voce. "Now he's on the phone."

Eli was so focused on what he was hearing from Irina's feed, he almost missed the faint sound coming from the door beside him.

He stopped breathing, hoping that would help him hear better, but the distant sound of voices coming through the earpiece made it hard for him to tell where sound was coming from. He took out the earpiece, closing it into his fist.

The sound came again, a *thump*, as if something had hit the door from the other side.

Eli stared at the door in horror. Should he move? He didn't know if Irina's plans depended on him staying where he was. He might throw the proverbial wrench if he left this spot.

Then again, being discovered here would raise questions they didn't want to answer.

Eli looked at the door. He had to squint, because there was no light in this short hall. The only illumination bounced from the fixtures around the corner into this dim little space. The door was drenched in shadow. Pulling his phone from his pocket with his free hand, Eli held it up, using the soft light of the screen, not the flash, to examine the door in detail. It was covered in layers of paint that had flaked away in places, revealing the strata of color choices and, in a few places, exposed metal that was weak with rust. This door was not often used. Based on the way the paint formed an unbroken seam along the edges, it looked like this door had been painted shut long ago, and not opened since.

Eli took two careful steps closer to the door, and leaned until his ear was almost touching it. There was another *thump*, tinged with the high ringing sound of metal. Something was hitting the door.

Legs tensed to bolt out of there, Eli held himself still and continued to listen. Now he could hear voices— faint, indistinguishable, like the muffled sound of a radio playing in a car two lanes over.

He stuck the earpiece back in.

"...make an announcement upstairs, and everyone we have is helping search." The man was back, talking to Irina.

"Thank you. I have to find it. I just have to. I'm going to call the police, just in case."

"You're of course welcome to do so, if that's what you feel is necessary, but let's just check and see if you dropped it."

Eli didn't like the tone the man was taking with Irina—patronizing and irritated.

"Asshat," Jasper whispered.

"Agreed," Eli replied in his softest voice.

Irina didn't respond directly to their comments, for obvious reasons, but said, "Thank you." There was something in her voice that made Eli think she was fighting a smile. "You're probably right. I probably dropped it..."

"The guards are doing something." Jasper's voice was crisp. "They're going out of a door or down another hallway."

Eli, still leaning toward the door, heard a few thumps, louder than before. The sound of voices was louder too. Eli strained to make out what was being said, but didn't catch any of it. The thumps sounded like they were moving things—there was a rhythm to it. *Pause. Talking. Thump, thump. Pause. Talking.*

It went on for what felt like half an hour, but was, according to his phone clock, only three minutes. Then there was a sound Eli could positively identify. The sound of a door closing.

"It was definitely a room," Jasper said. "I just heard a door close."

Eli blinked. He and Jasper were quite literally looking at two sides of the same issue. "Jasper, I think—"

"Now they're walking." Jasper spoke quickly, bowling over the top of Eli's comment. "They're gone. I'm going off com. I need fifteen minutes, Irina."

Irina didn't reply. She was talking to someone, but the conversation was muted, as if she'd covered her com in some way.

"Jasper?" Eli waited, but there was no reply. "Irina?" Again no reply.

Eli willed himself to calm down. His arm muscles were twitching again. Wherever Jasper was, he was able to see the outside of that door Eli heard close.

A radio squawked. A muffled voice spoke.

Eli's eyes widened. He took two oh-so-careful steps away from the door, covered his mouth and whispered, "Jasper, there's someone still in the room. Don't go. There's someone still in the room."

No response.

"Irina, what should I do?"

No response.

"What the hell is the point of this stupid ear thing if no one but me is using it?"

No response.

Jasper and Irina were both drastically better prepared to handle this situation than he was, so there was probably no need for him to do anything. He wasn't arrogant enough to assume that he—an academic—would be able to do something Jasper or Irina weren't.

Jasper was going to do...something, then bust open the door to the bad guy's room.

Eli blinked, then straightened. It wasn't just the bad guy's room. If there had, until a moment ago, been men at the door, and there was currently one person still in the room, this was the room where they were storing the art. In his panicked, adrenaline-addled state, he had lost track of what was really important.

The Rodin was on the other side of this door.

Filled with the godlike fury of a righteous academic, Eli grabbed the knob, put his shoulder against the door, and shoved.

Chapter Six

Jasper used the trusty credit card trick to open the door he'd been hiding behind. The door had been locked, but it was an older interior door, and popped open easily with the application of a flexible store loyalty card—he'd found they worked far better than actual credit cards for this particular B&E method.

The door popped open, and Jasper let it swing on its own, his left side pressed against the wall. There was no reaction to the open door, so he slid into the light.

After ten minutes spent in the dark, the hallway beyond seemed glaringly bright. Once his eyes adjusted, the reality was that sporadic low-wattage bulbs gave the hallways a sickly yellow cast. There were folding chairs at the far end of the hall, where another door, this one with a cracked glass panel, had been propped open with a toolbox. The floor was dusty, and that dust was like an archaeological record, telling the story of movement.

All along the hall were inset doorways. Each of them was a potential danger point—the alcoves were deep enough to hide a person. Hidden guards seemed unlikely. More dangerous was the possibility that there were cameras mounted in the shadows. Jasper used gloved fingers to make sure the mask was riding high on his cheeks, and pulled the hood forward. It wasn't the perfect camouflage, but it would have to do.

It was easy to identify the door he wanted, due to the unusually clean floor in front of it. Head down, he walked quickly but quietly to the door. His hands were in the pouch pocket of his sweatshirt, credit card in one hand, lock pick in the other.

He crouched, put his hand on the doorknob, and twisted. He wanted to listen to the sound the door made when the lock caught. If you knew what you were doing, the sound a lock made could tell you what you were up against.

But the doorknob turned under his hand. Jasper wasn't expecting it and lost his balance, tipping forward from his crouch onto his knees, effectively shoving the door open.

"Hands up!" There were three thudding steps and a guard appeared, gun already drawn. "I'm armed and will shoot you if you give me cause."

Jasper froze, head and hands rising slowly.

The room was packed with wooden boxes. Anyone who'd ever seen a heist movie featuring art would recognize the boxes for what they were—art crates. Packing and transporting fine art was an art form of its own. Jasper should know; he was a consultant for one of the larger packing and moving companies. Art crates were custom-made of specially fumigated wood, and lined with foam and anti-friction and anti-static fabric. The people who made the crates usually had training as furniture makers.

He'd been right about where the art was. He'd been wrong about all the guards leaving. A tall man, hair cut in the classic high and tight, pointed the muzzle of a gun at Jasper's head. His face was terrifyingly blank—the mask of a trained soldier.

"Stand up. Face the wall. Keep your hands above your head."

Jasper shifted his weight, planted his left foot on the floor.

Deep in the room, behind the stacks of crates, something thudded. The uppermost crate in a floor-to-ceiling stack wobbled precariously.

The guard flinched at the sound, and moved to keep Jasper in sight while he also examined the stacked boxes. He shifted to a one-handed gun hold, and raised his free hand to the radio on his shoulder.

Another *thud*; the top crate wobbled then fell.

The eighteen-inch square crate tipped off the stack, landing edge-first on the smaller stack in front of it. The box teetered there, balanced for a moment. Something moved near the back wall.

Yet another *thud*, and Jasper could see a thin wedge of dim light widening with each sound. There was a door back there.

The teetering crate tumbled forward, cracking against the guard's head. He staggered to the side, the hand that had been on his radio grabbing his head. For a moment it seemed that he might crumple from the blow to the head. The guard stumbled a few steps and braced himself on a table, leaning on the gun.

Jasper jumped up. This was no time for a fair fight—a concept Jasper found laughable at best and stupid at worst.

Grabbing the wrist of the hand on the man's head, Jasper jerked his arm back. The guard reared up, since his shoulder didn't give him the option of rotating with the movement.

Jasper used the shift in the guard's center of gravity against him, yanking hard on his arm and then jumping out of the way.

The man managed one stumbling back step, and if he'd had space might have recovered his balance, but he tripped over the box that had cracked him on the head.

When he hit the ground, the gun fell out of his hand.

That was what Jasper had been waiting for. He snatched up the gun then yanked the radio free from the guard's shoulder clip. A few quick twists and he'd separated the hand mic and cord, rendering it useless.

Pressing the gun against the guard's temple—the man was still conscious but in too much pain to do anything—Jasper looked up for the secondary threat. While he'd been disarming this guard, there'd been additional noises coming from deeper in the room. Jasper planned to hold the guard hostage to keep his partner in check.

But it wasn't another guard that had been making all that noise.

Eli looked like an avenging god. His jacket was gone, his dress shirt strained against his muscles, and his face was streaked with dirt or dust—whatever it was, it evoked war paint.

Jasper started to say something, stopped. He couldn't have been more shocked if Elvis had popped out of a box and started singing.

"Where's the Rodin?" Eli demanded.

Jasper winced. The guard was suspiciously still, his eyes closed. He wasn't unconscious. He was playing dead and listening. Eli had just given away why they were here. "Hopefully it's not in the box that fell on *this* guy."

Eli's gaze dropped to the man Jasper held at gunpoint. Eli's complexion didn't lend itself to blanching, but his eyes rounded in horror. "My God."

"Don't worry, he didn't lose consciousness. We just need to—"

"Did you check the box? What is in it?"

"And clearly you're worried about the art, not the man who almost killed me. Fair enough. There's duct tape in my backpack. Get it."

Eli pulled the blood-spattered crate into the light and examined it.

"Or don't be helpful. That's fun too."

Jasper shifted the gun from hand to hand as he shrugged out of the backpack straps. The roll of silver tape was easy to find one-handed.

Eli had gotten the box open. It was empty except for carefully formed foam and padding and a plastic sleeve mounted on the inside of the lid with an inventory sheet.

"Hey, you," Jasper hissed. He threw the tape at Eli. "Help."

With Eli's assistance, they bound the guard's hands behind him with tape. They did the same for his ankles and then hog-tied him by taping ankles to wrists. They wound tape around his head, gagging him.

Jasper looked at the guard and shook his head.

"What?" Eli asked.

Jasper tugged him to the corner. "We're out of time. It's been fifteen minutes."

"That's it? Feels like it's been hours."

"The other guards could come back at any time. We've got to leave, and we'll be coming out hot."

"Not without the Rodin."

"There's no time. The fact that there was a third guard we didn't know about—"

"I knew." Eli crossed his arms. "I heard him. I tried to tell you. Both of you. No one was listening."

Jasper whistled. "I fucked up." He frowned as he realized something. "You realized I was about to walk into what was effectively a trap?"

Eli didn't reply.

"Well shit. I *really* fucked up. Thank you." Just as he'd done at their binding, Jasper grabbed Eli and kissed him, hard and quick. "Let's get out of here."

"Not without the Rodin."

"There's *no time*."

Eli ignored him and turned to the crates.

Jasper considered pistol-whipping Eli, but he was too big for Jasper to move as a dead weight. Sticking the buds into his ears, Jasper said, "Irina, we have a bad situation. Buy us fifteen more minutes."

The chatter coming from Irina's feed seemed loud in the quiet room. "Ten," she whispered.

"Ten, if you get the car and meet us in the alley by the back door."

"Be there at nine twenty-one," she said.

Jasper checked his watch, then whipped around and got to work.

"Stop playing with it," Jasper snapped.

Eli was in the backseat, crate cradled on his lap. He set the lid back in place when Jasper yelled at him. He was holding a Rodin in his lap. A new Rodin. Well, it wasn't new, but it was new to the art world. Oh, the peer-reviewed papers he would write…

Eli grinned and hugged the box.

"I'm out," Irina reported via the com link.

Fifteen minutes ago, she'd raced Eli's car into the alley, then jumped out and run back into the party, leaving the car to Jasper and Eli, who had hauled their loot into the alley, thrown it in the car, and taken off.

"Let's get the story straight," Irina said. "Eli, I told them that you'd gone home to check for the bracelet, and that you'd called to say you found it. I then said I was taking a cab home. That explains your absence, but there are huge holes in the timeline."

Eli hadn't even thought about their "story," let alone worried about getting it straight. The giddy feelings inspired by the Rodin started to fade.

"We're about five minutes out," Jasper said. He was driving Eli's car, and Irina was driving Jasper's rental.

"In and out," Irina reminded them. "We wouldn't be going back at all if we could help it."

Eli's stomach clenched at her words. "What are you talking about?"

"We've got to get out of town." Irina's voice softened. "It's not safe here, Eli."

"Why?"

"Because we left a trail a mile wide for them to follow." Jasper braked for a yellow light. He was following every possible rule of the road. "It will take them less than ten minutes to connect the theft to you, Eli."

"And to me. I used my real name to register for the event." Irina sounded disgusted. "I was introduced to half the attendees as Eli's fiancée."

"That guard we taped up will be able to ID you from a picture." Jasper looked at Eli in the rearview mirror as he spoke.

Eli shook his head. "Wait, when you say it like that, it makes it sound like—"

"Like you just planned and executed an art heist." Jasper's voice was flat. "You RSVP'd at the last minute, with a woman who you claim to be engaged to but whom you'd never talked about before tonight. You asked questions about a specific piece of art. You were missing from the party during the time that same piece of art was stolen. The private security was pulled away by a crisis manufactured by your supposed fiancée."

Eli's whole body flushed cold then hot. "No, that's not..."

"That's exactly what it looks like. And it means either cops or private security will be at your house any minute now." Jasper pulled into Eli's driveway. "I'm going in. I will be out in three minutes. We will unload this car, and as soon as Irina gets here, load everything into the rental."

Jasper was out the driver's door, running into the garage, which he'd opened with the remote.

Eli looked down at the box in his lap.

"Eli?" Irina's tone was worried. "You okay? I'm coming."

He didn't answer. He couldn't. He'd just lost everything, and hadn't even realized it.

"Eli, say something. I need to know you're okay."

"Why?" he asked.

"Why what?"

"Why did you two do this?"

Irina pulled into his driveway. She jumped out at the same time that Jasper came out of the house, suitcases under his arms.

Irina yanked open Eli's door. "We're going to talk about this, but for the next ninety seconds we have to focus on moving. Will you agree to that, for the next ninety seconds?" Irina was calm and focused, the soft, inquiring tones of a moment ago gone, replaced by short, sharp questions to which the only answer was yes.

Eli got out, holding the crate with the Rodin. The sculpture was small, the crate roughly two and a half feet square. Eli crossed the few feet between his car and the rented SUV, climbing into the backseat and placing the sculpture beside him. He felt like he was moving underwater—his limbs were heavy, sounds muffled.

He saw Irina and Jasper exchange a glance.

If he were moving in slow motion, they were in fast-forward. Jasper loaded their suitcases into the back. Irina tossed Jasper's backpack from Eli's car into the rental, then opened the trunk.

"Uh, what else did we steal?" she asked.

There were painting crates and two small sculpture crates in the back of Eli's car.

"Eli insisted we take them."

Jasper drove Eli's car into the garage, closing the garage door as he turned off the car. Less than a minute later, he emerged from the house and ran to the rental car. It was already in gear, and Irina started reversing before Jasper had the passenger door fully closed.

Eli stared at his hands, rubbed the gold of his Trinity Masters' ring with his thumb.

Life as he knew it was over. He'd made his interest in the Rodin clear to everyone at the party. He hadn't been wearing a mask or hood like Jasper was. It had never occurred to him, because he'd gone there to look at a piece of art, nothing more.

Jasper had planned to steal it all along. Eli was his fall guy.

"Shock?" Irina asked Jasper. Her eyes were on Eli, who she could see in the rearview mirror.

"I think so." Jasper twisted just enough to look over his shoulder at Eli, who sat like a monolith in the backseat, staring at his hands.

"It's hard to imagine that having gone worse," Irina said.

"No one got shot." Jasper was trying for lighthearted but it fell flat.

"Was that a possibility?"

"Yes. I didn't realize there was a third guard who'd stayed behind in the room." Jasper rubbed his hands over his face. "Eli did. He was hiding on the other side of some back door no one seemed to realize was there. He heard the guard still in the room. Tried to warn us."

Irina clenched the steering wheel. "I took my earbud out so I wouldn't distract you."

"I wasn't on either. He realized I was walking into a trap and busted in through the back door. Him distracting the guard is probably the only thing that stopped me from getting shot the instant I opened that door. If he hadn't come busting through like some avenging art god, I would be in custody." Jasper sucked air through his teeth, leaned his head back. His next words were so low, Irina barely heard them. "And in exchange, I framed him for a felony and destroyed his reputation."

"You didn't frame him…at least not on purpose. I never would have suspected this operation would go sideways like this. I wish I'd been more prepared for it, but no one can be prepared for everything, all of the time." Irina knew she was right, and self-recriminations and second-guessing, though natural, weren't helpful. That line of reasoning did nothing to lessen the ball of anxiety in her stomach. Five hours ago, she'd been sure they were about to ID some bad guys, and in the morning they'd be on their way back to Boston to be formally bound.

Now they were on the run, no closer to their goal, and they'd destroyed Eli's very nice life in the process.

"But you got the Rodin?" she asked, trying to find the good.

"We did. And whatever is in those other crates."

"What if those are legally purchased pieces?"

"Then we fucked up. We didn't stop to run a pro and con list."

Irina shot Jasper an irritated glance. "I'm not saying you should have."

Jasper held up his hands. "Sorry."

There was silence as Irina navigated them south out of the city. Right now her only goal was to get away from Denver. The question was, which way to run. Interstate 70 ran east-west across most of the country. Interstate 25 crossed I70 in Denver and went through New Mexico almost all the way to the Mexico border, and north into Wyoming before joining with 90.

Going east offered them the best options as far as populated areas they could hide in, but she lived in D.C., so anyone after them might assume they'd head east. West meant going through the Rocky Mountains, which meant long stretches of road where there was nowhere to turn off, and sporadic small towns all the way through Utah. The route north was similarly isolated.

She got on I25 south. The car was filled with the ambient sounds of driving, just loud enough that the silence wasn't deafening. They could head to Albuquerque, but that seemed too obvious. They could jog east and head into Texas, but the rural northern part of Texas was fairly uninhabited and wouldn't provide options for hiding the way more populated areas would.

"I grabbed the computer."

Irina was lost in her planning, so it took her a minute to process what Jasper had said.

"What?"

"They were monitoring their supplementary security cameras via a laptop. I grabbed it."

"And you're just saying this now? That should tell us everything we need. Okay, maybe not everything, but at the very least we'll be able to figure out who the security company is. From there, maybe we can backtrack to the client, or maybe there's some client info on the computer."

"I just wanted to stop them from using the security video they have of me."

"Well, I can't guarantee that grabbing the laptop means someone doesn't have that information. Standard procedure for *my* company is to have all data backing up to an online server every fifteen seconds."

Jasper sighed. "These were professionals, so let's assume the worst."

"They have you on camera?"

"I only looked at the laptop screen for a split second, but there were four feeds. One for the back door, one in the lobby covering the guests. The other two were of what I assume was the second floor. Looked like a gallery."

"If they were recording the front door then they have Eli and me there." Irina pressed her lips together, then shrugged that off. "So they have a recording of us loading the crates into the car in the alley."

"No. I knew the camera was there from earlier, so before we went out the back door I cut the power supply for the camera, and as soon as the door opened, I yanked it down and trashed it. If it had a backup battery, the most they have is a video of my hand. Maybe my arm."

She processed that, then lowered her voice. "Eli will be the only person who's on video coming in the front door, but never shows up on video leaving."

There was silence for twenty miles. Irina kept checking on Eli in the rearview mirror. He was staring out the window, motionless.

"There's an address." Jasper's voice once more broke into her thoughts. "On the inventory slip."

"What inventory slip?"

"Inside the lid of the crate there's a piece of paper—it's got the information for the piece of art inside that box. When we were opening boxes looking for the Rodin, I realized there's an address, the same address, on every slip."

"You think it's the owner's address?"

"Doubtful. They're too security conscious for that. It might be the storage location, or an intermediary company."

"I can look into it." Irina felt a few faint strings of hope. "Get me the address."

"Now?"

"We need gas. We'll stop in Colorado Springs and I'll call it in then."

It was another twenty minutes before they actually stopped. She didn't want to use a gas station near the freeway. They'd cruised through a few residential neighborhoods, finally finding a massive shopping complex with several superstores.

It was nearly eleven, and the superstores were either closed or closing, employee cars scattered sporadically throughout the parking lot. The gas station was in the corner of the expansive parking lot, closer to the intersection.

"Pull up outside that store," Jasper said.

"I think it's closed."

"No, it's closing. I have ten minutes."

Jasper ran in, emerging a few minutes later with a bag and a large gas can. He jumped in.

"Don't pull up to the gas station. There will be cameras. We're going to park there, where it's dark." He pointed toward the center of the lot. It was far enough from the respective front doors of the neighboring stores that it wasn't a desirable parking location, and was deserted. "I'll walk to the station for gas."

Irina parked where Jasper had indicated then turned in her seat. She was going to ask Eli to hand her the lid of the box, but his body language hadn't softened. Hopping out, she opened the back door, then carefully lifted off a crate lid. Curiosity got the better of her and she peered into the box. There wasn't much to see in the faint dome light of the car, especially since most of the sculpture was cocooned in packing.

Irina powered on her phone. It was risky to do so, but she carried a new type of phone, which was harder to trace. She snapped a picture of the inventory sheet—just in case—then still holding the lid, she called the D.C. offices of Bennett Securities. After identifying herself, she was quickly connected to their information and research division. She read off the information and asked them to pull up everything they could on the address, especially the names of the owners or, if applicable, renters.

That done, Irina powered off her phone and looked at Eli. His hands rested on the back of the passenger seat and his head was bowed.

Jasper appeared at Irina's shoulder. He dug into the bag and pulled out some clothes. "Here, I got you something else to wear. I had to guess the sizes. Eli, I got you some too." Jasper held out a folded set of athletic gear to each of them.

For the first time since they'd left the Denver city limits, Eli spoke.

"I'm leaving."

Irina looked at Jasper, who slowly lowered his arms.

"What do you mean, Eli?"

"I mean I'm leaving. I can't...I won't do this." He opened his door and slid out.

"Eli, you can't just leave." Irina hurried around the back of the car. Jasper started to follow behind her, then changed course and snatched up the gas can, jamming the spout into the tank.

"Yes, I can."

"Well, what do you mean 'leaving'?"

"It's been less than forty-eight hours and my entire life has been destroyed. I'm going to go and do my best to put the pieces back together."

"You know what will happen if you disobey the Grand Master. If you think your life is ruined now—"

"We're not married yet. I know it's not common, but I have the right—we all do—to tell the Grand Master this trinity won't work. That's what the binding period is for. I'll ask the Grand Master to reconsider this trinity."

That stopped Irina in her tracks. Her heart clenched and her stomach curled from the rejection.

"My life may not seem like much. May not seem exciting. But I had to work very hard to get where I am. People look at me and expect me to be a retired athlete, a coach." He looked up, and anger and hurt were there, just under the surface of his face. The mild-mannered professor was gone, replaced by something raw and achingly sad. "When I say I'm a professor, they ask if I'm a professor of African-American studies. When I tell them I'm an art history professor, that I'm fluent in Mandarin, people are shocked." He tipped his head back, looking up at the stars, which seemed both closer and brighter here than they were in Boston.

"I've never really belonged before. Maybe that's why I wanted to join the Trinity Masters. I'm not black enough to be part of that community. Despite being fluent in Mandarin, I was never part of the Chinese community. I'm a man without a home. The Trinity Masters was supposed to be my home. My trinity was going to be a place where I belonged, but now…"

Irina blinked and the tears that had gathered in her eyes fell. He still wanted a trinity, just not one with her or Jasper in it. Her heart was breaking for him, and for the impending loss of him.

She knew, in that moment, that she could love him desperately if given the chance.

"I'll contact the Grand Master. If she says that I have to stay in this trinity, well, there are options. Not good ones, I know, but there are options."

Eli stuck his hands into the pockets of his pants. He looked elegant and tragic, standing in the starlight in his slacks and dress shirt.

"Goodbye, Irina, Jasper."

Irina watched him walk away with watery eyes. Beside her, Jasper began to curse creatively, most of the curses directed at himself. He yanked the empty gas can out and flung it away.

Irina was painfully aware of her part in fucking this up. She'd offered to create the distraction without thinking it through, without realizing that in doing so, she'd draw attention to Eli by association. Usually when she protected someone, she was anonymous—just another warm body playing a role in an expansive security net. The missing-piece-of-jewelry bit was a distraction technique she'd used before. Usually she did it to cause a commotion in one area, which drew attention away from another so that others on her team could escort the client out. She'd treated Eli like a client, making sure he was physically safe, but physical safety wasn't what he'd needed.

"How could I have been so stupid?" Irina's throat ached with suppressed tears. She fought the urge to race after Eli, who was almost at the edge of the parking lot.

"This is my fault. I thought I could get in, grab the Rodin, and get out, and it would be days before they figured out it was gone." Jasper turned and slammed his fist into the car. It made a sickening noise.

"Even if you had, they would have suspected him. He was the one asking people about it. And then his stupid 'fiancée' made a fuss. He was damned the minute we walked in there."

"I haven't worked with a team…I don't know how to be part of a team." Jasper was massaging his hand.

Irina swallowed her tears and shook her head. "We've got to stop. We're in fight-or-flight mode, and that's affecting everything we're doing or saying. And I'm including myself in that assessment. Now that the immediate danger is over, we're releasing emotions as a stress outlet. That's all this is—excess emotion. If Eli has never been in a violent confrontation before tonight his reactions are especially understandable. We need to get somewhere safe, and we need time to settle down, or engage in some physical activity, then we'll talk."

A corner of Irina's mind had been dispassionately processing and observing everything that was happening around them while she worked to master her emotions. That same unemotional corner of her mind was now sending up red flags.

"Jasper." His name passed her lips like a bullet fired from a gun.

He went dead still. "What?"

"Your phone. You turned it off, right?"

"Of course."

"Of course," she echoed. "Because if you leave it on, it can be tracked. I turned mine off before we left the warehouse, and I have an untraceable phone."

"Same."

Irina turned to face him, her already-knotted stomach starting to fall. "Did either of us make sure Eli turned his off?"

Tires screeched.

Irina whipped around in time to see a black panel van rock to a halt in front of Eli, who'd finally reached the end of the massive parking lot. He'd stepped over a low wall onto the sidewalk. Even from this distance, she could see the dot of light that was his phone screen. He must have pulled out his phone to call for a cab.

"Eli!" she screamed. "Run!"

Jasper took off at a run. Irina, still in her heels, started to follow, but stopped herself. Act, don't react, was the motto of security. Reacting meant you had no power. Acting meant control.

The side door of the van slid open and three people jumped out. Eli stumbled back a step, but it was already too late.

His attackers, clad in black, surrounded him. There was a small tussle. Eli held his ground, his physical size his best defense. An arm arched toward his neck.

Irina lost sight of the fight for a moment as she jumped into the driver's seat and slammed the car into reverse.

Three against one was nearly impossible odds, and when Irina could once more see what was happening, Eli was being pulled and shoved into the van. He wasn't fighting back—his head lolled forward.

Jasper was only halfway to the street when the door slammed closed and the van squealed away. He kept running, craning his neck to keep sight of the van.

Irina slowed, barely, as she pulled up alongside Jasper.

He jumped in. "Go!"

Chapter Seven

"Which way?"

"Left."

Tires squealed. Irina wished she were in one of the black sedans her company used when handling protection details, instead of the top-heavy SUV. She had a funny feeling she'd taken that curve on two wheels instead of four.

"There. Make a right." Jasper was leaning against the passenger window, tracking the car. "When we catch up—"

"I'm taking the lead." Irina's tone was harsher than she'd intended. "This is what I do. I'm perfectly aware that I'm the main reason everything went wrong back at the warehouse. If I hadn't forced Eli to stay hidden, if I hadn't been the distraction—"

"It's on me, not you," Jasper countered. "I romanticized the idea of having a team. And I underestimated what we were up against."

The kidnappers must have cut the power to the car's rear lights, because even when the van braked there were no red brake lights, let alone running lights. But they'd made a mistake. The small bulb illuminating their license plate was still on. It wasn't much to follow, but it was something. Irina sped into a turn. Every time she lost sight of the van, she was sure that was it, that they'd lost Eli forever.

"We'll get him back," Irina said, mostly to herself.

"Yes. And then we'll seduce him until he forgets all about leaving us." Jasper added a comical leer to his tone.

That startled a laugh out of Irina. That was what she'd needed. If fear was crippling, dry humor was like a shot of adrenaline. She grinned at Jasper, adjusted her grip on the wheel, and floored it.

"*Ave, Imperator, morituri te salutant.*" Jasper braced one arm against the dash.

"Don't lock your elbow like that. It'll break." Irina turned off the headlights.

"Uh, why would it—"

The van slowed to turn right—under the freeway—as the access road dead-ended.

Irina did not brake. She cut to the inside of the van's turn, and clipped the quarter panel in a modified PIT maneuver. The van spun, the rear tires squealing as they were forced sideways. Irina yanked the SUV into a turn. Jasper cursed fluently and inventively as she battled the car under control. The van shuddered to a halt, but Irina kept going. She didn't want to give them time to stop and regroup.

Irina once more wished for a sedan, where she could have stamped on the parking brake—which in some instances was safer than using the car's normal brakes. She couldn't risk that with this SUV.

"Irina, you're not going to—whoa, whoa, whoa!"

Jasper yelped as she maneuvered the SUV to face the side of the van, then slammed her foot on the gas. She T-boned the van, shoving it up against the wall and pinning it there. As she'd hoped, the front impact hadn't been enough to deploy the airbags in the SUV.

The tinted window in the driver's door cracked in the honeycomb pattern of safety glass, but held. They were blind as to what was happening inside the van, but she could make an educated guess.

"Duck." Irina grabbed Jasper's collar and yanked him down. Their seat belts prevented them from hunching down all the way, but it was enough to protect them from the shot that cracked the windshield.

"They've got guns," Jasper hissed.

"I know." Irina frowned. A shot from that close should have shattered the windshield. Plus, that hadn't sounded right. It wasn't the *pop* of a handgun. It was a deeper, louder sound. Closer to the *boom* of a shotgun.

Irina took her foot off the gas, and the SUV rolled back a foot or so. She stole a glance over the dashboard. The driver's door was mangled, meaning they probably couldn't open it. The barrel of a shotgun peeked out of the broken driver's window. They must have punched out some of the safety glass.

The barrel of the gun moved, catching the yellowed light of the security lamps high overhead. The stock and stops of the gun were bright orange. She ducked down.

"They're using beanbag rounds," she whispered.

There was a second *boom* and the windshield shattered and fell in. Pebbles of safety glass rained down on them.

"Definitely beanbag rounds," she said. Her ears were ringing, and the driver's ears would be ringing even worse than hers, unless he was wearing headgear. Either way, she wasn't worried about being overheard.

"That doesn't make me feel any better."

"Less lethal is better than fully lethal." Irina reached out and released Jasper's seat belt. "I'm going to ram them again. You jump out and go to the back door. All I want you to do is open it. Don't stand directly behind the door, in case they shoot through. Once you do it, retreat down by the back tire. You should be safe there, and relatively hidden by both cars. Do you understand?"

"I hate this idea."

"I'm going to be shooting at them." Irina slid her gun from under the seat where she'd stashed it. "They'll be distracted."

"Don't kill anyone."

"I will if I have to. Do you have a problem with that?"

"Yes, I do. If you kill someone there *will* definitely be cops. Cops are bad."

"Fair enough." Irina rolled down the driver's side window, twisting awkwardly to both keep herself hunkered down and aim. She squeezed the trigger. The crack of the shot made her ears ring, but her aim had been good. One of the security lights died, drenching them in shadow. "Go."

Her shot earned an in-kind *boom* response from the shotgun. The blast sailed through the space where the windshield should have been, cracking against the window in the quarter panel.

Jasper was already out, moving at a crouch. To cover the sound of his movement, she gunned the engine, ramming the SUV against the van. She shot the front of the van, hoping to hit something vital in the engine block. Fear and adrenaline rolled in her stomach, and it was training and sheer will that kept the lethal cocktail of emotions from causing her to curl up in horror or go completely bat-shit crazy and do something rash.

Right now, Jasper was in more danger than she was. If there'd been a way to do it, she would have switched places with him, but they couldn't risk losing their biggest physical advantage, which was the SUV pinning the van in place. But she had a plan.

Stretching, she grabbed what she needed from the backseat, then lifted her head enough to see out the side window. Jasper was at the corner of the van. He darted out of view around the back. Two shots—and these didn't come from the driver—boomed and Irina's heart stopped.

Jasper, hands over his ears, flung himself around the side of the van, dropping into a crouch in the corner created by the intersection of SUV and van. The van's rear door flapped open.

That was what she was waiting for. Irina took her foot off the gas, which let the SUV roll back a few feet. Pulling her legs up, she hauled her small, hard-sided suitcase into the front seat and jammed it under the steering wheel. It took precious seconds to position it so that one of the wheels was pressing on the gas. The SUV leapt forward, Irina's body bouncing like a Ping-Pong ball between the wheel, armrest, and seat. She'd be bruised tomorrow.

Slithering between the front seats, Irina wasn't surprised when pain exploded in her hip. Because of the height of the armrest, she'd had to raise her body above the level of the dash. The light color of her dress would have made it easy to spot her, and the driver had tagged her in the hip with a beanbag round.

Dropping onto the floor behind the passenger seat, Irina gritted her teeth against the pain. It hurt. Badly. But it must have been a glancing blow, because usually at this range, a direct hit would have been enough for her to lose feeling in the affected area.

Teeth gritted and eyes watering, she was still able to find the small black equipment bag she'd picked up from the Bennett Securities offices in Boston. Wishing she'd opted for a full kit, which would have included things like tear gas and gas masks, she had to settle for the stun grenade, commonly called a flashbang.

She opened the back passenger door, which was jerked out of her hand as the driver hit it with yet another beanbag round. This guy had suppressive fire down to an art. Sliding out the open door, Irina crawled under it then kept her back against the SUV, using it as cover until she could tap Jasper on the shoulder.

"Did you see Eli?" she asked.

He shook his head.

That meant she couldn't throw the flashbang into the back. Though they were designed specifically not to harm bystanders with shrapnel, they were still grenades. She couldn't risk it landing on Eli, especially if he was incapacitated.

"Take the gun. Shoot anyone who comes out the back door."

"What are you going to do?" Jasper's eyes were clear and steady. There was no panic or shock riding his mind. He'd been in firefights before. Clearly Irina had a sanitized idea of what an archaeologist's day was like. Or maybe the Indiana Jones movies were closer to documentaries than anyone would have guessed.

"I'm going to throw this in the driver's window." She held up the flashbang. "You need to be ready. Cover your ears, close your eyes."

Jasper shook his head. "It's too dangerous."

"I can do this. Do you trust me?"

Jasper's gaze searched her face. "You come back to me."

Irina's heart clenched. "I will."

Jasper palmed the gun, checked the safety, then dropped one knee to the ground, braced his elbow on his thigh, and raised the gun. It was the pose of someone experienced, but not formally trained. "Go," was all he said.

Irina kissed his shoulder, then slid away, back along the side of the SUV. Their opponents had been suspiciously quiet. Waiting. Waiting for what?

Irina's mouth went dry. If she were in their position, she'd be waiting for backup. Why risk engaging, especially when they had a less-advantageous tactical position for attack, when they could assume a defensive tactical plan and wait it out?

That meant they needed to move. Now.

Irina positioned herself at the back of the SUV. She could step out, take aim, and throw the grenade, risking a direct hit from the beanbag round. Or she could try a distraction to draw fire. She'd counted five shots so far, which probably meant there was one shot still in the gun in the driver's hands. Unless it was 37mm, which would have shot one round at a time. She was betting on it being a six-shot L8. If she was right, after the next shot, he'd have to either reload or switch guns, either of which would give her a very small window of opportunity.

Irina closed her eyes, forehead scrunching up as she ran through the possibilities. There wasn't one perfect idea, but several viable ones. Decision made, Irina crouched at the bumper, then reached up and hit the button to open the lift gate. She waited for a shot, but none came. Of course not—that would have been too easy, and if this was the last shot in the gun, the driver was being smart. He was waiting for a good target.

One suitcase lay drunkenly in the storage area of the SUV. Irina left it lying on its side, but extended the handle.

A few quick wiggles and she was out of her dress. The strapless design meant she was wearing nothing but panties under it. Her nipples puckered in the cold night air, and her confidence dropped a few degrees. It was hard to feel battle-ready wearing only underwear and heels.

Slipping her dress over the extended suitcase handle, Irina braced herself, then tipped the suitcase up. Her pale dress rose, hopefully appearing like she was climbing into the car through the open back.

Boom. The rifle thundered and her dress took a direct hit and the suitcase tumbled out of the vehicle onto the road.

Irina was already moving. Grenade in hand, she stepped out from behind the SUV. Three running steps brought her level with the driver's door. She pulled the pin. At this range, her aim was dead on. The grenade sailed through the rough-edged hole of the driver's window. She caught a glimpse of a surprised face— though whether the surprise was from the grenade or her nakedness, Irina would never know.

She turned, crouched, and covered her ears.

The night came alive with light and sound. The grenade detonated, the bang part of "flashbang" rattling her eardrums through the flimsy protection of her hands.

Her inner ear was reeling, which meant that when she opened her eyes and stood, the world shifted dizzily around her, her balance thrown off. Her vision had escaped mostly unharmed.

Keeping one hand on the vehicle as an anchor, she stumbled back around the SUV to where Jasper was. He was still crouched, eyes closed, hands over his ears, gun in one hand. She tapped his shoulder.

He raised his head and the gun at the same time. He looked at her naked body in confusion, then leered, lowering the gun.

Irina bit back a smile and jerked her head at the van. Jasper rose and tried to go first. Irina shook her head and held him back. She raised her hands in the classic surrender posture and stepped around the open back door.

She braced herself, expecting an attack, but none came.

The back of the van was one large compartment, with a wire screen partition between the front seats and the rear area. A bench seat ran along the left wall, with gun and equipment racks mounted above it. The right side had the sliding door, and in the space between the sliding door and back door was a storage cabinet. She could see the driver was slumped forward over the wheel. He'd taken the brunt of the flashbang, and being that close to the grenade had probably knocked him out.

Three men, all in military contractor black uniforms, were hunched over in the back. One rested his head on the bench seat, the other was vomiting against the wall—a common reaction to having one's inner-ear fluid blended like a margarita.

The third man, the one closest to the back, had fared the best. He caught sight of Irina, raised his arm, and pulled the trigger. She managed to jump to the side, out of the way of the stun gun prongs. Irina couldn't hear the telltale hiss and crackle of electricity through the ringing in her ears.

Eli was slumped on the floor, his head wedged against the sliding door. His big body took up most of the floor space in the back of the van. Irina's heart clenched—what if he'd been injured in the crash she caused?

That was a later problem. Now what they needed was to get Eli and get away.

Jasper appeared at her side. He stuck the gun in his pants then grabbed Eli's legs. The one lucid guard reached for another weapon.

Irina grabbed a stun gun from the convenient wall rack. She shot the guard, who twitched and fell back, landing on his vomiting compatriot.

Jasper had Eli propped in a sitting position. Irina slid into place under one arm. Together they lifted him. He was dead weight. Irina staggered, but they managed one step, then another. Eli's feet dragged on the ground.

Please God, let him be alive.

By unspoken consent, they headed for the lift gate. Together, they rolled Eli to the trunk space. Irina pointed at Jasper then pantomimed driving. He nodded.

Jasper picked up the suitcase and her dress and tucked them in next to Eli. Wanting to buy them more time, Irina ran back to the van. She jumped in, surprising the non-tasered guards, who were starting to recover. Ripping two more stun guns from the wall, she shot them in tandem. The driver still seemed to be out of it.

Irina groped one of the guards, checking pockets for ID. Then she checked his neck for dog tags. Nothing. No convenient clues.

She grabbed a beanbag shot gun off the floor, plus the last unused stun gun, and jumped out of the van.

Jasper was in the driver's seat. He'd backed the SUV up enough to free it from the van. It was eerie to see what was happening without the expected sounds of screaming metal.

Irina jumped in the still-open rear passenger door, then slid over the bench-style seat into the back with Eli. Looking up, she caught Jasper's gaze in the rearview mirror. She gave a thumbs-up; he nodded. She felt rather than heard the engine roar to life.

Irina spent five agonizing minutes looking out the back window, watching for followers.

When she was sure they were not being followed, she turned her attention to Eli.

"Please," she whispered. "Please be okay."

Chapter Eight

"Eli, can you hear me?"

Eli groaned, which made the banging in his head worse. Reaching up blindly, he groped for the speaker's face. Identifying lips by feel, he covered them with his hand, then said, "*Shhh.*"

The lips moved against his palm. Kissing him.

Kissing. *Hmm.* He hadn't realized this was a kissing sort of situation. Plus he would have sworn the speaker was male.

"Here, this will help." Now it was a woman talking.

Hands slid behind his shoulders and head. He was lifted and something pressed against his lips. Water. Cold, clear water. He gulped it thirstily. When someone said "open," he did. Pills dropped onto his tongue and he swallowed them down with more water.

His head and shoulders were lowered once more onto something soft. A pillow. A bed.

Some part of his brain had been trying to rouse him to panic, insisting they were in danger, but as his head touched the pillow, that lingering feeling settled down and faded away. He was safe.

"Water?" He kept his eyes closed. He didn't know where he was, and didn't want to risk opening his eyes. His head no longer pounded, but felt both fragile and heavy, like a thick glass globe.

The hands were back, lifting him from the bed, holding a straw to his lips.

"How are you feeling?" the woman asked.

He knew her. "Irina."

"Yes, it's me. Oh thank God, Eli."

There'd been a man here earlier. "Jasper?"

There was a pause, then the male voice answered. "Yes."

Eli opened his eyes. Color and light danced slowly and elegantly before him. He hummed a waltz under his breath, imagining the streaks of light as Ginger Rogers and the colors as Fred Astaire.

"Eli? How are you feeling?"

Irina's face appeared above him. There was something different about her face, and her hair swung loose. She looked younger and more vulnerable.

"Am I drunk?" he asked idly.

"Is that how you feel?"

"Yuppers."

Irina's head turned, her hair swaying. Eli reached up, sliding the glossy locks through his fingers.

Another face appeared beside Irina's. Jasper reached out to take Eli's wrist. He looked down at something, his brows knit in a frown.

"It hasn't actually been that long. He's probably still under the influence of whatever they used to drug him. We could pour coffee into him and—"

Eli's focus shifted from Jasper's words to his surroundings. The lights and colors had resolved into distinct objects. A room with cream walls. A TV resting in a dark armoire. Two tall lamps, one on a desk, the other beside a large armchair.

Jasper and Irina were standing beside the bed. Irina wore a T-shirt. Jasper wore loose pajama pants, his chest bare. There were scars on his chest and one arm.

Eli had seen those scars before. He'd seen both of them naked before. That was important.

Eli's eyes drifted closed as he tried to remember.

He'd seen them naked at their binding ceremony. They were his trinity. He finally had a trinity.

They were his and he was theirs and they were mostly naked. He was on a bed.

Eli opened his eyes. "Take off your clothes."

Irina and Jasper, who'd been talking to one another, both swiveled to look at him.

Jasper's lips twitched.

Irina's eyebrows rose. "What?"

Eli tried to raise his head, but couldn't. He did manage to raise his hand and point at them. "Take off your clothes."

"Why?" Irina asked.

"Because you're mine."

Irina glanced at Jasper, who shrugged.

Irina looked between them then pulled the shirt off. She wore underwear nearly the same color as her skin.

Jasper backed up a step. Eli moved his hand, including Jasper in the pointing. "You too," he demanded.

Irina grinned. Jasper looked unsure, his eyes crinkling.

Eli frowned in irritation. This was taking too long, and pointing was making him dizzy. He closed one eye. "Take his pants off."

Irina slid around behind Jasper and worked his pants down and off.

"Her," Eli said. He'd meant to say, "Now take her underwear off, I want you both naked." But that was a bit too complicated. The furniture and walls were starting to soften and melt into nothing more than color and light.

He blinked to focus, and was glad to see that Jasper had understood. He dropped to his knees beside Irina. Hooking his fingers in her panties, he slid them slowly over her hips, down her legs.

"Now what?" Jasper asked, and his voice sounded different, husky.

"Come here," Eli demanded.

They climbed onto the bed, naked and pale. He reached out, fingers brushing against bare flesh, the contrast of his dark hand against the extra-pale flesh of Irina's breasts making her gasp.

Or maybe it wasn't their contrasting skin tone that made her gasp as his fingers closed over her breast, squeezing gently.

"Eli, we shouldn't do this, you're...ah..." Irina's voice trailed off as Eli managed to get coordinated enough to stroke her nipple. That had taken more energy than it should have. His hand dropped to the bed.

"Jasper, you do it."

"Do what, Eli?"

"Play with her."

The bed dropped as Jasper moved, positioning himself behind Irina, who was crouched at Eli's hip.

Irina gasped again as Jasper grabbed her hips, jerking her so she was no longer sitting back with her ass on her heels, but kneeling up.

Eli lay before her, his gaze heavy-lidded, his voice low and husky. They'd pulled into this out-of-the-way motel a few hours ago. They had gotten some aspirin and water into him, figuring he'd sleep off whatever the bad guys used to drug him.

But it seemed sleeping was the last thing on his mind.

"Jasper," she whispered. "We shouldn't. If he weren't drugged…"

"We won't take it too far. But he said we're his. And that's true. Until the Grand Master says otherwise."

"Don't you think we should—"

"Spread her legs," Eli growled. His dark gaze raked over her naked body.

Jasper shifted behind her, then used his knee to force hers open. His naked body was warm at her back. His cock pressed against her ass. Irina shuddered in pure arousal.

"Does this turn you on?" Jasper's words were low, whispered into her hair. "To have him ordering us to perform for him? Do you like him ordering me to touch you?"

No. Say no, some rational part of her mind argued. If you're ever going to hold your own with two husbands, showing any sign of sexual submission is a bad idea.

"Yes," she breathed. "I shouldn't, but…"

"You belong to us, don't you?" Jasper was no longer whispering. His words were for Eli as much as her.

Eli rumbled in agreement. He lifted his hand, which waved in the air before dropping to the bed. Jasper reached out, taking Eli's hand in his.

"Where do you want to touch her?" he asked Eli.

"Everywhere."

Jasper brought Eli's hand to Irina's breasts. Her arousal was so acute that Irina shuddered from that simple touch. She reached up to push their hands away.

"Hands down," Jasper snapped. "Do you need to be tied up?"

"No," Irina said.

"Yes," Eli replied.

"Take off his belt, then give it to me," Jasper said.

Irina held still, the proverbial deer in headlights, unsure that she was hearing this right, that this was really happening. She always imagined that when she first met her trinity, they would spend some time talking through their sexual history, discussing preferences, and then maybe planning out how they would have sex the first few times, since there were more logistics involved with a ménage.

Jasper's free hand slid under her hair, his thumb and forefinger settling into the spots just behind her ears. He forced her to bend forward.

"Take off Eli's belt and give it to me."

Eli's hand, cradled in Jasper's, squeezed and stroked her breast. Irina slowly unbuckled the belt, then worked it free of Eli's slacks.

Doubling it up, she raised it over her shoulder, passing it to Jasper. He released her neck to take the belt.

"Put your wrists together," he said. Irina started to slip her hands behind her back, but Jasper stopped her. "No, in front."

The belt was looped around her wrists until the buckle and holes aligned. It wasn't tight, it wasn't even secure. But it wasn't really about that, and the symbolism was powerful.

"Arms up, on your head."

Irina raised her arms, resting her bound wrists on top of her head. This left her torso bare and defenseless. A point shoved home by Eli's sudden pinching of her nipple. Irina gasped and hunched forward.

"What?" Jasper asked.

"He pinched me. Hard."

"And did you like it?" Jasper asked.

Irina didn't answer, not wanting to reveal that she *had* liked it. They were her trinity, her husbands, yet she was having trouble bringing down her walls. She was afraid.

Eli grasped her nipple and twisted slightly, wringing a small cry from her. Her pussy clenched in reaction, and she tried to close her knees. Jasper's leg between hers prevented the move.

"She likes it," Eli said. "I want to check."

Jasper guided Eli's hand from her breast down her belly to her spread thighs. Ten fingers slipped between her legs, over her swollen, wet labia. Irina shuddered, overwhelmed. There were fingers on the outside of her sex, fingers spreading her open, fingers searching for her clit, and two fingers sliding down, searching for her entrance.

Her highly sensitized body, which hadn't yet come down from the adrenaline high of the fight, reacted as if the foreplay had been going on for hours instead of minutes. Her pussy clenched, her teeth gritted, and she rocketed perilously close to coming as fingertips massaged and rubbed her clit.

"Fuck her," Eli demanded in the bass rumble that did nothing to lessen her arousal. "I want to watch you fuck her."

Jasper bent her over, pushing her down so her head lay on Eli's chest. Irina started to shift, to lift herself up, but they were there, anticipating the move. Eli raised his free hand, the one not buried in her pussy, and reached for her bound hands. Jasper reached out to help him. Eli grabbed the belt, dragging it across his body and pinning her hands on the far side of the mattress.

Jasper slid his hand from her pussy and spread her legs. She could feel his cock, resting hot and hard on her ass. His fingers feathered along her hip. Irina buried her face against Eli, breathing in his scent. She couldn't stop herself from moving against his fingers as she waited for Jasper to thrust into her, to fill the aching need that sat molten hot at her core.

"What do you want, Eli?" Jasper's voice was ragged.

"Fuck her," Eli demanded.

"And then?"

"I'll eat her out."

The crude phrasing sent a wave of arousal through Irina as her mind's eye painted an image of her sprawled on the bed, Jasper twisting her nipples as Eli licked her clit. Her pussy clenched.

"Then?" Jasper's fingers once more joined Eli's at her pussy, but now he was coming at it from the back rather than the front. He toyed with the entrance to her body, stroking and pressing, then wiggling one of his fingers in, adding them to the two fingertips Eli already had in her.

"Then I'll fuck her pussy and you fuck her mouth."

"Then?"

"I'll fuck her ass, while you lick her pussy."

Irina gasped and whimpered against Eli's stomach, aroused and terrified all at once. Or maybe she was terrified by how aroused she was.

"Then?" Jasper demanded, his voice a prod, driving them all deeper into this dark sexual world that Eli's words were painting.

"I lick her pussy while you suck my cock." Eli's voice was stronger, his words more lucid.

Irina felt Jasper still, and realized this was the first time Eli had mentioned directly touching Jasper, or vice versa.

"Then?"

"I'll fuck you while licking her."

"Then?"

"Stop!" Irina cried. She couldn't wait anymore. "Fuck me, please."

Jasper's weight shifted the mattress under her knees, and Irina sobbed in happy anticipation.

Cold air washed over her as Jasper slid off the bed. Irina raised her head, looking around frantically. She tried to rise, but Eli still held her wrists, keeping her pinned across his body.

"Jasper?"

"It wouldn't be fair to do anything more without him." Jasper was standing at the foot of the bed, hands on his hips. His shoulders were hunched, and his cock was thick, hard, and glistening. Irina had never considered cocks particularly attractive, but the sight of Jasper's made her mouth water. She wanted him in her mouth, her pussy.

"Please," she whimpered. "He's right here."

Eli's fingers slid over her clit, and Irina stopped talking, focusing.

"I don't want to fuck up our relationship with him any more than we already have." Jasper pulled on the sweats he'd been wearing, wincing.

"Fuck her," Eli said again.

Jasper came around to Eli's side of the bed. He bent and kissed him. Irina twisted her head to watch. A shudder of fresh arousal rocked through her.

Jasper broke the kiss, rested his head against Eli's. "I hope you don't hate us in the morning."

Eli frowned. "You're mine. That's all that matters." His hand clenched in Irina's pussy, fingers pressing deeper into her, thumb dragging over her clit. "Mine."

Irina shuddered and thrashed.

"You're right. But you need to rest, and frankly, I don't think your body is up to this."

Eli frowned, lifting his head to look over Irina at his crotch. There was no telltale bulge in his pants. "Well damn."

"We should wait, until we can all...participate," Jasper said.

Irina took a fold of Eli's shirt in her mouth and bit down to hold back the begging that was waiting on her tongue. Jasper, damn him, was right.

Jasper detangled Eli's fingers from her bindings then helped her roll off Eli, onto her back beside him. Irina closed her eyes and tried to calm her body. They were done. They were stopping.

"I'm not done with you." Eli's voice was a growl in her ear.

Irina tensed, eyes snapping open.

"Jasper," Eli said.

They must have used some secret boy telepathic connection to have a conversation Irina wasn't privy to, because Jasper lay on her other side, tight against her—the queen bed wasn't big enough for the three of them. He took her wrists and unbuckled the belt. Irina expected him to unwind the quasi-bindings, but instead he forced her arms over her head and looped the belt through the rungs of the shaker-style headboard. He wound the belt not only around her wrists, but between them, turning the loose symbolic ties into functional bindings.

"What are you doing?" Irina arched and twisted.

Beside her, Eli chuckled. He rolled on his side to face her then dropped his arm onto her belly, hand sliding toward her pussy. Irina clenched her knees together and twisted her hips.

"Stop," Eli growled. "Spread your legs. I want your pussy."

Irina could have sobbed from arousal and frustration. Yet she spread her legs, wanting, needing to have him, to have both of them, touch and own her. This was the hottest, sexiest thing that had ever happened to her. Perversely, the frustration was making her even hotter.

Eli settled his hand on her pussy, wiggling his fingers until her labia were being held open by three thick fingers, his middle finger lying tight across the top of her clit. Eli closed his eyes, apparently happy and relaxed.

Jasper adjusted his pillow, scooting down the bed until his head was level with her breasts. He draped his arm across her abdomen, his forearm lying alongside Eli's. He settled his hand on her breast, middle and index finger on either side of her nipple. He squeezed and plucked. It was an idle, lazy motion.

Jasper closed his eyes.

Irina lay tense and tight, ready and waiting for the next move, for the touch that would send her over the edge into orgasm. Seconds built to a minute, a minute into two. Her husbands' breaths evened out, falling into a deep rhythm of sleep.

"Oh you have got to be kidding me." But she whispered it, unwilling to wake them. Irina closed her eyes and prepared for a long night.

"Jasper, wake up, I have to pee."

Jasper opened one eye. A lovely breast, topped with a rosy nipple, waited to greet him. He flexed his hand, feeling a second breast under his palm. The nipple trapped between his fingers tightened in response to the movement. Jasper plucked it idly as he yawned.

"Ohhh, Jasper…"

Irina's body arched into a taut bow, her breast lifting into his hand. Jasper shifted his gaze lower. Eli's hand still cupped her pussy, and based on the way her hips where moving, she was doing her best to either fuck herself on his fingers or get off by rubbing her clit against him.

He twisted her nipple, watched her shudder in reaction.

"Have you been aroused this whole time?" he asked.

"Please," she pleaded.

"Please what?" Eli rumbled. He propped himself up on one elbow, gaze roaming over both Irina's naked body and Jasper's bare chest.

Eli's hand moved against Irina's pussy. Her teeth clenched in reaction and she moaned. Jasper cupped her breast, squeezing the base and offering it to Eli.

Eli bent his head, taking her nipple in his mouth. Irina sobbed, her body thrashing between them, her eyes squeezed shut. She was utterly vulnerable, open to them. Theirs.

Eli released her nipple, then laid his head on her breast and closed his eyes. His hand still moved between Irina's legs. The tight muscles of her thighs were twitching, her teeth clenched. The only sound was the wet slide of Eli's fingers, but the pace began to taper off, even as Irina's moans grew louder.

"Eli, are you going back to sleep?" Jasper asked.

The only response was a further slowing of his fingers' torment of Irina's pussy.

"No, no, don't stop," she begged.

But Eli was once more asleep.

Jasper reached up and unbuckled the belt. Irina looked at him, her eyes pleading.

He shook his head. "Not without him."

Irina's eyes flashed. She wiggled out from under Eli's hand, then slid her own hand down to her pussy. She closed her eyes, clearly prepared to finish the job herself. Jasper turned away, not because he didn't want to watch, but because watching might destroy the self-control he was clinging to so desperately.

"Damn it." Irina's voice was heavy with resignation.

He turned. She lay on her back, arms flat on the bed. She pressed her legs together and drew her knees up.

"Not without him. Together." She rolled off the bed, standing stiffly. "I'm going to shower."

Chapter Nine

The room was surprisingly nice, given that they were at an otherwise unremarkable motel just off the freeway. It was one of those motels where the parking spaces were right outside the door of each room, and based on the smattering of cars, it was mostly unoccupied.

Jasper checked on their vehicle through the front window, which looked out onto the parking lot. They hadn't been able to go far with the windshield-less SUV, so when he'd seen a small used car lot outside Pueblo, he'd pulled over. Irina had stripped the SUV's plates while he broke into the office and snagged the keys for the five-year-old gold, four-door sedan that now waited outside their room. They'd loaded everything, including the Rodin, into the surprisingly large trunk, then swapped the SUV's plates for those of a red compact. They'd taken it a step further and traded the gold car's plates for those of a similar gold vehicle at the back of the lot. Jasper hoped the elaborate switching of plates would buy them some extra time. They'd dropped the SUV off near the front entrance of a less-than-savory-looking body shop. If they were lucky, the shop might "borrow" some pieces and make it disappear.

They'd managed to put a hundred and fifty miles between themselves and Denver before concern over Eli, and the need to sleep, had them pulling over. They'd paid cash for the room and ditched Jasper's outfit and Irina's dress in the Dumpster. The bags of clothes Jasper had gotten for them had survived the transfer between vehicles, and they'd brought those in. The laptop he'd taken from the security people had not. It had a massive dent punched into it, so Jasper had broken it open and pulled out the important-looking pieces—he wasn't great with computers, but he knew just enough to get the hard drive—then tossed what remained. Maybe Irina could do something with it, but it would take time and equipment. Their best lead was no longer looking so promising.

Toothbrushes and their own clothes were steps away, in their suitcases, but it was better to keep the suitcases closed as long as possible, making sure nothing identifiable, or covered in trace evidence, was left behind.

Jasper pulled on the generic sweats he'd gotten for himself only eight hours ago—though it seemed like days had passed since then—and jogged down to the motel front desk. He bought a cheap toothbrush and toothpaste from the night clerk, who was getting ready to leave. The sun was streaking across the sky as he hustled back to their room.

Irina was out of the shower and preparing to pull on the exercise clothes he'd gotten her. Jasper put a hand on her bare lower back, turning her to the light. Her left hip and buttock bore a spectacular bruise blooming to the size of a small plate.

They'd both showered as soon as they'd gotten here, removing any GSR, as well as the sticky sweat they'd built up. He'd first seen the bruise then, but it hadn't been nearly this big. He released her, saying nothing, and watched as she continued to dress. After this second shower, he was struck again both by how lovely Irina was and how young she looked, face bare of makeup and wet hair loose.

"Toothbrush?" He offered it to her.

"You first. There's a burner phone in my kit. I want to call in."

Jasper nodded, then checked the bedside clock. "We'll find the local morning news, see what they're saying, if anything, about last night."

Irina put on socks, then slipped out the door. Just to be safe, Jasper watched from the window as she rummaged in the trunk. When she was safely back in the room, he took his turn in the shower.

Eli was awake and sitting up when Jasper exited the bathroom wearing nothing but a towel. He looked at Jasper, then at Irina, who had her back to the room, phone pressed to her ear. He blinked. Gone was the aggressive sexuality, replaced by the slightly baffled-professor demeanor.

"Welcome back," Jasper said. He tried to smile, but it faded quickly. He had no idea where they stood with Eli.

A lot had happened in the darkness of the night, and this was their first real conversation since before the attack.

"Did I get kidnapped or did I dream that?" Eli looked disconcerted, as if being kidnapped was puzzling rather than terrifying.

"Yes."

"And…then we, uh…" Eli looked around the hotel room, as if searching for evidence of the raw sexual encounter.

Jasper couldn't help it, he laughed, but it wasn't mocking. "There are some pieces you're missing. Stuff happened in between the kidnapping and the sexy times."

Eli looked down and cleared his throat. "I thought I was dreaming part of it. A really vivid dream."

"They drugged you. You were out cold when we got you back."

Eli's head snapped up. "Got me back?"

"This is going to sound dramatic, and frankly it was. We rescued you."

"Rescued me?"

"How much do you remember? I mean before the sex."

"Not much. We were in the parking lot." Eli frowned. "Oh. We had a fight."

"Actually, you left us. Not without reason, but you made it clear you wanted nothing to do with us."

"The Rodin—"

"Safe. And the other boxes."

"But I'm… Oh God. Everyone is going to think I stole the Rodin."

"Well, technically you did…" Jasper couldn't help himself.

Eli glared at him, then dropped his head into his hands.

Jasper's heart broke a little as, for the second time, he watched Eli crumple under the weight of the consequences of last night. He wanted to reach out and touch him. After the interlude they'd shared, after the raw and visceral truth of what they'd done, he wanted to assume things were, if not fixed, at least better between them.

"I was going to turn on the news, see what the reporters are saying, but I won't if… I don't want to upset you."

"Just do it," Eli mumbled.

Jasper grabbed the remote, turned on the TV. They suffered through the last ten minutes of an infomercial before the early bird local news came on.

There was nothing in the morning breaking news, and nothing in the scrolling announcements.

"It might not break until later in the day," Jasper said as he turned off the TV.

Eli looked at Irina's back. She still had the phone pressed to her ear.

"Jasper, is she…is she okay?"

"A bit banged up. The shot to the hip is going to hurt for a while."

Eli whipped around. "She got shot?!"

"Maybe I'd better give you a play-by-play."

"I just wanted to know if she was okay after…after what I did to her. You know, uh…"

"You mean mercilessly teasing her and never letting her orgasm?" Jasper raised a brow.

Eli cleared his throat. "Yes. That. Wait. After all that, we didn't…she didn't?" He frowned.

"That was not anywhere close to being an actual sentence," Jasper pointed out. "We didn't have sex. I mean no one had sex. I touched her…when and how you ordered me to." Jasper's voice grew husky and his cock twitched. He looked away, getting his body under control.

"I'm…I'm so sorry," Eli said. "I'm not normally like th—"

Jasper whipped around, voice hard with anger. "Don't. Don't apologize. Don't make that cheap. Don't make it less than what it was."

Eli straightened, meeting Jasper's anger head on. "And what was it?"

"It was the first time we were a real trinity instead of three strangers. And the whole time I had to remind myself we'd never have anything more than last night, because you were already gone. As soon as your walls went back up, you'd be out of our lives." Jasper let out a sharp laugh. "The first time our trinity came together it was already broken."

Eli's face was inscrutable. They stared at each other, neither willing to back down, yet there was something lying unsaid between them, the connection they'd forged last night, a connection forged as they'd put their hands on their wife.

"Oh fuck."

Jasper whipped around, looked at Irina. Her words were soft but vehement in a way that made his muscles tense. Her bare face was etched stark with some expression he couldn't name.

"Irina." Eli pushed to his feet.

Jasper stood shoulder to shoulder with him. "What is it?"

Irina placed the phone on the table, then carefully picked up the lamp and brought the base down on the phone, smashing it to bits.

"We need to run. Now."

Irina, this is Price Bennett. You asked for information on an address that belongs to a VIP Bennett Securities' client. The request triggered an internal flag, which is why I'm calling. I'd like you to call me back, on my personal line, so we can discuss the source of your request. Your supervisor says you're on personal leave.

Irina, this is Price Bennett again. I'm getting after-action reports from an engagement by our high-risk division in Colorado. Call me back, immediately.

Irina repeated the carefully memorized voicemails for a second time. She'd listened to each message five times, memorizing them before destroying the burner phone. Jasper white-knuckled the wheel and cursed both inventively and at length.

Eli leaned forward from the backseat. "You're sure this Price Bennett guy is in the Trinity Masters?"

"Yes. I've met him a couple of times and saw his ring. It's this sort of open secret that he lives with both a woman and a man. Clearly they're his spouses, though officially I guess they're just his roommates or something. The man, Gunner, is an FBI agent, and Denise is a renowned scientist, doing cutting-edge research in genetics. I've met both of them a few times at work events."

"That's an interesting trinity," Jasper remarked.

"Price is rich and powerful. He can do what he wants." Irina grimaced. "After we saw that address on the sheet inside the box, I called it in, asked the research office to look into it. That's what the first message is about. Whoever owns the art is a VIP client." She made air quotes with her fingers as she said "VIP."

"You think that means a member of the Trinity Masters," Jasper said.

"Yes."

"But we already knew that." Eli shrugged. "We knew the owner of the Rodin was a member."

"No." Jasper drew out the vowel. "We suspected. Now we know. Not only are they a member, they're a well-connected member."

Irina nodded. "Bennett Securities' High Risk Division is, as far as I know, exclusively overseas. They handle stuff like security in war zones. If the owner of that," Irina pointed at the Rodin, "has enough pull to get an HRD team at short notice, at an art fundraiser…"

"Oh." Eli sat back and pulled the Rodin protectively onto his lap. "You're saying Irina's boss—"

"Reporting directly to Price is above my pay scale. More like my boss' boss."

"—is in on it? He's one of the purists?" Eli finished.

"And he's got to be the owner of the art. Who better to hide something like that than the owner of a massive private security firm?" Jasper's tone was grim.

"The real question is," Irina said, "why bother kidnapping Eli?"

"And were they targeting him specifically? Or was he just the easiest to grab?"

"I'm offended by that, I think." Eli frowned. "Er, should I be?"

Irina winced out a smile. "The thing is, Jasper and I both turned off our phones, because we knew we could be tracked by them."

It didn't take Eli long to see where she was going with that. "And my phone was on."

"And you'd walked away, all by yourself. It was very dramatic. Stupid, but dramatic."

"Thanks, Jasper," Eli grumped.

"You're welcome, husband."

Eli did that blinking thing and Irina laughed.

Scenery whipped by the windows. The imposing Rocky Mountains were behind them as they headed south and east. Before them lay expanses of forest intersected by bare ridges of barren, rocky soil. They'd hustled into the car and gotten on the freeway, putting miles between the burner phone and themselves before Irina finally relayed the messages that had been waiting for her when she'd called in to her personal phone's voice mail service.

For safety's sake, they were completely off the grid. They'd tossed Eli's phone—which they'd found in his pocket after they'd rescued him—into the back of a pickup going the other direction after turning it back on. Jasper's and Irina's phones were in a lead-lined pouch in the bottom of Irina's suitcase. They were traveling old school, using a map Jasper had picked up at a gas station. With no phone, and by using only cash, they were doing their best to minimize their digital footprint.

No phones meant no GPS, and they had no way to check where they were real time, but Jasper had a destination in mind. The last sign they'd passed said 150 miles to Amarillo, Texas. They'd changed highways since then, and were now on a narrow two-lane road that aspired to be a real freeway.

"Stupid question." Eli sat forward again. "Doesn't this mean we did it?"

Irina and Jasper shared a surprised look.

"We were supposed to find one of the pieces in the ERR album." Eli ticked the points off on his fingers. "We did that—though, to be fair, I haven't had time to make a definitive identification. We don't know for sure who owns it, but we know that this Price Bennett guy is at the very least protecting it. Why don't we just call the Grand Master and tell her?"

Irina looked at Jasper. "He has a point."

"He does," Jasper agreed.

Irina smiled. "And if the Grand Master steps in, we'll be safe. Even if Price Bennett is a member of the purists, I'm sure she can shut him down. All we need to do is stay safe until he's…dealt with."

Jasper grinned. "I have an idea about where we can hide out."

"Veto," Eli said.

"What?" Irina glared at Eli. "What are you vetoing?"

"Whatever he has planned. I don't trust that smile on his face."

Irina examined Jasper's expression, noticed the way his eyes sparkled with some hidden mirth. "You may have another point, Eli."

"Oh come on, you'll love it."

"Uh, does that sign say we're entering Oklahoma?" Irina asked. "I thought we were in Texas."

"We were. We turned north about thirty miles ago."

"What's in Oklahoma?" Eli asked.

Jasper laughed.

"There's a fetish hotel in the Oklahoma panhandle." Eli's voice was flat.

Irina bit her lower lip to hold back the laugh that bubbled in her throat.

Jasper slung an arm around Eli's shoulders. "No one will look for us here."

The two-story concrete structure was nondescript from the outside. The front door was dead center in one of the end walls. The parking lot was to the right, and surrounded by an eight-foot-tall fence. From the parking lot you could see the long wall of the building and the evenly spaced square windows, five on each floor. The security bars on the windows looked like a large X, with smaller Xs inside the triangular spaces made by the larger main arms. It was the only decorative touch on a building that otherwise looked like a storage facility.

"Why do you know this is here? *How* is this here?" Eli's voice remained comically resigned. "I thought Oklahoma was conservative?"

"It is. This hotel is one of the only businesses in this county, a county which a huge amount of bribery by the owners—a lovely Dutch couple—helped create.

They're their own county and their own town. She's the mayor, he's the sheriff. It works. I heard about it at one of the galas."

"Why can't we hide out in a big hotel? You know, a normal one."

"Because this place is entirely off the grid. No security cameras that can be hacked, no digital anything. They're an all-cash business. That is very hard to find."

"I'm sure those are the only reasons," Eli grumped.

Irina lost it, laughing so hard she had to lean against Jasper.

They left their luggage in the car, secure within the parking lot's protective fence. The automatic car gate had opened to admit them only after Jasper gave the password—"Amsterdam." Apparently that was the name of the hotel.

They were empty-handed as Jasper pressed the doorbell beside the solid metal front door. There was a mail slot above the doorbell, but there was no business name, street numbers, or any identifying information. It was clearly one of those places where if you had to ask the name, or what it was, you would never be let in.

A small window within the large steel door opened, and Irina was reminded of the gate into Oz. That thought had her biting back another smile.

A woman peered out at them. She didn't speak.

"Hello. My name is Sigmund," Jasper said. "I've been here before."

Irina could see the corners of the woman's eyes crinkle, in what was probably a smile. "Sigmund. Welcome."

The window slid shut and there were heavy metal clanks as the door was opened.

"Sigmund?" Eli asked.

"This place is positively Freudian," Jasper responded.

Eli groaned.

The small foyer was intensely modern—the walls were concrete, but had been coated in something that made them glossy, as if there was a layer of glass over the rock composite. The front desk was a gleaming white block, and two molded plastic chairs made up the entirety of the waiting area. Behind the reception desk was the hotel logo—a stylized door—backlit in indigo fluorescent light.

The woman who'd let them in wore a loose black smock dress. She was barefoot. A gold chain necklace had two longer chains coming off of it, disappearing under the dress. When she turned to move around behind the counter, the thin, crepe material molded to her body, and it was clear she was wearing some sort of nipple jewelry. Irina's mouth went dry as she flashed back to an image she'd once seen of nipple clamps with chains coming off them that attached to both a collar and another set of clamps…

She jerked her gaze off the woman's breasts, only to find that Jasper had caught her looking. He grinned.

Crap.

Jasper stepped up to the counter. "Which rooms do you have available?"

The woman grinned. "Many choices, Sigmund. There is only one other couple. What would be pleasing to you and your lovely…companions?"

They drove an hour and a half north, deep into Kansas, to make the call to the Grand Master.

They'd debated going together versus splitting up. There were disadvantages to both, but the factor that tipped the scales over into "staying together" was that if for whatever reason the person or couple making the call had to go on the run, there would be no safe, quick way to let whomever was left at the hotel know what had happened. No one wanted to be left behind, or left out of the loop, so they went together.

If they had gone east out of Pueblo they would have hit Garden City, Kansas. They hadn't gone east, they'd gone south, so by backtracking north into Kansas, Irina hoped that if they were spotted or traced, their presence in Garden City would lead their pursuers to assume they were on a straight eastward route, working their way toward Wichita. That might prevent anyone from thinking to look for them in Oklahoma.

They ate at a small diner on the outskirts of the city named Wheatland Eats. Their group earned more than a few stares. Or to be precise, Eli earned a few stares. Irina and Jasper wore the workout clothes Jasper had picked up for them, Irina in skintight leggings, a sports bra top, and a thin zip-up hoodie. Jasper wore knee-length basketball shorts and a tight exercise top with long sleeves. The construction of the shirt and stretch material did delicious things to his chest and biceps. Eli hadn't had a chance to change. His slacks and dress shirt were badly rumpled.

Their trinity looked mismatched and out of place.

Eli's shoulders tensed up as they slid into a vinyl booth and looked at menus. "Someone in here is going to call the cops."

"No, they're not," Jasper said.

"A big black man with a nice white couple? Yes, they are."

Irina looked around, caught two men at the booth on the other side of the long, narrow diner looking at them. She smiled, and the couple looked away.

"We'll eat, make the call, and go," Jasper said.

"First, we need to decide exactly what we're going to say."

The waitress came over. They ordered, then flipped over one of the red, scalloped-edge paper placemats and hashed out the message they wanted to leave using a battered crayon that had been left behind and tucked into the sugar caddy. Sebastian had given them a number to call before they'd left headquarters, but it would only allow them to leave a message. Their food arrived just as they finished editing. Irina popped a few fries in her mouth then stood. "Be right back."

When she asked the waitress for the phone, the woman threw a look at Eli then ushered her behind the counter, where an ancient corded phone rested on a shelf. Irina crouched down, picked up the phone, and dialed.

It rang once, then beeped.

"This is Irina Gentry. We think we found what you sent us to find, and more. It was protected, more heavily than it should have been, by my employer." She put stress on "my employer."

"He called, personally, to say that we were asking questions and doing things that angered one of his VIP clients. We do not have a name for the client, but *he* will, if one exists." Here, Irina paused, letting the silence add weight to what she'd just said. "We are safe. What you sent us to find is safe. To remain safe, we are going to retreat, and hope the information we've given is enough to solve the problem. I will check my email on Wednesday, three days from now."

Irina hung up and stood. The server hustled over as soon as she did. "Honey, is everything all right?"

Irina wanted to snap at her, tell her that Eli was the kindest, gentlest man imaginable. That *she* was more dangerous than he was. But this was not the right moment to make a scene. Yet she couldn't bear the suspicious glances people were throwing Eli's way.

Irina crooked her finger, inviting the woman, whose lipstick had settled into the smoker's lines around her lips, to lean in.

"We had to get him away from his little brother, give the kid a chance to enjoy the Wildcats' recruiting activities. He's overprotective, and wasn't going to let the kid have any fun. Plus, he was a Cyclone." Irina shook her head sadly. "We needed a fair shot at his brother."

"Ohhh." The server's eyes flickered to Eli. She nodded sagely. "I thought I recognized him. I always watch the games. Looks like you put him through the ringer."

"We got 'lost'." Irina made sure the other woman could hear the quotes around the word.

"Oh, honey, that's just bad." The Kansas was thick in her voice as her whole body relaxed a bit. She grinned conspiratorially.

Irina had gambled on several things: that this woman was a Kansas State Wildcats fan—at least when it came to the famous Kansas State, Iowa State rivalry; that implying Eli was a former athlete would allow the woman to slot him into a comfortable stereotype; and that she'd enjoy the idea of thwarting Iowa State, even in a small way.

Irina winked and went back to her table.

"Did you do it?" Jasper asked under his breath.

"Yes."

They tucked into their burgers and fries, which were delicious. Or maybe they were just okay, and the fact that none of them could remember when they'd last eaten made them delicious.

The waitress bustled up, three frosty chocolate milk shakes on her tray.

"Here you go, honey." She set the first milkshake in front of Eli. "I heard you're having a rough day. A milkshake will help that. Here in Kansas, we always help somebody out. You remember that."

Eli looked suspiciously at the milk shake, then at the waitress. "Uh, thank you."

The waitress winked at Irina as she set down the other two shakes.

Irina sucked up a mouthful of cold, creamy chocolate.

Eli looked at her and sighed. "I don't even want to know what you said to that woman." But he drank his shake, and the tension eased from his shoulders.

When they were done, Irina put a hundred dollars cash on the table, and as they left, she and the waitress shared conspirators' nods.

"What next?" Eli asked as they got back in the car.

"We have three days before Irina needs to check her email." Jasper backed out of the parking space and twisted the wheel, pointing them toward the freeway.

Irina, who'd slid into the backseat to give Eli the added legroom in the front, sat forward. "I think we're overdue for a couple different conversations."

"I can think of another way to resolve our issues," Jasper cajoled.

"Sex is not going to fix anything," Irina pointed out.

"If you do it right, sex fixes everything," Jasper countered.

They continued to snipe at each other until Eli held up his hands. "Enough, you two."

They fell silent. Eli cleared his throat. "Talk first. Then sex."

Irina sat back, surprised and thrilled by Eli's words. It was a long drive back to the hotel.

Chapter Ten

"Aw, hell no. I'm out." Eli turned on his heel.

Jasper slid in front of the open doorway, blocking Eli's retreat. "Calm down, it's the biggest room they've got. And trust me, this is mild in comparison to some of the other rooms."

Jasper had chosen it for the oversized bed. They needed a good night's sleep, and the custom-made, orgy-sized mattress would take all three of them easily. But right now, neither Eli nor Irina could see the bed, which was on the second floor of the two-story suite, and accessed by a spiral staircase partially obscured by layers of swagged fabric.

Sultan's Delight was decked out like a fantasy imagining of a harem. The walls were hung with panels of umber, rose, and gold fabric. The floor was laid with marble tiles covered with indigo, green, and red rugs. It was undeniably meant for fantasy sex and role-play.

There was a cushion-strewn seating area in one corner with a low wooden ottoman in the center. Fabric hung from the ceiling around it, creating a tent-like feel for the seating area. A low bench mounded with pillows ran along two walls, while huge pillows were tossed on the floor, creating the rest of the seating. The large ottoman at first glance seemed like it might be a coffee table, but coffee tables didn't usually have cushioned, easy-to-clean vinyl fabric on the top, or gold chains dangling from the legs, waiting to be used to secure a "concubine."

In another corner was the auction and sale block—a small wooden stage with a horizontal bar mounted to two adjustable legs. More brass-colored chains lay coiled on the stage and dangled from the ceiling overhead. There was a chest on the back corner of the stage. Two low-backed chairs of rich, dark wood with gold cushions were positioned in front of the stage.

The lower floor had a bathroom, but this bathroom had no walls. Instead there was a sunken tub and multi-headed shower, both of which were completely open to the rest of the room. A small lip edged the jewel-blue tile floor, keeping the water from splashing into the rest of the room. There was enough square footage, and enough showerheads, to host an orgy. Even the toilet, tucked into a corner of the tiled bathroom area, was completely exposed.

Jasper wondered idly how many people were necessary to qualify something as an orgy.

The final corner of the room had a series of wooden cages, four in all. One was waist-high, about the size of a large dog cage. The one next to that was tall but very shallow. Beside that was a large one about the size of a phone booth, and finally the largest cage had enough room for two people in it...or one person with their arms and legs spread wide, and secured by the padded restraints that waited in the corners.

Jasper went over to the smaller wooden cage and swung the door open. "We'll put the crates in here."

Eli didn't move. Irina had grabbed the laminated guidebook from a slot on the wall beside the door. If it was like the guidebook that had been in the room Jasper previously stayed in, it would have suggestions for how to use the various equipment and areas of the room.

"Okay, I'll do it," he said to no one in particular.

Jasper tugged the luggage cart into the room and unloaded the crates. There were five in all. Three were clearly sculpture boxes—one of which was the Rodin. The other two were larger, flat boxes—they were for framed art. There really was no reason to take them, except he and Eli had been able to tell by the weight that there was still something in them.

Jasper had asked for a new lock at the front desk, and the proprietress had pulled one out of a stock behind the counter. He ripped open the packet and tested the heavy silver lock. It wouldn't stop someone, merely slow them down. He snapped the lock closed and hooked the key into a dangling tassel on the wall.

Jasper unloaded the suitcases and Irina's black bag "kit" and then shoved the cart into the hall. "I'll take these up to the bedroom." Jasper waited for one of them to offer to help. Neither paid any attention to him.

The bedroom upstairs was sumptuously decorated, with more rich fabric drapes and a gold bed cover. The massive bed took up most of the floor space. The bathroom—with a standard shower-tub and blessedly private toilet—took up one corner of the room, and created an alcove that was completely lined by closets. Instead of doors, the closet had heavy drapes. He pushed the drape aside, only to find the closet was already full—of costumes and "toys." He tried a different drape, this time finding empty rods and folding suitcase racks. He tossed the suitcases behind the curtain.

There was an entrance to this room, which led into the second-floor hallway. The proprietress had explained that if they needed to use the elevator to go between floors of their room, they'd have to use the main elevator, since there hadn't been space to fit a private elevator into the room. He double-checked the locks on the door and then jogged back downstairs.

Eli hadn't moved, but Irina was up on the stage, peering into the chest. Bells jingled as she riffled through it. Jasper cleared his throat and she snapped the lid closed like a kid caught with her hand in the cookie jar.

"Shall we?" He gestured to the seating area.

Irina followed him over, and Eli finally moved, trailing after both of them, hands in his pockets. Irina chose a seat where her back was against the wall and she could see the door. Jasper settled himself into the corner where the walls met, and Eli sat catty-corner from Irina. He groaned as he stretched out his long legs, then tugged his glasses case from his pocket. Luckily Eli's glasses had been safely at his house when they went to the art exhibit, and Jasper had seen them on the table and snatched them up on his mad dash through the house.

"How did you know about this place?" Irina asked him.

Jasper adjusted the pillow at his back. "That's actually a good place to start this conversation. I came here with a guy I was dating."

Both Eli and Irina looked surprised. "Guy?" Eli asked.

Jasper nodded. "When I joined the Trinity Masters, I realized that there was a possibility, maybe even a probability, that I'd end up with a husband or two. I tried to keep myself open to either gender—just be with people I had chemistry with. When I met a man I was attracted to, I started dating him. I'm enough of an anthropologist to know gender is a social construct, as are the labels of 'gay' and 'straight.'

"One of the guys I dated was very into leather. There's a leather room here, so we came for a romantic weekend."

Irina crossed her legs, rested her elbow on her knee, her chin on her hand. "That's smart; to try dating all different kinds of people, I mean."

Jasper sighed. "It sounds nobler than it was. I was having bad luck with relationships with women. I thought maybe I'd be better at it with men. I'm not. I'm terrible at it, no matter who I'm with."

Irina laughed softly.

Eli leaned his head back against the wall. "Why did you say that this would be a good place to start our conversation?"

"Because we should know each other's pasts. What kind of relationships, if any, we've had."

There was a beat of silence, but it wasn't a hard silence. It was an invitation.

"For me, the Trinity Masters was an excuse." Eli stared at the fabric draped from the ceiling. "I could focus on my career, my research, the paper I was writing. It was my free pass to ignore this massive part of my life. My parents worry about me, so occasionally I'd go out on a few dates. I'd take a picture or two, put it up on Facebook, so my mom would stop worrying.

"I think I said it before, but I was really starting to think that I was never going to get called to the altar. Most of my colleagues are married, have kids."

"And do you want kids?" Irina asked softly.

"Honestly, I do. I didn't think I would, but the older I get, the more I realize what we sacrificed to join. Maybe if I hadn't joined the Trinity Masters I'd be married with kids. Maybe I'd still be single, but I would have had the option to adopt. I had this vague idea that maybe I'd one day petition the Grand Master to let me adopt, so I could have a kid when I was still young, if I didn't get placed in a trinity until later."

"There's a reason they recruit us when they do," Irina said. "When you're in college, getting married and having kids sounds boring and unadventurous. Why be like everyone else when you can be different and interesting?"

"Is that why you joined?" Jasper asked.

Irina smiled sardonically. "I'm your classic child of divorce. I spent my childhood being shuttled between parents. I had to partition my life into two pieces. I couldn't ever talk about what happened at Mom's house when I was with Dad, and vice versa. I dressed differently at each house. I went to soccer practice when I was with Mom, ballet when I was with Dad. I was never good at extracurriculars because I only did half of everything."

Irina looked into the middle distance, clearly lost in a past that sounded, in its own way, as traumatic as Jasper's.

"Our custody exchange location was outside the art department of the local college." She laughed bitterly. "Because that had the easiest parking. I spent a lot of time hanging out in the courtyard, watching students sketch and paint."

She shook herself. "The one thing my parents agreed on was that I had to excel academically. I could do academic work no matter who I was with. When I got old enough, I started to take on academic work beyond class assignments. I wrote science papers and short stories. Competed in essay contests. Wrote code for a photo-scanning app meant to detect cancer on X-rays. Academically, I looked like an amazing renaissance scholar. That's how I got into Harvard. In reality, it meant I didn't love anything."

She paused there and pursed her lips as if she were going to say more, but she shook her head and when she started talking again, it left the sense that she'd shifted her story deliberately to avoid something.

"I didn't know what I wanted to do when I was in college. Joining the Trinity Masters gave me some direction. Plus I knew I never wanted to get married, not the kind of married my parents had been. For other people, the arranged marriage and no possibility of divorce is probably a deal breaker. For me, it was a way to escape the fate of my parents."

That settled over them, and they each took a minute to digest the revelations so far.

"Relationships?" Eli asked her.

Irina smiled and wiggled her eyebrows. "I took advantage of the fact that I was free to do whatever I wanted before I was called to the altar. Always casual. Plenty of experimentation. I can't claim anything as fancy as having come to a fetish hotel. But I tried to embody GGG."

"What's that?"

"'Good, giving, and game.' Be good in bed, be giving in bed, and be game to try anything and everything."

Jasper smiled at that. Damn he liked this woman. "Now that we're talking about sex—"

"Are we?" Eli looked a bit panicky.

"Hold on." Irina held up her hand. "We can't talk about sex."

"I agree," Eli said, "but, uh, why not?"

"Because first we have to decide if we're in this together." Irina focused on Eli. "If you're still planning on leaving, then say so now."

Eli raised his gaze to the faux-tent ceiling. He couldn't ignore their focus. Their regard—and the accompanying expectation—was practically a physical weight, like one of those lead blankets dentists use to protect the body during X-rays.

He was gathering his thoughts, but apparently he took too long, because Jasper cut in.

"I don't want to spend my life with someone who resents me and the relationship."

Eli turned his head, looking at Jasper. Jasper's eyes were crinkled in the corners, not with mirth, but with concern, maybe regret.

"You and I," Jasper waved a hand between them, "were never going to be an easy match. And that was before Denver. I'm not denying I screwed up. Frankly, we all did. But I'm not going to spend the rest of my life with someone who hates me, or who is waiting for me to fuck up so they can blame me."

Eli looked to Irina. She nodded her agreement as Jasper spoke.

When Jasper fell silent, she added, "If you don't want to be a part of this trinity, then when we get back to Boston, tell the Grand Master. I've heard that when you go back for the official marriage, you can say you're not a good fit. Maybe, because we have the Rodin, the Grand Master will just break this trinity. She'd want us to be strong, and if we explain that you'd rather suffer the wrath of the Trinity Masters than be with us…"

Irina's voice cracked slightly toward the end of the sentence. Jasper leaned to the side, stretching out his arm to capture Irina's hand. She laced her fingers between his as she cleared her throat, clearly fighting back tears.

Eli looked at them—their bond was formed. Unsurprising, given what Jasper had told him about their rescue of him. Maybe they'd go back to the Grand Master and she'd keep Jasper and Irina together, give them another third. Eli would be assigned to a different trinity.

And he'd never see Irina or Jasper again. Never touch or kiss them. Never argue with Jasper about art, or get knocked on his ass by Irina. Never know what it was like to lay between them, to grow old with them.

He cleared his throat, drawing their attention. "What I said, in the parking lot, was true in that moment. I worked hard to get where I am, and while being an art history professor might not seem like much, it's important to me. I'd given up on being called to the altar, so my career was all I had to focus on. In that moment, I did blame both of you.

"But I was grieving. I was in shock. I was not emotionally prepared for what happened." Eli took a deep breath. "You're mine. The two of you. We belong to each other."

Irina scrambled off her seat, leapt across the low ottoman, and threw herself onto Eli's chest. Eli stroked her back as she tucked her head under his chin. Jasper slid over, wrapping his arm around Irina's back and resting his forehead against Eli's shoulder.

"We'll make it right," Jasper said. "I have an idea. We'll fix your life, and then you and Irina can be the married couple and I'll—"

Irina's head snapped up so fast she clocked Eli's jaw, making him bite his tongue. He grunted and slid Irina off his lap, onto Jasper's. "You're dangerous. Here, you take her."

"So when she's dangerous, she's my responsibility?" Jasper's eyes sparkled with mirth.

"Yep." Eli dabbed at his tongue with his finger. No blood.

Jasper's eyes slid to the coffee table. Eli followed his gaze, wondering why a piece of furniture was making Jasper leer in that manner. Then he saw the chains dangling from the legs.

Oh. *Ohhhh.*

"We will come back to what you two just said, and I will kick both your asses," Irina threatened. "But first we need to address what Jasper said. What are you talking about? What does that mean, that Eli and I will be the married couple?"

Jasper frowned. "My parents—my foster parents, I mean, the people who took me in—were members of the Trinity Masters. Two women and a man. I lived with Alan and Becca. They were legally married, on top of being married under the laws of the Trinity Masters. As far as the rest of the world knew, they were a normal married couple, but Becca's best friend, Annie, who never married, was a very close family friend. I called her Aunty Annie, but she was also my mother. In a lot of ways, I was closer with her than with Becca. Annie was an artist. She understood my passion for art and archaeology in a way Mom and Dad didn't.

"My parents didn't have any biological children. Dad was an FBI agent and injured on the job before he was married. He couldn't have kids. That's why they fostered. But Aunty Annie—because she was pretending to just be a family friend—never got to be the mom who woke up in the middle of the night with the kids, or went to parent-teacher conferences. I lived with Annie on and off once I graduated high school. That's why I know she always regretted not getting to experience that. She told me how hard it had been for her. She warned me about that part of being in the Trinity Masters. In her words, it was hard, really hard, to be the one on the outside.

Jasper picked up Irina's and Eli's hands. At his urging, they laced their fingers together. Jasper kissed their linked fists.

"When I heard you," he kissed Eli's knuckles, "call you," now he kissed Irina's, "his fiancée, I suddenly saw myself in Annie's position." He leaned his head back against the wall. "Saw myself spending my life part of a family in private, but to the outside world, I'd always be alone."

Eli felt sick to his stomach. "That's never…never what I'd intended. I didn't even think about it like that."

Jasper shook his head. "It makes more sense for it to be the two of you."

"No, no. It should be the two of you. I'm—"

"Hold it." Irina detangled herself from the two of them and slid off the cushions to perch on the edge of the table. Jasper's eyes darted from her to the chains and he sat forward a bit, like a cat lowering his shoulder before the pounce. Eli wondered idly if he should warn her of the peril. But in this analogy, he was Jasper's fellow predator, rather than an ally of the prey.

Irina frowned at Jasper. "Your dad was an FBI agent?"

"Yes."

"What was your mom? The one married to him, I mean."

"She was in local politics."

"Local?" Irina prodded.

"She was the city manager of New York."

"Local politics…" Irina shook her head, clearly exasperated. "Your parents both had jobs that made their personal lives subject to scrutiny. Of course they had to pretend to be married."

Jasper shook his head, but Irina held her hand up, stopping him.

"Do either of you have morality clauses in your employment contract? What would happen if anyone you work with found out you lived in a house with a woman and another man?"

Eli paused to consider. "They might think it's weird, but I don't think I'd get fired. I mean it hardly matters, since I stole a Rodin and I'm *already* fired, but I take your point."

Jasper had stopped shaking his head. "Uh, actually, nothing would happen to me."

"Do you even have a job?" Eli asked.

Jasper grinned. "I do, and if you knew what it was, you'd be pissed."

Eli felt a growl rumbling in his chest. Jasper must have heard it, because his grin widened.

"So really, I'm the only one with a traditional job. I'm based in D.C. now, and I'm assuming I'll be relocated to one of your cities. When I do, I'll just keep quiet about my personal life. I'm in the private sector, and the owner of my company is living openly with his trinity." She spread her hands. "I say we do the same." Irina's expression shifted to a frown and she muttered, "Except that I probably don't have a job anymore. I keep forgetting that."

Jasper looked stunned. "I just always assumed... Well damn. That could work."

"I agree with her." Eli was done with this topic. There were more pressing things to discuss. "What is your job, Jasper?"

"I'm not going to tell you."

Maybe he was a professor too. An archaeology professor? No, that wasn't possible. If he was running around stealing things, when would he have time to publish?

"Eli, we're talking about our future here..." Irina poked him with her foot.

"Live together. Fuck people's opinions. Check." Eli grabbed Irina's foot, pulling it into his lap, but kept his gaze on Jasper. "What do you do?"

Jasper pursed his lips, then inched away from him. "Irina, you can stop him, right?"

"I could, but you're both annoying me right now, so I'm going to let him hit you."

"You wound me, woman. You do."

"*I'm* going to wound you if you don't tell me," Eli growled. "I'm normally not a violent man, but you inspire me to it."

Jasper grinned, his blue eyes sparkling. "I'm a scholar-in-residence at the Smithsonian."

Eli blacked out for a moment from sheer horror. "They... I... You..."

Jasper hummed and rubbed his hands together like a cartoon villain. "I have credentials that get me into all the archives and storage areas. All that lovely art, just waiting to come home with me."

Eli lunged for Jasper, who leapt up, putting Irina between them.

"Stop torturing him," Irina chided. "Eli, I'm sure he's joking about taking the art home with him."

Jasper doubled over with laughter. Eli took a minute to compose himself. Hands on hips, he dropped his head and blew out a breath. Irina threw up her hands and wandered over to the stairs, heading to the second floor of their strange accommodations.

"Are you actually a scholar-in-residence at the Smithsonian?" he finally asked.

"I'm so sorry, but I really am." Jasper had stopped laughing, though his eyes still sparkled. "You recognized my name, right? Where did you first hear about me?"

"When I was... When I spent three months at the Smithsonian." Eli paused. "Wait, do they *know*?"

"The director is the one who nicknamed me Indiana Jones."

Eli was having trouble with this. "And they trust you? Not to, uh, steal art from the museum to hang in your house?"

"Well…" Jasper pursed his lips again. "I have an A. Culver hanging above my toilet."

Eli's muscles tensed with the need to strangle him, but he forced himself to relax. "I know you're joking, but I still want to throttle you."

"Actually, this time I'm not joking."

"You stole a piece by A. Culver, a seminal American contemporary artist, from the Smithsonian, and hung it over your toilet?" Eli realized his voice was getting louder, but couldn't stop himself.

"You know A. Culver?"

"Now you assume that just because I'm an art historian, I don't know about contemporary artists?"

Jasper shrugged. "I was just surprised."

"Stop changing the subject. Which painting did you steal?"

"Who said anything about steal?"

Eli growled.

Jasper laughed. "I'm sorry. You're just too much fun to tease. I didn't steal it. A. Culver. Anne Culver…" Jasper's voice trailed away.

Eli frowned, but it didn't take long for him to put the pieces together. "Anne Culver is your Aunty Annie?"

Jasper nodded. "I don't talk about it much, but people know. That's part of why I'm where I am. Her name opens doors."

"I'd say so." Eli was jealous of Jasper, growing up with one of America's most outspoken and brilliant artists as a parent. Then he immediately felt guilty and disloyal to his own parents. "Oh, we never talked about what we were going to tell our families."

Jasper shrugged. "Mine won't be the issue. Maybe don't tell them anything."

Eli snorted. "You ever tried to keep anything from an old Chinese woman?"

"No, can't say I have."

"Then trust me, we'd better have our stories straight." Eli grimaced. "*Lao lao* is the one we need to worry about."

"Terrifying grandmother. I'll put it on the list of things to worry about."

They spent a few minutes comparing notes on mutual acquaintances, before a sound from the second floor paused their conversation.

Irina coughed delicately, then called out, "Are you two done?"

Jasper and Eli exchanged a look. "Yes," Eli replied.

Irina's footsteps were soft, almost inaudible as she came down the stairs on bare feet. The hanging fabric obscured her until she was halfway down. She took another step and cleared the fabric, appearing like Venus before them.

Irina wore sky blue, the silky fabric held up by a gold band of embroidered ribbon fastened just above her breasts. From there it fell to the top of her thighs, where a short, beaded fringe pulled down on the fabric, the weight at the hem molding the garment to her breasts, revealing the stiff peaks of her nipples. Swags of the same beaded fringe as on the hem dropped from the band at the top, across each of her arms. From the breasts up and the thighs down, she was delightfully naked. Her hair was pulled into a loose braid, the color darker than normal—she must have showered.

She stood before them, chin raised in a challenge, and yet her eyes were vulnerable. Light that touched her was filtered through a gold drape, painting her with the glow of the golden hour.

"She's like a Maurice Shapiro," Jasper said.

"Or George Inness," Eli whispered.

There was another beat of silence, yet Irina didn't cower or flee. She was the brave one among their trinity, of that there could be no doubt.

Jasper took Eli's hand, led him across the room to the stairs.

Irina's eyes widened as they approached. Eli tried to imagine what she must be feeling—she was as good as naked, offering herself to not one, but two men. Jasper stopped at the foot of the stairs, looked at Eli.

Once more he felt the weight of their gazes.

Eli prided himself on being mild-mannered. He was, in many ways, the archetype of the absentminded professor.

Yet that was a ruse, a front. One he'd cultivated to minimize his physical presence, and the depth of his passion. Yet he'd revealed himself to them the other night. When the drugs had, like a drink or three, stripped away his inhibitions, he'd revealed his raw, demanding core. They hadn't run. They hadn't mocked. They'd reveled and enjoyed.

"Upstairs," Eli said. It was a command.

Irina and Jasper started up and Eli followed them, shedding both pretense and restraint with each step.

Chapter Eleven

Irina shivered, but not from cold, though the air was chilly enough and this crazy piece of lingerie she'd found in the bedroom closet was hardly keeping her warm.

She'd showered—and shaved and moisturized—and it wasn't until she found herself digging through her makeup bag to pull out neutral-tone eye shadow and pale-pink lip gloss—the kind of cosmetics you wore when you wanted to look like you weren't wearing any—that she acknowledged what she intended to do.

Now that she'd done it, now that she'd made herself the impetus for intimacy, she was doubting the bold move.

Hands settled on her bare shoulder blades, warm on her chilled skin, and Irina gasped. He was at her back, and she didn't know which "he" it was. There was something erotic and terrifying about that.

Hands slid over her shoulders and down her chest. Now she could see those hands, and knew who was touching her. Eli's palms skimmed over her distended nipples and Irina moaned.

"Watch him," Eli whispered into her ear.

Irina obediently looked at Jasper, who was examining Irina and Eli with a hooded gaze.

"Take off your clothes, Jasper," Eli said.

Jasper wasted no time, pulling the snug exercise shirt up and off. He toed off his shoes, lifted each foot in turn to strip off his socks, then shucked his shorts. He was naked underneath.

Eli thumbed her nipples as she looked at Jasper's naked and erect body. It was almost as if he was conditioning her to be aroused at the sight of their husband.

Jasper's cock was hard, the tip glistening. Once more Irina was struck by the scars that marked his chest and arm, yet now wasn't the time to ask about them.

Eli's thumbnails scraped against the fabric directly over the tips of her nipples. Irina arched her back and let out a sob. Her sex was pulsing with need.

"Jasper, take her clothes off."

Irina waited eagerly as Jasper approached, but he bypassed her to reach for Eli, forcing him to let go of Irina.

"I'm not going to pretend having you play puppet master isn't hot." Jasper unbuttoned Eli's shirt. "But this time you're not going to be the only one giving orders."

Jasper pushed Eli's shirt off his shoulders. He reached up, plucked Eli's glasses off, and walked away to drop them on the bedside table.

"Irina," Jasper ordered, "take off his shoes."

Irina wanted to protest—why was *she* the only one not giving orders? That was plainly sexist and unfair.

On the other hand, this was incredibly sexy, and at this point she didn't care about fair. She wanted to be fucked. She wanted to touch and be touched.

She wanted to feel their power. Wanted to be a leaf riding the turbulent winds of two battling tornadoes that would slowly merge into one. Because there was no doubt in her mind that these two very different, yet equally sexy and powerful men were forces of nature. Social custom and refinement had muted the raw core of them. That was about to be stripped away. Until they were just three people, three beings, coming together.

Irina dropped to her knees. Eli shifted his weight to his right foot, allowing her to remove shoe and sock from his left foot. She repeated it on the right, then sat back on her heels.

"Now his pants," Jasper said.

Irina reached up and unfastened his dress belt—the same one they'd used to bind her last night—then undid his slacks. Her fingers brushed over the hard ridge of his cock. She worked his pants down and off, leaving him in dark blue boxer briefs.

Irina considered waiting for someone to order her to finish the job, but the thread of her patience was wearing thin against the sharp edge of her desire.

She slid her hand into the slit of Eli's underwear, wrapping her fingers around his cock. Eli groaned. His hands, which had been loose at his sides, now curled into fists. She squeezed gently before removing her hand and sliding his boxers down and off.

Eli stepped out of his puddled clothes, kicking them aside. Irina was still on her knees. Her mouth temptingly close to Eli's long, hard erection.

Jasper joined them, standing at Eli's shoulder, so now she was confronted with two hard cocks. Irina waged an internal battle. On one hand, she could take those cocks, pull them close together, and taste her men. On the other hand, she wasn't that giving of a person—her body was humming with the need to be touched. She held up her hands, one to each of them, and together they pulled her to her feet.

Eli ran a finger through the fringe draped over her upper arm, making the beads click. Jasper slid his fingers along the gold band that held it up, finding the button hidden under her arm.

He unfastened it. Irina lowered her arms to her sides, and the weight of the beads pulled the garment down and off. As it slid, the heavy gold band raked over her nipples, making sure that they were hard and ready for her husbands.

Jasper reached for her nipples but before he could touch them, Eli had scooped her up, carrying her to the bed. Irina had never been carried like this before and it was intensely erotic. It was all too easy to imagine she was the pretty concubine being carried off by the sultan.

Jasper rolled onto the bed as Eli set her down.

Make that *sultans*.

Eli came down on her other side, and for a moment they lay there, Irina on her back between them. The quiet before the storm gave way, and like the tornadoes she'd likened them to, they caught her up, held her in the force of their desire.

Jasper closed his lips over one nipple. Eli pinched the other as he leaned down to kiss her.

Eli's mouth was wet and hot. His tongue slid between her lips, demanding she open herself to him. Irina did so willingly, letting him invade her, her attention split between the kiss and the delicious tugging at each of her nipples.

Jasper bit her nipple gently, raising his head to distend the sensitive tip of her breast. Irina gasped and bit Eli's lower lip.

A hand trailed down her stomach and pushed her thighs apart, baring her wet, aching pussy to the cold air. Irina wiggled her hands free and grabbed their heads. She tangled her fingers in Jasper's hair and pushed his head down, toward her pussy. She was no longer content to wait and obey. She needed to be touched, now.

Jasper said something she didn't hear, but Eli raised his mouth from hers. His eyes were dark in the dim light of the bedroom. She knew they were blue, made brighter by the contrast between their light color and his dark skin, but right now they were dark pools—not the bright blue of the day sky, but the midnight blue of the night ocean.

Jasper shifted, sliding between her legs. Eli reached down and grabbed her knee, pulling her leg up and to the side, opening her to Jasper's touch.

Irina slid her fingers through Eli's hair, but it was too short for her to grab, and apparently Eli was, unlike Jasper, in no mood to be commanded. He manacled her wrist with one hand, then forced her arm above her head. He pinned her to the mattress—one hand on her wrist, the other on her knee, mindful of the bruise that still decorated her hip. She strained, tried to move her arm and leg out from under his control. Eli's muscles tensed and her rebellion was short-lived. She paid for it as he nipped her neck, her shoulder.

Jasper's breath fanned over the wet lips of her sex. Irina arched her hips, begging him with both body and words to touch her.

"Please, please."

"Please what?" Jasper asked.

She felt his words and puffs of air against her pussy, which only made her more desperate. She tugged Jasper's hair.

"Stop teasing. Touch me. Fuck me."

Eli released her arm and shifted on the bed, until his upper body was at her hip.

"Spread her labia," Eli said. "I want to see her."

155

Jasper's fingers stroked her pussy lips before his thumbs opened her, exposing the pink core. Irina again tugged on Jasper's head, desperate to feel his lips on her.

"Ow," Jasper said.

Eli grabbed her wrist, forcing her to release Jasper. "Arms over your head. Keep them there while we learn your body."

Irina eagerly obeyed, not because she didn't want to touch them, but because she would do anything that would bring her closer to the sweet release she craved.

Jasper stoked her clit, a single sure pass of the pad of his finger, and Irina's whole body quaked.

"I'm not going to last," she sobbed out. "I'm close."

The mattress dipped and shifted. Irina looked up to see Eli crawling toward the headboard, his cock bobbing along under him. He settled himself with his back against a stack of pillows.

"Come here, Irina."

Rolling over, she slid reluctantly away from Jasper and crawled up the bed, toward Eli. He leaned back and spread his legs. When she paused, he beckoned her with an imperious wave of his hand.

When she was on hands and knees between his legs, Eli grabbed her under the arms and hauled her up, flipping her over so she lay with her back against his chest. His cock was nestled into the crevice of her ass, the tip poking against her lower back. She swallowed at the thought of having him inside her.

Eli bent his knees, digging his heels into the bed, then grabbed her legs, forcing them up and over his raised knees, so she was spread wide.

"This way I can watch," he growled in her ear.

Jasper crawled up to them. He raised a hand, caressing first Eli's cheek, then Irina's.

"Play with her nipples," Jasper said.

Eli's fingers closed over the tips of her breasts, plucking and pulling. Irina dug her nails into Eli's wrists. She wanted to stop him. She wanted to beg him to be rougher.

Jasper watched for a moment, his cock twitching in response to the show they were putting on. Then he lay down, belly on the bed, and kissed her pussy. His lips slid along the smooth lips of her sex, then he opened her with his fingers and finally, finally he licked her clit.

Irina sighed in relief that it had finally happened, but that relief was washed away by a wave of arousal. Her head twisted side to side, seeking something. Eli captured her lips in a kiss, his tongue once more burrowing into her mouth, giving her the oral stimulation she wanted.

Jasper set to work on her clit, his tongue rubbing rather than flicking. She couldn't help but grind herself against his mouth. Each breath brought her closer. The combined sensations of the tongue on her clit, tongue in her mouth, fingers on her nipples, fingers on her labia, all pouring together into a seemingly endless well of arousal.

Yet she was rising, her body clenching tight, like a vise closing. She should tell them, warn them, but Eli's kiss was relentless.

And she was afraid if she said anything, they might stop.

Irina held the orgasm at bay, strangely reluctant to end this moment of bliss. But the pleasure they were giving her couldn't be stopped. Eli twisted her nipples in tandem with a hard stroke of Jasper's tongue and that sent her over. She screamed, wrenching her mouth from Eli's so she could clench her teeth. Eli plucked her nipples, making her breasts dance, and Jasper pressed his thumbs against her inner thighs, holding her still as he continued to lick her.

The orgasm kept going long after it should have stopped. It was a like a lightning strike that didn't flash and fade but stayed, electricity crackling along her nerve endings, making her so sensitive that her toes curled. Her lower body shook, the muscles of her thighs twitching uncontrollably.

"I can't, I can't," she said.

Jasper surged up, his face a snarl of desire.

Eli released her breasts, grabbed her by the waist, and lifted her. Irina had a moment of relief as the orgasm finally faded. She breathed heavily, but her respite was short-lived.

Jasper reached under her ass and grabbed Eli's cock. Eli's fingers dug into Irina's waist as Jasper stroked him. Irina watched, entranced, as Jasper expertly manipulated their husband's cock. When Jasper slid two fingers into Irina, she arched her hips against his hand—at least as much as Eli's grip would allow.

Jasper ran his fingers, wet with the proof of Irina's recent orgasm, over the head of Eli's cock. When he angled his cock toward her pussy, she gasped, realized what they had planned.

"Jasper, Eli…"

"I got to taste you first; he gets to be inside your sweet pussy first." Jasper stroked the tip of Eli's cock one last time, then pressed the head between Irina's pussy lips.

Reaching up, she grabbed the headboard, using that as an anchor point to tilt her hips. As she did, the head of Eli's cock found the entrance to her body.

Eli used his hold on her waist to press her down, at the same time as he flexed his hips.

Stars danced behind Irina's closed eyes as Eli's cock opened her, tunneling into her orgasm-tight body. He was hard as steel, and relentless. He pushed her down and flexed his hips until Irina was sure she couldn't take any more.

And then he kept going, demanding that she take more. That she take all of him.

When he finally stopped, holding still now that he was fully embedded within her, Jasper reached out. He first stroked the entrance to her body, which was stretched tight around the base of Eli's cock, then massaged her clit. He didn't stroke it directly—he was clearly well versed enough in women's bodies to know that right now she would be too sensitive to deal with more direct stimulation. Instead he pressed two fingers to either side of her clit and massaged not the exterior tip of her clitoris, but the nerves buried under the plump flesh at the top of her pussy.

"Hold on," Eli warned her.

Irina tightened her grip on the headboard, and it was a good thing she had, because when Eli began to fuck her in earnest—sliding his cock out before thrusting in hard—her whole body shook from the force of it.

She raised her head, watched Jasper watching Eli fuck her, and that added another layer to her arousal.

A follow-up orgasm had just started to awaken deep inside her when Eli abruptly stopped and lifted her off his cock.

"What? Don't stop," she begged.

"Jasper needs a turn."

Eli reached down, shifted his cock to one side, then tapped her clit with two fingers, which made her jump.

Jasper slid into place. Her pelvis, raised off the bed by Eli's body, was at the perfect height and angle. Jasper couldn't reach the headboard, so he braced his hands against Eli's shoulders as he started to work his cock into Irina's pussy.

She moaned, tipping her head back. She was trapped, caged. Eli was at her back, his legs forcing her open, his fingers spread over her breasts, squeezing and massaging them, but not touching the nipples.

Jasper's arms pressed in on her, ensuring that if she'd wanted to let go of the headboard and lower her arms, she couldn't. His cock slid into her, thicker than Eli's but not as long. She felt each inch as he entered, and when he lowered his upper body, releasing Eli's shoulders to brace himself on the bed, Jasper's chest raked against Irina's exposed nipples with each thrust.

Jasper kissed her, then stretched his neck and kissed Eli, who'd raised his head. Irina released the headboard so her arms wouldn't be in the way. This meant she had no purchase, that she was entirely at their mercy, and she was more than okay with that.

Jasper's lips moved from Eli's to hers, then back again. She closed her eyes. She didn't know who kissed her, couldn't tell whose lips rubbed over her own or whose jaw she nipped.

But she knew it was Jasper's cock thrusting in and out of her. She could feel the steel of Eli's cock when Jasper's thrusts pressed it against her. From the sounds he was making, she was sure that each time Jasper thrust, Eli's cock was being stimulated.

Irina lost herself in them. She'd imagined what it would be like to be with her trinity, but the imagining didn't come close to the reality. She was theirs, they were hers.

When Jasper's thrusts sped up and he dropped his head against her shoulder, Eli said, "Finish. Come in her."

Jasper shuddered and thrust once, twice. She could feel his cock twitch deep inside her.

For a moment they were still, then Jasper pulled out, leaving Irina feeling both exposed and empty.

But they weren't done with her. It was Eli's turn.

Together they shifted her, and once more Jasper guided Eli's cock into Irina's pussy.

Eli fucked her faster this time, relentlessly. Jasper pressed the heel of his hand against the top of her pussy, so the thrusting of Eli's cock made her hips rock and her pussy rub against Jasper.

Irina gasped as the direct, rhythmic stimulation rocketed her toward orgasm.

"I'm going to come," she warned them. If they replied, she didn't hear it. Pleasure ripped through her—a deep, muscle-tightening orgasm turning her inward, until all she could do was feel.

Eli's thrusts sped up, then he too came, groaning in Irina's ear.

Irina didn't realize she was crying until Jasper helped ease her off Eli's cock then lifted her stiff legs, straightening them.

"Shh, beautiful. It's okay, you're okay."

Jasper lay down and she curled against his chest.

"I, I d-don't know why, why I'm crying."

"That was pretty intense." Jasper stroked her back.

"No, don't," she begged. "Too sensitive."

"I'm just touching your back."

"Too sensitive," she repeated.

"Okay."

The mattress dipped, and Eli loomed over her. His glasses were back on and he blinked at her. "I'm sorry, Irina." He awkwardly wiped her tears with a wet washcloth.

"No, no." She rolled onto her back. "Don't you dare apologize. That was beautiful." Another sob welled up. "So beautiful."

Eli looked confused. "You're...happy?"

"Of course I am, you idiot." Irina burst into sobs, grabbed both of them, and pulled them to her.

"I don't understand women," Eli said.

"Why do you think I started dating guys?" Jasper teased softly.

"Is she really okay? That was pretty depraved," Eli said.

Irina slapped his shoulder. "Don't you dare say that."

"That's it. I give up. I don't understand what's going on right now."

"This is great; usually I'm the one who gets slapped." Jasper's tone was laced with both that familiar hint of amusement, but also a deep satisfaction. "Worry about figuring it out later, Eli. Just lie here with us."

After a moment, a blanket settled over them, then Eli lay down on one side of her, Jasper on the other.

Irina smiled through the hiccupy end of her crying jag. Her men. Her trinity. Her loves.

Chapter Twelve

The hotel served brunch and dinner. The people who came to stay here weren't coming for the fine dining experience, and the location—the middle of nowhere—meant that it wasn't exactly easy to nip out to a restaurant. The food was far from gourmet, but not terrible. Charcuterie, crudité, and fruit were set out on black plastic platters—the kind that came from grocery story catering. There were some cold salads, many of which featured mayo rather heavily, and for something hot, a tureen of soup.

The dining room was on the first floor, just behind the small lobby. Given that the hotel itself wasn't very large, it wasn't surprising that the dining room wasn't large either. The food was laid out on a buffet, and there was a beverage cart in one corner, with liquor on the top shelf and bottles of soda and water on the lower. There were four two-top tables and a stack of extra chairs in one corner. Two small couches and a large armchair were crammed together around a gas fireplace. A framed sign by the door said, "Due to health code, underwear must be worn at all times in the dining area. Thank you for your understanding."

Jasper had fallen asleep, but woke up around 11:30 p.m. when Irina rolled over and elbowed him in the ribs. He'd scooted to safety—out of range of her elbows—but hadn't been able to fall back to sleep. After lying in the dark, he heard a change to the rhythm of Eli's breathing, and at his whispered inquiry, Eli confirmed that he too was awake.

They'd tried to slide out of bed without waking Irina, but she popped up as they'd fumbled for clothes. She confirmed that she was hungry, and so they'd headed out for a very late dinner together.

They stumbled into the dining room just after midnight. A couple, both with dark hair, sat together on one of the couches by the fire. The woman wore a short black robe, open to reveal a leather bustier and black lace panties. The man wore only dark brown pants made of some loose, lightweight fabric. He watched their trio as they walked in, and Jasper moved a bit closer to Irina, shielding her. The man wasn't exactly threatening, but he certainly didn't give off a "harmless" vibe.

While Eli and Irina picked up plates, Jasper shoved two of the tables together and gathered silverware and napkins for them, setting the table. When he came back with a bottle of water for each of them, Irina was sliding into the seat Eli held out for her. Jasper held out a seat for Eli, who did that startled/confused blinking thing Jasper was coming to love, and he too sat down.

"I wanted to get you a plate," Irina said to Jasper, eyes pinched with distress, "but I didn't know what to get you. I don't know what you like to eat. Are you a vegetarian? Vegan? Are you allergic to peanuts? We're going to be married and I don't even know if you have food allergies." Irina's voice was soft.

Eli reached his long arm across the table, taking her hand in his. Jasper returned to the bar, rifling through the bottles on the top shelf until he found a nice bottle of red. He grabbed that, a corkscrew, and three stemless wineglasses. The dark-haired man on the couch watched Jasper's hands, narrowing his eyes. As Jasper returned to the table, the man leaned over to say something to the woman, who twisted to look at them, tapping her champagne flute against her lower lip.

He left the wine and glasses at Eli's elbow, then quickly filled a plate, taking the seat beside Irina. Eli passed him a glass.

"To us," Jasper said.

"To us." Eli raised his glass.

Irina took a deep breath. "To us."

They clinked, sipped, and then tucked into their food. The silence between them was comfortable. As soon as the first piece of cheese passed his lips, Jasper realized he was ravenous. Their irregular sleeping and eating schedule was taking its toll. They'd started their day around dawn in a motel in Colorado. It seemed as if days had passed since then, and even the burgers in Kansas seemed long ago.

Once the first flash of hunger had been satiated, Jasper set down his fork and picked up his glass. "I'm not allergic to anything. Though sometimes walnuts make me feel itchy."

"I was lactose intolerant growing up, but grew out of it in my twenties. I don't really like the taste of cheese, but love ice cream." Eli pointed at his cheese-less plate.

Irina's shoulders were starting to relax. "I normally don't eat red meat, unless it's something like earlier, where a burger seemed to be the safest option. Or if I'm in Texas I'll eat brisket. For some reason I love smoked brisket, but I don't like steak."

"I hate wearing underwear." Jasper gestured toward his crotch with a spear of asparagus.

"That explains the bacon boxers." Eli's voice was dry.

Irina laughed. "I wondered. Figured it was you showing off your irreverent sense of humor. Which is accurate."

"Let's say it served two purposes. One, it let my triad know what they're in for." Eli rolled his eyes and Irina giggled. "Two, they were the only boxers I could find."

"What about pets? Anyone have one?" Irina asked.

"You know I don't." Eli popped an olive into his mouth.

"I have a cat. Well, I got a cat from a shelter, and then he decided he liked my next door neighbor better, so it's more like there's this cat that hangs out with me sometimes when I'm home."

Irina shook her head. "No pets here."

"Hobbies? Sports?" Eli looked pleased with having come up with the questions.

"I don't know about hobbies," Jasper said, "but my sport of choice is cycling. I ride to work when I'm in D.C."

"Krav Maga," Irina answered. "There's an amazing studio on Eighth Street, near Eastern Market."

Eli frowned. "You both live in D.C."

"We haven't really talked about that." Jasper watched Eli, who was poking a piece of salami dissolutely. "And I for one don't have to be in D.C."

"But that's where the Smithsonian is."

Jasper shrugged. "I spend as much time in New York with Annie as I do in D.C."

"And like I said before, I can transfer anywhere." Irina frowned. "That's assuming I still have a job. I wonder what happens to the company once, uh, you-know-who deals with Mr. Bennett."

The scrape of chair legs on the wood floor halted their conversation. Jasper's, Irina's, and Eli's heads whipped around.

The dark-haired couple was standing beside their table. The man pulled over an extra chair, placing it beside Eli. The woman, who seemed either unaware or unconcerned that her robe hung open, showing off her lingerie, sat with the unhurried grace of the supremely confident.

"Oh come on, you three." The woman propped her elbow on the table, chin on her fist. Her eyes sparkled. "She's not Voldemort. You can say 'Grand Master.'"

Shit.

Jasper tensed. Irina shoved her chair back half a foot, bracing herself to leap into action. The man, who was standing at the end of the table, assessed Irina and Jasper's movements and shifted his weight onto his back foot, making it clear that he too was ready to engage.

Eli leaned toward the woman, peering at her boobs.

"Eli," Jasper snapped.

Eli sat back, adjusted his glasses, and raised the wine bottle in the direction of the newcomers. "Would you like a glass?"

Irina and Jasper were looking at him like he was cracked in the head. Eli glanced at the dark-haired woman, who raised one brow at Eli, indicating that it was up to him to clue in the other people at the table.

Her companion went, not to get glasses for wine, but to retrieve a short glass of amber liquid and a champagne flute from a side table near the couch they'd been sitting on.

The dark-haired man pulled up a fifth chair, situating himself at the head of the table, between his companion and Jasper. Jasper flicked his gaze between the newcomers and Eli, eyes wide, and a "what the fuck?" expression written large on his features.

Eli should just tell them, but over the past few days, he'd regularly been the one who didn't know what was going on, who had to ask what was happening. They weren't dumb, they'd figure it out in a minute, and Eli's advantage was proximity to the woman, but he was going to savor the moment nonetheless.

It felt good to have the tables turned.

"To the Grand Master." Eli raised his glass.

"Long may she reign." There was a rueful note to the woman's voice as she raised her flute.

"And may wisdom find her." If the woman's tone had been rueful, the man's bordered on cutting and snide.

They each took a sip. Irina and Jasper didn't move. Irina in particular was starting to look at Eli suspiciously, so before she could fully panic, he decided to relent.

"Look at their jewelry," Eli said.

The woman obligingly dropped her forearm to lie atop the table, leaning back so the small gold charm dangling just above her cleavage caught the light. That's what Eli had been looking at. It was partially hidden by the black choker she wore, meaning Eli was the only one who could really see it. The man saluted them with his glass, then set it down and twisted the ring he wore, so the embossed signet caught the light.

Eli watched, knew the moment Irina and Jasper realized that their new companions each wore the triquetra, the symbol of the Trinity Masters.

"You're...you're..." Irina stumbled over the words.

"We're members of this great experiment's oldest and most ruthless society." The man's smile was sardonic. "I'm Caden, this is Darling."

The woman set down her glass and extended her hand, first to Eli, then to the others. They introduced themselves and shook hands in turn.

Jasper looked at them. "Of all the gin joints."

Caden snorted. "True. Though there are few places that offer this level of anonymity and privacy."

"And, to be fair, I did learn about this place from another member at one of the galas." Jasper looked a bit sheepish.

Darling nodded. "Considering, I'm almost surprised this is the first time we've run across other members."

"You, uh, come here often?" Irina asked.

Darling looked to Caden, who answered, "There are other places we frequent more—better ambiance, better food. But this is our favorite for privacy. And there are no stupid games."

"I couldn't help but overhear—" Darling started.

"You were listening as hard as you could," Caden broke in. Darling ignored him.

"—but are you a new trinity?"

"We were just called to the altar a few days ago," Eli answered.

Darling raised one brow. "And the Grand Master sent you here? I'm sorry. It used to be that people went to a suite at the Plaza in Boston. Perhaps not all the new Grand Master's changes are for the better."

"We *were* there. It's a bit of a long story how we ended up here." Eli was about to launch into the details of their adventure so far, but Irina spoke first.

"Are you married? I mean trinity married?"

Darling's face blanked. Caden shook his head. "No. We're not."

"Oh, I'm sorry. I just assumed…"

There was an aloof intensity about Caden that was both intimidating and faintly irritating. In a blink, that was gone, and in its place was the face of a man haunted. "Darling is the love of my life."

"Caden, don't…" Darling reached out for him. He took her hand, forcing it down onto the table.

"Until a few months ago, we thought Darling was going to be called to the altar to be with two other people." Caden picked up his glass and tossed back a mouthful. Eli wondered how much of what he said was because he was drinking. "A trinity that didn't include me. That…changed with the new Grand Master. We're enjoying the stay of execution. Another few months, maybe another year, of stolen moments and weekends of kinky sex. No tenderness. No love."

Darling had lowered her head, shaking it slightly. Caden raised his glass and drained it.

Silence sat heavy on the group, and Eli felt as if the floor had shifted under them, as if they were now players in an entirely different game.

"You, my friend, need another drink." Jasper went to the bar, returning with a bottle in each hand. "Irish or Scottish?"

"Irish."

Jasper poured Caden two fingers.

Irina's eyes were soft with sadness. "You're in love, but you won't be in the same trinity? Why do you assume that?"

Darling shrugged delicately. "It's a relatively common practice among some of the legacy families to ask the Grand Master to agree to certain trinities, family alliances, that sort of thing. My family wants me to be in a trinity that is politically and financially advantageous to them."

Irina frowned, but Jasper nodded in understanding.

Caden considered Jasper. "Are you a legacy?"

"Somewhat. I was adopted by people who were members, so I knew about it all, growing up."

Darling hummed in understanding. "My whole family, going back generations, are members. In fact, our families were founding members of the Trinity Masters." Darling gestured at Caden.

"I don't understand," Irina said. "Why can't you be together now if you're in love?"

"If you all are done eating, let's move by the fire," Caden said.

Since Caden was shirtless, and Darling in lingerie, it was clear why they'd want to be closer to the fire. Drinks were refilled, small plates piled with fruit and cream for dessert, and then everyone selected seats. Caden and Darling returned to the same couch, Eli and Irina settled on the other love seat, and Jasper took the armchair.

Once everyone was in place, Eli looked at Caden and Darling, who were looking at each other.

Darling held out her hand. Caden raised it to his lips. He kissed her reverently, with his eyes closed and a slight furrow to his brow. Darling made a noise, like a wounded animal—part pain, part distress.

She pulled her hand away from Caden and pressed her fingers—the ones that had just been kissed—over her mouth.

Caden sighed, twisted his Trinity Masters' ring around his finger. "Maybe I should tell you my story. My life story. Darling's life story."

Darling raised her hands. "No, Cade, don't. They're happy. They're on their honeymoon. They don't want to be dragged down by this."

"They should know what can happen. What generations of power and perversion can lead parents to do to their own children." Caden's voice was harsh, and his gaze seemed to bore into Darling.

Then Caden's gaze roved over their little group, before returning to the woman he loved.

"Darling." His voice dropped half an octave and rang with command. "Remove your robe."

Jasper and Eli both tensed, and Irina gasped.

Darling didn't protest. Didn't slap his face. She shrugged the robe off her shoulders.

"On your knees," Caden commanded.

Without protest, Darling dropped to her knees, facing Caden. She kept her chin up, staring at his chest, her hands resting palms up on her thighs.

"Strip," he commanded. Caden didn't look at Darling as she obeyed. He was watching Eli, Irina, and Jasper.

Darling pulled at the bustier, undoing the hidden hook-and-eye closures at the front. She slid it off, exposing her bare back to them. She folded the bustier and held it up to Caden, who took it, tossing it over his shoulder to the other side of the sofa, ensuring it was out of reach.

"May I stand, Master?" she asked softly. Her thumbs were hooked in the edges of her lacy panties.

"I don't know what you're trying to prove," Irina said angrily.

"Stop it," Eli demanded. This should have been sexy, but instead he just felt uncomfortable, and protective of Darling.

Tension was mounting—until Jasper burst out laughing. "Are you two seriously trying to blame your kinky preferences on your parents?"

Eli looked at Jasper, who didn't seem concerned by what Caden and Darling were doing. Caden looked shocked by Jasper's reaction, then a reluctant smile spread across the dark-haired man's face.

"Darling, you may put on your robe and sit on the couch."

"Thank you, Sir."

When her robe was on and belted, Darling rose and plopped down onto the couch. She looked worried, but not by what had just happened. She was looking at Caden, her worry clearly for him.

No one spoke for a moment. Eli caught Jasper's eye, and Jasper winked. Eli relaxed, but that feeling didn't last long.

"Without knowing our story, our Dom/sub relationship isn't shocking," Darling said quietly. "It shouldn't be."

Caden nodded. "Maybe you know a bit about power exchange play in sex, or BDSM in general. Most people learn about kinks when they're in their twenties. They match up these vague feelings they've had their whole lives with an adult kink that makes sense to them. They choose to explore it."

The way he emphasized the word "choose" made dread pool in Eli's stomach.

"We didn't choose this," Darling said quietly. "Caden's parents…"

"My parents started training us, her as a submissive, me as a dominant, when we were teenagers. One of my fathers has a theory, a pet theory, you could say. He thinks in every trinity there has to be a submissive, a dominant, and a switch."

"When you were teenagers?" Eli asked, horrified. He hadn't touched a naked boob until college. There'd been some under-the-shirt fumbling in high school, but that was it. He certainly hadn't been learning about sexual power dynamics.

"What do you mean 'training'?" Irina asked. "He didn't…I mean, they were your *parents*."

Caden's jaw clenched so hard the muscles bunched under his skin. He looked between the glass in his hand and the fireplace, as if he were planning to throw it at the flames. When he didn't respond to Irina, Darling leaned to one side and stroked his jaw. The muscle unclenched and his shoulders relaxed.

"Our families are old friends," Darling said, "and have been for generations. When my mother died, and my father and other mother couldn't take me in for political reasons, Caden's parents adopted me. I spent most of my time with them anyway. When I say trained, I truly mean trained. Caden's fathers kept a submissive in an apartment in the city. They'd take Caden and his brother to her to train them how to touch a woman, how to treat a submissive, how to always be in control."

Darling spoke to them, but kept a hand on Caden, as if he were a horse she was afraid would spook without the reassuring touch. "Caden's father—one of them—wanted him and his brother to be the dominants in their relationships. He wasn't sure which role I'd have to play in my trinity, so he trained me as a switch."

Caden snorted. "Darling he was willing to train himself. Magnanimous, wouldn't you say? To take your fifteen-year-old adopted daughter and make her your sexual submissive."

"Oh my God, you poor thing," Irina whispered.

Darling merely shook her head. "They're so out of touch with reality, with how real relationships should be, that I'm not even sure they know how screwed up what they did to us was. They were legacies, and *their* parents were legacies. To them, the family, and the Trinity Masters, is far more important than the happiness of a single person."

"Oh, they know how screwed up they were," Caden growled. "They knew exactly what they were doing. What they *are* doing."

Caden stopped speaking, and in a complete reversal of what had happened moments ago, he slid to his knees before Darling, dropping his head into her lap.

She stroked her fingers through his hair. "It's okay, love, it's okay."

The silence was so thick it was like a sucking, sticky fog seeping into everyone's skin.

"Why didn't you go to someone?" Jasper asked. "You were children."

"There were...extenuating circumstances. Reasons we didn't, and don't, say anything."

A moment passed before Irina, who looked as if she were about to burst from the effort of holding back her comment, said, "Why do you still let him do that to you?"

The question was made absurd by the fact that Caden was kneeling at Darling's feet, his head on her lap. It reminded Eli of a tableau from one of the Romantics' paintings—perhaps a Waterhouse.

Darling raised a brow. "Let him what? Be my master? Because I like it. Because it's what I am. It's who I am. Submitting—submitting to *him*—is where I feel safe."

Irina looked like she wanted to argue the point. Caden rose to his feet and held up his hand. It was easy to see why Darling felt safe with him. He gave off an air of quiet, grim authority.

"Maybe the Grand Master will put us together in a trinity with someone lovely and normal and we'll change. But for now, this is what we have. This is the best way I have to show her that I love her." Caden looked at Darling. "Show her that I'll always keep her safe."

His face hardened, and once again Eli tensed. The way Caden was looking at Darling, as if she were a bunny and Caden a hungry wolf, made Eli very, very worried for her. Yet Darling looked unconcerned—she smiled at Caden, reaching her hand up to him.

Instead of lacing his fingers with hers, Caden grabbed her wrist, jerking her forward a few inches.

"She's mine. And will always be mine."

Chapter Thirteen

Irina opened one eye, peering around the room. There were no clocks, and she wasn't wearing a watch. Their phones were powered off, so she had nothing on which to guess the time but a narrow band of light that pierced the murky darkness via a small opening in the heavy blackout curtains. The light was gold more than silver, which meant it was after dawn, but she had no idea if it was eight in morning or one in the afternoon.

Irina sat up, shoving aside masses of puffy gold duvet.

"Good morning."

Irina yelped, whipping to her right. The mounds of pillows and covers had camouflaged Jasper, who tossed a few pillows to the floor as he too sat up. Irina had slept in the middle of the ridiculous bed, Jasper on her right, Eli on her left.

She looked to the other side. Eli was already up and gone.

"How did you sleep?" Jasper asked.

"Not great. It took me a long time to fall asleep."

"I think that happened to all of us."

After the conversation with their fellow Trinity Masters, Irina, Jasper, and Eli had trudged back to their room. They'd gotten ready for bed—changing into PJs, brushing their teeth. It had been strangely domestic, all of them piled into the bathroom, taking turns using the sink.

Then they'd climbed into bed, close enough to touch, but not cuddling. Irina had lain awake, arms stretched out so she held Eli's hand and rested her fingers on Jasper's shoulder.

"If you'll excuse me." Jasper slid out of bed and padded to the bathroom.

Irina threw open the curtains, blinking at the light. It was mid-morning by her guess. She stretched a few times—her hip no longer ached, but the bruise was still there. She found her suitcase, flipped it open, and pulled on clean clothes—jeans and a black sweater with a deep V. She usually wore the sweater to work, over the top of a button-up shirt. Without the shirt, the V cut deep enough to almost reveal the edge of her bra, and showed off plenty of cleavage.

Jasper, wearing only sweatpants, exited the bathroom. They stopped for a moment, admiring each other. A little shiver of arousal shook Irina. That feeling was followed immediately by relief. After Darling and Caden's stories last night, she worried she'd never find anything arousing again.

Then her bladder protested, so she walked past Jasper, trailing her fingers along the bare skin above his waistband. He hummed in approval and stretched to give her ass a quick squeeze.

Laughing, Irina slid into the bathroom. She used the toilet, brushed her teeth, and pulled her hair up into a ponytail, then scrubbed her face before applying the same "look, I'm not wearing makeup" makeup she'd used the day before.

Finally ready to face the day, she left the bathroom. The bedroom was empty, so she headed down the stairs to the lower level. Her libido perked up, wondering if they were going to take advantage of the room's amenities, even while the rest of her was having a violently negative reaction to the idea of any sort of power exchange play, because of Darling's story.

She was rehearsing what she wanted to say on the topic of sex and kink when she rounded the last curve in the stairs, leaning to the side to see her men.

My men. I like that.

Turned out she didn't need to worry about discussing sex, because Eli and Jasper's attention was focused on the one thing they found more interesting than sex.

Art.

Eli, who unlike Jasper and Irina, still wore PJs, was sitting cross-legged in the middle of the floor. He was wearing latex gloves and using the corner of a brilliant ruby scarf to hold the edges of a thin gold frame. The canvas within that frame was an explosion of colors— deepest violet, blood and ruby reds, and golden yellows. If she'd been standing closer, Irina might not have realized what it was, but from a distance it was clear that the painting was of flowers, rendered in oil and the expressionist style.

They'd opened the other crates. She sucked in a breath and hurried over.

Jasper was sitting beside Eli, hands over his mouth as he gazed at the painting.

Irina circled around until she could see both of their faces. Eli's eyes were damp with tears, and Jasper looked like he was in shock.

"Eli? Jasper?"

Eli carefully passed the painting to Jasper, who also wore gloves and used a scarf to hold the frame. Jasper propped the painting against its crate, leaning it there so they could look at it.

Eli shook his head. "There's no way they didn't know."

"Not after what happened in Sweden," Jasper replied.

Irina looked at the painting. She was fighting outside of her weight class when it came to art, but she took a stab in the dark. "Is it...a Van Gogh?"

The bright colors seemed Van Gogh-like, but the flowers didn't look like the paintings of irises or sunflowers, the only two Van Gogh flower paintings she could think of.

Eli snorted and Jasper shook his head. Irina fought the urge to curl into a ball of embarrassment for having said something that was clearly dumb.

"Emil Nolde. This is an Emil Nolde oil painting." Jasper shook his head again. "This is unbelievable."

"Eli," Irina said piteously.

He cleared his throat and adjusted his glasses. "The expressionists aren't my area of specialty, but you can't study the effect of Nazi Germany on art without talking about Emil Nolde."

"The irony." Jasper shook his head. "Nolde was a member of the Nazi party, but Hitler condemned what was at the time modern art. He called it 'degenerate art.'"

Eli picked up where Jasper left off. "More of Nolde's art was removed from museums than that of any other artist. He appealed to the Nazis not to pull his art down. Instead, starting in nineteen forty-one, he was forbidden from painting. Some of his paintings went into what they called the Degenerate Art Exhibition."

Eli fell silent. Irina looked at the painting, and her initial thought that the reds looked like blood seemed even more appropriate. "What does it mean that it's here?"

Jasper cleared his throat. "This makes everything a bit more complicated, wouldn't you say?"

Eli nodded in agreement. "The Rodin would have been confiscated by the ERR. It had value to them. Pieces like this," he gestured to the Nolde painting, "were considered disgusting. In nineteen thirty-eight and nineteen thirty-nine, many of the most valuable pieces of modernist art were sold at auction to international collectors. Joseph Goebbels famously said that at least they should be able to make some money off the 'garbage.'"

"A Picasso. A Van Gogh. That's what they were auctioning off as garbage." Jasper surged to his feet and began pacing.

Eli continued in his calm professor tone. "Dealers tried to sell off the rest, but no one who otherwise might have liked the art dared go near Berlin, and everyone in Germany now firmly believed the art was garbage." Eli paused once again, collecting himself. "On March 20th, 1939, nearly five thousand pieces of art were burned in the courtyard of the Berlin fire department. It is probably the single greatest loss of modernist art in history. But we know not everything the Nazis took and labeled as degenerate burned. Pieces started showing up after the war. Despite the party line about modernist art degrading good German society, high-ranking Nazi officials took pieces for their own private collections. Some of it was smuggled out by art lovers."

Irina shifted to lean against Eli, who wrapped an arm around her.

"Whoever owns the Rodin owns this piece too?" Irina asked.

"We should assume so. And we can assume they know its provenance, otherwise they wouldn't have bothered to pull it from the exhibit."

"It would have been risky to hang it at all." Jasper plopped down beside Irina. "A Rodin is actually less likely to raise any alarms. Something like a Nolde... I'm an archaeologist, not an art historian, but if I'd seen it, first of all I would have known it was a Nolde, and secondly, I would have wondered how it survived. How it got out of Germany."

"I agree," Eli said. "A charity event with art scholars in attendance is not a smart place to show off such a recognizable piece."

"Then why did they offer this art up as part of the exhibit?"

No one had the answer to that question.

"Have you opened the others?" Irina asked.

"I don't think my heart can take it," Jasper said. He moved the Nolde to the side, then lay the crate flat and carefully fitted the painting back inside, replacing the lid.

Eli climbed to his feet, but not before kissing Irina's head almost absently. Ah well, at least he remembered she was there. Considering the magnitude of the art discovery they had, that was actually quite the compliment.

Eli slid the second frame-sized box out of the cage-turned-storage-locker. "If this is the missing Metzinger or Gleizes, I'm going to... I'm not actually sure what I'll do."

Jasper made semi-incoherent noises of agreement. Eli laid the box flat on the floor then carefully undid the small latches on all four sides, before lifting the lid.

They crowded around, all of them on their knees.

"Huh." Jasper sat back. "Well that's anticlimactic."

This crate held a faded line drawing that looked like an architectural schematic. Lines over lines, as if the paper had been reused, or as if the drafter had changed their mind halfway through, and decided to go with an entirely different design. The blueprint was mounted under glass, held in a thin gold frame.

Irina pointed to the frame. "The frames match."

Eli nodded. "You're right."

"That means that, at some point, these were displayed together." Jasper sat back, eyeing the three remaining crates.

"Maybe this is a map of somewhere in Germany. Berlin?"

"Wait, is that a signature?" Irina pointed, then bent down to peer at it. "No, it's initials. C...CFM?"

Eli and Jasper started listing off artists it could be or places the blueprint might represent. Irina, slightly bored, snuck out to get some coffee. She held her breath when she reached the dining room, but it was empty. She poked around until she found a room service tray in one of the buffet's drawers. She filled the tray with plates of brunch food and cups of coffee, returning to their room.

Eli and Jasper had moved on to the sculpture crates. The Rodin was out, set carefully on top of its crate. Beside that was a second sculpture. It was a tall, slender figure, wearing a robe or coat that fell in angular folds to the figure's feet, which were incredibly detailed, each toe perfect. It had exaggerated features, with vertical slashes for eyes, yet somehow it was delicate and subtle. The way the head tilted and the hands lay over the chest made her think the figure was female.

"It's a Barlach. It has to be," Eli whispered, as if he were afraid to wake the sculpture.

"So is this one." Jasper had the top off the final box. Eli crawled over to peer inside.

Irina carried the tray over to the low ottoman, setting it down. "I have breakfast," she called out.

They continued to mutter to each other. Irina fiddled with the food for another second to see if they'd respond. When they didn't, she made her voice as sultry as she could. "I'm naked and waiting for you."

Conversation paused, and in the next second they were both there, jerking aside the tent-like hangings.

"You're cruel, woman," Jasper said when he saw her fully clothed and eating a pancake.

"I brought you bacon and coffee."

"Hmm, you're forgiven."

Eli looked back at the art.

"Sit," she said. "Eat."

Eli dropped down onto a cushion and started shoveling food into his mouth like a little kid rushing through dinner so he could go back outside to play before the sun went down.

When Irina and Jasper's plates were half empty, and Eli's nearly cleaned, Irina raised her hand, like she was a student in class.

"Professor Wexler, I believe there's a question."

Jasper grinned at her.

Eli looked up, chunk of melon halfway to his mouth. He lowered his fork. "Yes...Miss Gentry, is it?"

Irina clasped her hands together just below her boobs, making them swell above the neckline of her top. "Oh my gosh, your class is just like, my favorite."

Jasper snort-laughed. Eli's lips twitched. "You had a question?"

Irina dropped the act. "Does what's in those crates change anything?"

Eli frowned. "I'm not sure. We were supposed to identify pieces from the ERR album. I want to compare the Rodin against the image, but I'm ninety percent sure we're right." He ate the melon, thinking. "We assumed that the security detail was there protecting the Rodin, but the Nolde and the Barlach pieces are actually far more controversial. On one hand, they might have been smuggled out of Germany by dedicated art lovers. On the other, they might have gone into the private collections of Nazi leaders, and then after the war, they were hidden or smuggled out of Germany by their families or by sympathizers."

Jasper was nodding. "If it was me, I would have been protecting those pieces, not the Rodin."

"Then why bring them to the warehouse at all?" Irina asked.

Eli shook his head. "That doesn't make any sense. And why let a picture of the Rodin be included in the event invitation?"

"The Rodin is safe to show off. Without the ERR album, there's no evidence of where the Rodin came from. It's not one of his large pieces."

"True, true." Eli slid his plate onto the tray. "We need more information."

"Let's wait until the Grand Master takes care of Price Bennett." Irina spoke slowly to emphasis her point. "It's not worth the risk."

Jasper and Eli looked at her. Then at one another.

"What about a library computer?" Eli asked.

"Works for me," Jasper agreed.

"What did I *just say*?"

"You can come with us, keep us safe." Eli grinned at her.

Irina was prepared to keep them there—by whatever means necessary—if she really thought there was extreme danger, but they'd been careful so far. And another few days stuck in this room would drive her nuts. She was already feeling a bit antsy. Better to take a chance on going out now.

They must have seen acquiescence in her features, because Eli jumped to his feet. "Good. Let's go."

"How about you put on some real pants there, big guy," Jasper said.

Eli looked down at his pajamas.

"Pants. Good idea."

Chapter Fourteen

Jasper adjusted his grip slightly and angled the Nolde canvas toward the light from the window. Eli, hunched down to minimize his shadow, snapped away with the small disposable camera Irina had picked up. While they'd been at the library, she'd run into the massive craft store that shared a parking lot with the library, a park, and several other businesses. They'd driven nearly an hour away from the hotel to a rather haphazard small town on the Oklahoma/Texas border. Eli and Jasper had hunkered down in the library while Irina ran to pick up cotton gloves. The rubber ones they'd used that morning weren't ideal for handling art.

Irina ended up buying two massive bags of stuff at the craft store, but had been weirdly cagey when Jasper asked what she got. When they made it back to the hotel, Irina had pulled out the cheap digital camera and handed it to them. Eli had looked like he was about to cry with happiness.

He and Eli were doing their best to take archival shots. They needed to talk about what they'd discovered with the surface-level internet searching.

Jasper would have given several toes to be able to turn on his phone and have the internet at his fingertips, or even better, to have his computer, which had access to Alexandria, one of the massive art databases used by museums.

Those things would have to wait. They'd decided taking the photos was priority number one, so that's what they were focusing on. Once that was done, they'd talk.

They'd considered taking the Nolde out of the frame to photograph the edges, but they didn't have the right equipment. The plan had been for Jasper to work the camera while Eli held the frames, but Eli got too nervous.

Jasper didn't point out that being afraid to touch the art was not a good trait in an art thief. It was almost as if Eli didn't want to be an art thief... Jasper smiled to himself.

"I think I've got it." Eli peered at the tiny screen of the camera.

"The blueprint next?" Jasper flipped the painting around as he carried it back to the crate. Eli made a distressed noise as he watched Jasper, reconfirming their decision to have Jasper handle the pieces.

The line drawing, which Irina had referred to as a blueprint, was the last item to photograph. Because it was behind glass, it would also be the most difficult to take pictures of.

Jasper sealed the Nolde in its crate, then put that crate back in the cage with the others. He was briefly distracted by Irina, who was doing either Pilates or yoga, wearing nothing but tiny little shorts and a sports bra with lots of thin crisscross straps. She had an old iPod shuffle—which she assured them wasn't Wi-Fi enabled—clipped to her shoulder, the white headphone cord dangling. She braced her hands on the floor then tipped forward until her whole body was balanced on her hands, her upper arms tight along the sides of her body. With exquisite control, she extended her left leg, tucking her right in until she braced her foot flat along the inside of her left thigh.

Jasper realized he was staring, and turned back to his task. Eli was watching Irina too. He had to nudge Eli with his elbow.

"Huh?"

"Art."

Eli hummed. "That right there is art."

Jasper huffed out a little laugh. "True. Let's get this done. Then we'll ask her to do that again, but this time naked."

"Naked yoga…" Eli shook like a dog after a bath. "Hurry up."

Jasper reached for the blueprint, which was propped against the wall, when there was a knock at the door. Jasper froze and looked at Eli.

They both looked at Irina, who was frowning at the door—body still balanced on her hands. Whatever she was listening too must have been quiet enough that she'd heard the knock too. With almost frightening control, she lowered her feet to the floor and stood. Barefoot and silent, she crept toward the door. She stopped there, seeming to consider. There was a peephole, but anyone on the outside would be able to tell when she looked through it because of the change in the light. She waved for them to go upstairs.

Eli shook his head and crossed his arms. Jasper raised his eyebrows and tipped his head to the side in a "you can't be serious" gesture.

She waved again, more empathetically. Eli folded his arms, face set in a stubborn expression, and Jasper crept towards the wall, where he'd be out of sight of the open door.

The knock sounded again.

"Irina, Eli, Jasper? It's Darling." The voice was faint through the thick door.

Irina popped up from her crouch, looking at Eli and Jasper. Jasper frowned at the door, unsure how he felt about a second visit with those two.

He shrugged, then tossed the large scarf he'd been using earlier over the cage where they were storing the art. It didn't completely cover it, but it did a good enough job. Irina lobbed a few pillows to Jasper, who propped them along the bottom of the cage, covering some of the areas the scarf didn't.

Irina opened the door.

"Darling." Irina's voice cooled several degrees. "Caden."

Caden looked down at Darling, eyebrows raised in an "I told you so" expression. Why ever they were here, it was Darling's idea, not Caden's.

"Would you three like to join us for brunch?" Darling asked.

"Actually, we just ate."

"That's fine." Darling smiled and took a half step forward. "We'll talk here and eat after."

Irina hesitated just long enough to let Darling know she wouldn't be cowed, but then stepped back to let the couple in.

By daylight, Darling and Caden seemed like different people. Darling was self-possessed and almost regal. She wore a fitted sheath dress in deep royal blue. Her arms were slim and toned. Her hair, which last night had been sex tousled, today hung in a perfect black bob. Behind her, Caden wore all black—black slacks, black tailored dress shirt. His belt was black, as were his shoes. His shirt had French cuffs, and the cufflinks winked in the light—onyx. He had strong features and thick dark brows. His eyes were framed by equally thick lashes. He was handsome in a way usually associated with male models in perfume commercials—ridiculously masculine.

Jasper was well aware that out of his trinity, he was the least good-looking. Irina was lovely, and Eli handsome. Jasper was, at best, charming. But all three of them were outclassed by Darling and Caden. It was disconcerting, but also made Jasper almost absurdly grateful for his triad. He'd known, from almost the moment he met them, that he could love Eli and Irina.

He doubted he would have had the same feeling if Caden and Darling had been the ones in the altar room with him. God help whoever ended up as their third.

"I wanted to apologize for last night." Caden took a few steps into the room, looking around with mild curiosity. "And to offer you something."

Irina had her hands on her hips. If she was discomfited by having this conversation while wearing what amounted to underwear, she didn't show it. "Why would you apologize?"

"I worried that our rather unorthodox childhood, the training we talked about, might turn you off of," Darling smiled and wiggled her eyebrows, "taking advantage of all your room had to offer."

Jasper warmed toward Darling. He'd been hoping for a little—or a lot—of sexy times, and after last night that had seemed like a dim possibility.

"We didn't come here to have kinky sex," Eli said.

Caden looked at him. "Then why are you here?"

No one answered. The silence stretched to the point of awkward.

Jasper cleared his throat. "Besides the fact that you're not practicing safe, sane, and consensual play, you certainly scared us off having kids." Jasper's intention was to change the focus, put them on the defensive, especially when Caden's gaze drifted over to the cage they'd concealed with the scarf. But what came out of his mouth was the truth. Jasper frowned, head tipping to the side for a moment before his gaze shifted back to them. "We just talked about how we'd planned to live openly as a triad, but now I think I understand why people don't."

Jasper kept talking, wishing that Darling and Caden weren't here, so he could have this conversation with his spouses in private. But now that he'd started, he couldn't stop—he needed to say what had been percolating since last night. "If you raise your kids as either a single parent or a couple, then you have the option of never telling them about the Trinity Masters. You can protect them from..."

Caden barked out a laugh, the sound completely unexpected. "From ending up like us?"

"Yes." Irina took a step closer to Jasper. He held out his hand and she took it. He pulled her into his side. Eli came up behind them, laying a hand on each of their shoulders.

Caden looked at them, a sardonic twist to his mouth, but Darling looked distressed.

"That's why I wanted to come here." She sighed. "Caden and I are not typical. But I can't stand the thought that you three won't explore every aspect of your sex lives because you're worried you'll turn into us."

"You won't turn into us." Caden's voice was dry. "You're all clearly too well adjusted."

"Uh, thank you?" Eli said.

"Jasper, Irina, do you believe me?" Darling asked.

Irina shifted her weight. "Will you promise me that you'll tell the Grand Master how you feel about each other? At least try to be happy?"

"Yes," Darling assured her. "We will. I will. I'll tell her."

"If you're embarrassed, I'd be happy to say something."

"No." Darling looked at Caden. "There are other things we need to tell the Grand Master."

"I would not want to end up as the third person with the two of them," Eli whispered.

"Mmmhmm," Jasper murmured.

"Shh," Irina hissed, then to Darling. "I really do hope the two of you end up together. And in couples' therapy."

This time Caden's laugh burst from him, rich and without malice. Darling looked surprised then smiled as she watched him hold his stomach. When he didn't stop, she rolled her eyes. Walking over to one of the chairs near the little stage, she flipped it around to face the room and sat, crossing her feet at the ankle.

"Ignore him," she said. "In case you haven't figured it out, he's really quite weird."

Caden laughed harder as he staggered over to Darling. He grabbed her out of the chair, spun her in a circle, kissed her, then plopped down and pulled her onto his lap.

Darling crossed her legs, feet dangling. "As I was saying…"

Jasper felt Irina relax. Eli squeezed his shoulder then dropped his hand. Darling and Caden had changed again, now seeming like perfectly ordinary, if alarmingly pretty, people.

Irina cleared her throat. "I was…reluctant to try anything kinky after our conversation last night. Especially since we sort of, uh, veered down that path once before. But I'll stop projecting. Thank you for that."

Darling looked at Caden, then back at Irina. "I actually came here with a specific conversation in mind. I want Caden to show you his party trick."

"It is not a party trick."

"Yes, it is."

"What party trick?" Jasper asked, interested.

Darling pursed her lips. "Caden and I are members of several...clubs."

"Sex clubs? Are sex clubs a real thing?" Eli sounded only mildly curious.

"Yes, they are. But of course the really good ones are secret. And members only. And expensive."

"Figures," Irina muttered.

Jasper glanced at her. She sounded resentful, as if she were irritated she wasn't a member of a secret sex club. She must have felt him looking because she caught his gaze, then blushed and studied the pattern on the carpet.

Jasper felt his neck prickle in a way he knew meant someone was watching him. Caden was staring at him and Irina with an intensity that made Jasper think he'd seen the body language byplay.

Jasper's curiosity, already aroused, jumped up a few levels.

"You're members of BDSM clubs, dungeons," Jasper said, hoping to restart the conversation.

"Yes," Darling agreed. "Caden—or more appropriately, Master Anderson—is the one they call when a sub is misbehaving, or a Dom is having trouble making a connection."

Irina eyed Caden with a mix of suspicion and inquiry. "And why is that?"

Caden tapped Darling's arm and she slid off his lap to stand by the chair. He rose to his feet. All trace of laughter was gone. "They call me because I can tell what people really want. What they really need. I see what they try to hide, even from themselves."

"That's your party trick?" Eli sounded doubtful.

"When a sub is pouting and begging to be spanked, I can tell what she really wants is to be fucked roughly in front of a crowd. Or if she panics at the sight of a gag, what it really means is that she hasn't fully given up control, or doesn't fully trust her Dom." Caden stalked forward, eyes on Irina. "The facades people build are the enemy of true pleasure, true acceptance of what and who you are. That is my 'party trick.' I can look at someone and know exactly what they want. What they need."

Jasper stepped in front of Irina, getting between her and Caden.

Caden met his gaze and tipped his head slightly.

"What is it you think I need?" Jasper asked, wanting to pull attention away from Irina.

Caden looked from Jasper to Eli and back. He circled around them, and Jasper had to resist the urge to turn. Irina did pivot in place, keeping Caden in her sights at all times.

"You've had sex, but not enough to really know each other," Caden declared.

None of them responded.

"You're wary of one another, because each of you knows, even if you're afraid to admit it, that you're all holding back." Caden peered at Eli. "Or maybe you've hinted at what you really want. Have you, Eli? Have you told your husband and wife exactly what you'd like to do to them?"

"What are you, like the Sherlock Holmes of sex?" Eli yelped. He was blinking hard behind his glasses.

"Lucky guess," Irina hissed to Jasper, but Caden heard.

"You'll be the last one to admit what you really want. You're strong, but you also feel...defensive." Caden examined Irina's face as if he were trying to pick out words on a faded manuscript page. As if all this information was right there for the taking if you knew how to find it. "You're aroused by the idea of submitting to both of them, of being used by them, but you're afraid of it too. You're scared you'll be outnumbered, or overpowered, when it comes to the rest of the relationship. You need to have some authority, so you won't admit that you'd like to be gagged and...no, not that."

Caden circled her again, and the sound of Irina's breathing was loud in the suddenly quiet room.

"Irina?" Jasper asked, worried about her.

Caden stepped up behind her, in her personal space, but not touching her. "Tell your husbands what you want. Tell them you want to be displayed on that stage, to be stroked and kissed—inspected as if you were a pleasure slave for sale. That you want them to be rough while they worship you. Tell them you want to know what it's like to have one of them in your mouth while the other one fucks your pussy—"

"Enough," Eli snarled. He shoved Caden away from Irina. Eli seemed to tower over the other man. "No one talks to my wife like that."

Caden's eyes gleamed with satisfaction. "There he is. I knew that gentle giant thing was a facade. A big man like you, you've been hiding your dominant streak your whole life. You want to take control of your sex life. You want to finally, just once, be completely honest without worrying what people will think later. You want to tie him down," Caden's head jerked toward Jasper, "and make him watch as you fuck her. Torture him with it, then sit back and watch as he fucks her, once he's been driven crazy by lust."

Eli's hands curled into fists. Jasper and Irina both sucked in a breath, and it wasn't because they were scandalized. Eli's shoulders bunched at the noise.

"Tell me I'm wrong," Caden said.

Eli didn't say anything.

Irina stepped forward, laid a tentative hand on Eli's shoulder. "Eli?"

He flinched away from her touch. Jasper looked at Caden, who met his gaze but offered no insight or advice.

Running on instinct, Jasper joined Irina at Eli's back, and slid his fingers up under the hem of Eli's shirt, finding smooth, warm skin. "We've done a little bit of that, but didn't take it all the way. Is that what you want, Eli? Because it sounds really fucking hot to me."

Irina hummed in agreement.

Eli whirled. "You...you're not..."

Irina pulled his glasses off. "No, we're not."

Eli started to reach for them, then paused, looked at Caden. "And what about him?" he asked the other man, pointing to Jasper.

Caden considered Jasper, who tensed.

"He's the gasoline to your fire. Every time you get...complacent. Every time you think you've found a rhythm or a rut, he will light you up until you burn white-hot." Caden shifted to watch them. "Jasper will push you, he'll demand that you please one another, that you not stop until each of you is exhausted and spent. Until you own one another, body and soul."

Jasper wanted to shake his head, to deny it. What Caden said sounded so intense that it couldn't possibly be a good thing. People liked simple, they liked predictable. Eli and Irina wouldn't want to feel like he was always harassing them and prodding them. Jasper started to take a step back, as if to prove that Caden was wrong, but Eli caught his hand. Their gazes met.

"Good," Eli growled.

Irina nodded quickly, her eyes bright with desire and her nipples visible through the material of her sports bra.

Caden was gazing at the wall, frowning. Darling came up beside him. He whispered something in her ear then she melted away again, walking toward the wall. Before Jasper could question that, Caden's voice broke into their little moment.

"Eli, you begin. Take them to bed. Demand their obedience. Give yourself permission to use them. Trust them. Trust them to tell you when it's too much. Use a safe word if you want.

"Then it's Irina's turn. Fulfill her fantasy. Put her up on that slave block. Test her skills as concubine. Inspect her. Play with her. Don't let her come.

"Then, Jasper…"

Caden leaned toward Jasper, whispered in his ear. Jasper's eyes widened, then he nodded.

"We'll leave you to it. Goodbye, Jasper, Eli, Irina."

Caden took Darling's hand, kissing her fingers as he led her to the door. Just before they walked out, Darling looked over her shoulder, not at Eli, Irina, or Jasper, but at the sheet of brocade fabric that only partially obscured the blueprint they'd been planning to photograph. A flash of emotion crossed her face. The door closed behind them with a *thunk*.

Irina and Jasper stared at one another. Eli was looking down, his hands braced on his hips. He raised his head, oh so slowly.

"Upstairs," he growled. "Now."

Chapter Fifteen

Jasper went willingly to be bound. Eli secured his husband to the head of the bed—seated with his back resting comfortably on a pillow. Jasper's arms were stretched to either side, and secured to the restraints bolted to the headboard. Jasper was still completely clothed, his casual button-down shirt stretched taut across his chest.

Eli finished buckling Jasper's right hand in place and slid off the bed. Jasper's eyes were heavy-lidded as he tracked Eli's movements, before switching his gaze to Irina.

Irina shivered, still wearing nothing more than her exercise clothes. Eli examined her head to toe, taking in the glossy ponytail, the taut lines of her waist, the sweet curve of her ass. He was gripped by a mad urge to grab her, push her face down on the bed, rip down those shorts and fuck her—quick, hard, and dirty, all while Jasper looked on.

His hands twitched with the need to take hold of her, but he held himself in check.

At least for now.

Not trusting himself to stand, Eli sat on the edge of the bed. "Take off your clothes, Irina."

Her gaze darted between him and Jasper. She hesitated, but he didn't say anything. Just waited.

Her arms rose, slowly, slowly. She reached up and pulled the band from her hair, freeing it. She ruffled her fingers through, until it brushed her shoulders in tousled waves. Next she tossed away the headphones and music player.

She turned her back to them, crossed her arms, and pulled the sports bra up and off. It left faint impressions in her creamy skin. Hooking her thumbs in her shorts, she pulled them down and off. As she bent, he caught a glimpse of her sex. Eli's cock, which had been semihard since they were downstairs, swelled to fully erect.

Naked, she faced them. Her hands were loose at her sides, her shoulders back, chin raised. She looked confident and powerful.

Yet...

Yet Eli could see her fingers trembling, and she was breathing fast and shallow. She was either scared, aroused, or both.

Rather than speak—he didn't trust himself to speak—Eli crooked his finger at her.

Irina rounded the bottom corner of the bed, tossing her hair in a feigned show of nonchalance. Eli held perfectly still, waiting until she was a foot away.

He grabbed her by the hips, jerking her forward so she lost her balance, falling against him. Rather than fighting it, Eli accepted the momentum and rolled back onto the bed, Irina lying atop him. She braced her hands on the mattress, lifting herself off of him. Eli took advantage of the movement to sweep his hands from her waist to her breasts. He rubbed her nipples with the flats of his palms and Irina shuddered, her head falling forward, her hair spilling over his face.

"Are you aroused, wife?"

"Yes."

"Good. Then lie on the bed and spread your legs."

Irina's eyes popped open. That clearly wasn't what she'd been expecting. Eli grabbed her ass, pinching gently. She yipped and scrambled off him, crawling toward the center of the behemoth bed.

Eli bounced to his feet and started pulling off his clothes. Out of the corner of his eye, he saw Jasper watching them. The easy willingness that Jasper had shown when Eli had told him what he'd planned seemed to be ebbing. Jasper looked significantly less calm than he had five minutes ago.

Irina was on her hands and knees in the middle of the bed as Eli finished undressing. She sat, but hesitated in the act of lying back. That gave Eli an idea.

"Crawl over to Jasper, put your nipple in his mouth."

Irina moaned softly, her eyes dark pools of arousal. Jasper, who'd been sitting with his legs crisscrossed, stretched them out. Irina crawled between his legs, her hips rolling with the movement. Chain clanked as Jasper tried to touch her, only to be brought up short by the restraints.

Irina grabbed the headboard, leaning forward until her nipple was a breath away from Jasper's lips. He opened his mouth, leaned forward, but Irina twisted her shoulders, moving her breast. Eli watched as she teased Jasper, watched him try and fail to capture one of the sweet pink buds.

Eli idly stroked his cock. He could see the bulge in Jasper's pants where his husband's cock was reacting to their play.

"Enough," Eli said when he couldn't stand waiting any longer. "I told you to put your nipple in his mouth, not to tease him."

Irina held still, waited for Jasper, but Jasper leaned his head back, lips curved in a smile. Irina darted a look between Jasper and Eli, eyes slightly widened.

"Irina," Eli growled with exaggerated menace.

Irina grabbed her breast and pressed her nipple against Jasper's mouth. She rubbed the budded peak across his lips.

"Jasper!" she admonished.

He twisted his face to the side before saying, "Beg."

Irina leaned away, her eyes hot. "I'm not going to beg."

Eli knew a cue when he heard one. He climbed onto the bed and knee-walked to where Irina was. "Oh, you're going to beg."

Eli knelt in the space between Jasper's calves, his back against Irina's chest. He forced her upper body forward, and at the same time he curled his fingers in Jasper's hair, holding his head still. "Play with her nipple," he told Jasper. "If you can make her moan and beg, I might free you earlier, instead of leaving you there all night with nothing to do but watch as I fuck her."

Jasper's tongue darted out, flicking her nipple. Irina arched back against Eli. He crowded into her back, his cock riding the crease of her ass. He watched Jasper tease and torment her, his tongue licking and flicking, lips engulfing and teasing, until finally Jasper captured her left nipple between his teeth and tugged, distending her nipple slightly.

Irina moaned, her nails digging into Jasper's and Eli's arms.

"I'm going to fuck you now," Eli rasped in her ear. She shivered and he felt it every place their naked skin touched. "But I'm feeling generous, so I'll let you pick. How do you want to be fucked? On your back or on your knees?"

"Back. I want to see you."

Eli ignored the way his heart clenched. He was not going to be distracted from his mission by mushy feelings.

"Lie down. Spread your legs."

He got out of her way, gave her space. She lay with her head toward the foot of the bed. When she spread her legs, Jasper and Eli were treated to the sight of her pink core, wet with need.

"More," he barked. "Spread your legs more. I want Jasper to see what he can't have. I want him to see your pussy and know that I'm going to fuck you while he has to watch."

"Damn it, Eli, enough. Let me go." Jasper leaned forward, pulling at the restraints.

"No," Eli said simply. "Irina, spread your pussy lips. Beautiful. Now play with your clit."

Irina obeyed, moaning, hips rising slightly as she spread her pussy lips with two fingers, and stroked her clit with the index finger of her other hand.

Eli grabbed her legs, turning her so that her side was facing Jasper. He wanted Jasper to see exactly how hard, how deep, he was going to thrust into Irina.

Eli lay between her spread legs, his cock resting between her pussy lips. He braced his upper body on his elbows and looked down at her. Her hair seemed inky dark around her head, and her pupils were wide with arousal.

"Kiss me," she demanded. This time *he* obeyed.

The kiss was rough and wet—tongues dueled, breath washed hot over greedy lips.

"Let me go. I need to touch you. Both of you." Jasper's words broke their kiss. Eli and Irina both turned to look at him—their third, their husband. Irina's face softened. She reached out a hand toward Jasper, brushing his bare foot.

Eli lifted his hips, positioned his cock, and thrust into Irina's pussy.

Irina screamed in pleasure.

Eli closed his eyes, reveling in the feeling of her heat around him. She was tight and hot. Her heels dug into his ass with surprising strength, yet he was also achingly aware of how slight and fragile she felt beneath him.

He withdrew completely, lifting his hips so that Jasper got a side view of his cock, wet from Irina's pussy. Irina was having none of it, and yanked him down with her legs.

"More," she demanded.

"Beg," Eli growled.

Irina bared her teeth. "Fuck me."

"Like this?" He pressed just the tip of his cock into her and moved in tiny rocking motions.

"No. No." Irina dug her nails into his shoulders. "Jasper," she pleaded, turning her head to the side.

"Undo these and I'll fuck you," Jasper rasped. "I'm going mad watching this."

Irina wiggled, as if she were going to roll across the bed and unbind Jasper. Eli stopped that with the simple act of pinning one arm to the mattress beside her head.

"You're not going anywhere. Did you forget who was in control?" Eli lowered his upper body until his face was an inch from hers.

Irina's pupils dilated. "No. I didn't forget."

"Good." Eli slammed his cock into her once more.

Irina's free hand scored Eli's shoulder and her mouth opened and closed, almost as if she couldn't draw a deep breath.

"My God, look at what you're doing to her," Jasper purred. His eyes were heavy-lidded.

Eli twisted to look at Jasper, maintaining eye contact as he fucked Irina with brutal efficiency. He kept his body weight on his upper arms, his knees braced in the mattress as he pumped into her.

Irina gasped, then reared up, smashing her lips against the corner of Eli's mouth. He turned to meet the kiss. She bit his lip hard enough to make his eyes widen, and he realized she was either orgasming or incredibly close to it. Eli freed his mouth from hers and arched his back so he could still fuck her, but opened up some space between their lower bodies.

"Play with your clit," he rasped.

"I...I can't, I'm too close."

Eli frowned, not really sure what that meant.

"He ordered you to play with your clit, Irina," Jasper purred. "Do it."

Irina's nails scored Eli's stomach as she slid her hand between them. Her fingers fluttered around Eli's cock, adding pressure as he continued to thrust. Then her fingers moved, and he watched her lick her lips, her closed eyelids fluttering slightly.

Eli knew the moment she came; he felt it in the way her legs and abdomen tensed, yet her neck relaxed and her mouth softened. Heard it in the low moan that vibrated through their bodies.

He continued to thrust, hard, deep and steady, until her legs went limp, sliding from his back.

"Eli." Her eyes were unfocused in the post-orgasm high. She then turned her head. "Jasper."

Eli pulled out. "On your hands and knees."

Irina stretched, then wiggled out from under him. She rolled onto her hands and knees and scooted back toward Eli, her pussy tempting and pink.

"No," he said, spanking her gently.

She yelped, twisting to look over her shoulder at him.

"You're going to suck Jasper's cock while I fuck you," Eli told her.

Irina shivered and Jasper hissed out a breath.

"Now." He let his hand hover near her ass, teasing her with the idea of another smack.

Irina crawled to Jasper, who was clenching his teeth as if he were in physical pain. She reached for the button of his pants, but because of the way he was sitting, she couldn't get them undone.

"You have to undo the cuffs," Jasper said.

Eli snorted. "I'll undo them when I'm ready to use you, too."

He helped Jasper scoot down so he was lying on his back, his head nearly touching the headboard. He had to be close to the head of the bed due to the restraints. Once he was lying down, the ridged line of his erection was readily apparent. Eli reached out and stroked his husband's cock through his pants.

Jasper groaned, "Oh, fuck yes."

"Irina, take off his clothes."

She pushed the fabric off his chest. The shirt would never be the same since, in her haste, she actually ripped off two of the buttons. Eli had to back up, climbing off the bed, because the sight of her, so overcome with lust that she was ripping Jasper out of his clothes, was testing Eli's ever-thinning control.

"What happened to you?" Irina asked.

It took Eli a moment to realize she was asking about the scar that was visible on Jasper's chest. "Someone tried to blow up a car I was sitting in. Some of the gas splashed on me."

"When? Why?" Eli asked, as Irina gasped.

"A long time ago, because I made the mistake of trying to go back to my old life. My uncle and some of my cousins were less than thrilled to see me."

"I'm so sorry." Irina touched the smooth, pale flesh of the scar first with the pads of her fingers, then with her lips. She kept stroking and kissing until Jasper's breathing grew ragged.

Irina worked Jasper's pants down and off, leaving him naked except for his arms, still covered by the sleeves of his shirt. Eli opened his mouth to issue more orders, but there was no need. Irina positioned herself between Jasper's legs, dropped down so she was propped on one elbow, and then wrapped her other hand around the base of his cock.

He grunted, chain clanking as his arms flexed. "I'm not going to last long," he said through gritted teeth.

"Yes, you will." Eli jumped back onto the bed. The slight of Irina's ass raised so temptingly in the air was too much for him to pass up.

He spread Irina's ass open with his hands, let the head of his cock brush over her anus.

She froze. "Eli, please, I'd need—"

"Trust me." He slid his cock down to her pussy, sliding just the head into her. "Are you sucking Jasper's cock?"

"No, she's not." Jasper sounded aggrieved.

"Tattletale," she whispered.

Eli leaned to the side and gave Irina's nipple a punitive pinch. "His cock should be filling your mouth."

Irina's head lowered, and Eli realized he wouldn't be able to see due to his position directly behind her. But he could watch Jasper's face. He could see the relief that washed over his features as Irina's head started to bob. Could see Jasper's skin flush and heat from the pleasure.

Eli surged into Irina's pussy. Her muffled moan made Jasper moan in turn. Eli smiled with savage delight that he could pleasure both of them this way.

Gripping Irina's hips, he used the improved leverage of this position to hammer into her. He was rough and fast, his hips slapping against her ass, the sound drowning out Jasper's moans and curses of pleasure.

Eli was close, he could feel it, but he wasn't ready for this to end. Not yet.

"After I come," he growled, "Irina, you're going to ride Jasper's cock until you both come. If Jasper comes before you do, then you'll sit on his face and he'll lick your pussy while I play with his cock."

"Oh fuck yes. Yes." Jasper raised his head and looked at Eli. Their gazes met. It was intimate and intense. Eli maintained the eye contact as he came, pumping into Irina's sweet pussy with mad, brutal thrusts.

Eli finally slowed and stopped. Post-orgasm lethargy wanted to drag him down, and a little voice whispered that he should just relax and watch them. But he wasn't ready for that.

He pulled out of Irina, then reached beneath her, cupping her breasts and lifting her up, off Jasper's cock.

"Damn it, no," Jasper snarled.

"Irina, I want you to fuck Jasper."

"Wait, in that case, yes," Jasper said.

Irina's lips were glossy and wet. She smiled at Eli, and it wasn't a sunny girl-next-door smile. It was a knowing, sensuous smile. Irina threw her leg over Jasper's hips, prepared to straddle him, but Eli stopped her.

"Oh, one more thing," he purred in her ear as he casually tugged her nipples. "Face the other way, because you're going to suck my cock while you fuck him."

Irina's nipple pebbled under his fingertips, and she made a soft sound that was almost a whimper.

Eli waited until she was positioned—facing Jasper's feet, her hand braced on his bent knees—before climbing to his feet. He was tall enough that he could brace one hand on the ceiling. The other he stroked through Irina's hair before winding a few locks around and through his fist.

His cock had softened, but at the first brush of Irina's fingers, he sprang to full hardness. She drew him toward her mouth even as she sank down. Eli watched Jasper lifting his hips to guide her, his stomach and chest muscles tensing and straining. Irina's lips hovered near Eli's cock, and when she was fully seated—Jasper buried inside her tight core—Eli felt the long, slow exhale against his heated skin. The look of relief on Jasper's face made Eli grin.

"She feels good, doesn't she?" he asked.

"Oh God yes. Hot, tight, wet."

Eli twitched his hips, brushing his cock against her lips. "I can't wait to feel her sucking me."

Irina looked up, maintaining eye contact with him as she opened her mouth and guided his cock in. She kept her fingers wrapped around the base of his cock, squeezing rhythmically, as she took the head into her mouth, swirling her tongue around the tip.

Eli cupped her head—not forcing more of him into her mouth, but grounding both of them, keeping them connected.

Then she started to bounce up and down on Jasper. For a moment they were out of sync, then Irina figured out the angles. She adjusted her position on Jasper, then urged Eli to bend his knees, lowering his hips to the point where she could easily have both his cock and Jasper's sliding in and out as she rose and dropped.

Once she found her rhythm, Irina worked them both mercilessly. Last time Eli had all the control, but now Irina did. Both Eli and Jasper were trapped. Jasper by the chains, Eli by the need to keep his feet braced and one hand on the ceiling. Irina alternated her rhythm, changing up what she was doing. At one point she lifted off Jasper's cock, leaving him cursing and desperately raising his hips, so she could focus on kissing the head of Eli's cock. Then she sank down on Jasper, grinding on him while she worked Eli's cock with both hands.

"Fuck, don't stop. Don't stop." Jasper braced his heels and thrust up into Irina, his eyes closed, mouth twisted in a snarl. Then he groaned, falling back on the bed.

Irina looked over her shoulder at Jasper, then whipped back to look up at Eli. "Your turn."

Eli regretfully shook his head. "Too soon for me to come again. But you need to."

Her eyes lit. "Yes, I do. But I don't want it to be just Jasper. I want *you* to lick my pussy too."

Eli walked carefully to the edge of the bed and hopped off. He reached out and released Jasper's right arm, then circled the bed and released the left.

"Lie back," Eli told Irina.

Jasper rolled out of the way and Irina lay down, her head on a pillow, glossy hair spread out around her. Jasper wasted no time sliding down the bed and burying his mouth in her pussy. Irina gasped and grabbed his hair. Eli started on her breasts, licking and nipping.

There was a tap on Eli's shoulder, and he looked over to see Jasper motioning for them to switch.

Eli took his place between her legs. He pushed two fingers into her, fucking her with them and watching her pussy clench in reaction, before pulling his fingers out and setting to work on her clit. She moaned, her hands sliding over Eli's head and face. Eli looked up to see Jasper kissing her while massaging her breasts.

It felt like it had only been moments, but Irina tensed and said, "I'm coming."

Eli licked her softly as she came on his tongue. Irina's fingers scrabbled at Eli's head and Jasper nipped and licked her breasts to extend the orgasm. They were relentless, leaving no inch of her body untouched, extending the pleasure until she shook from it.

"Too much," she said through gritted teeth. Eli pulled back, giving her clit one last stroke with his finger. Even that gentle touch made her gasp.

Irina curled onto her side, propping her head on Jasper's chest.

"Well, that will make you believe in the divine," Jasper murmured. His eyes, like Irina's, were closed.

Eli padded into the bathroom. He was sticky, and had to pee, so he took a few minutes to clean up. When he emerged, Irina and Jasper were curled together. He grabbed his glasses and put them on.

They looked vulnerable and battered, two pale forms in the great expanse of the bed.

Eli crawled gingerly onto the bed. "Are you two okay? Do you, uh, need something?"

"Okay? No, I don't think that's how I would describe it." Jasper didn't bother to open his eyes.

"Oh, uh. Do you want some water?"

Irina rolled over and opened one eye. "Eli, what's wrong?"

"I'm worried about you. You look..."

"Like we're exhausted from having our brains fucked out?" Jasper asked.

"From being ordered to have at least three different kinds of kinky sex?" Irina's lips twitched. "Ordered by you, I should add."

"Exhausted from being tied down and forced to watch while your husband fucked your wife and it was making you crazy?" Now Jasper opened his eyes.

Eli adjusted his glasses and blinked. Embarrassment heated his cheeks.

Irina started to laugh.

Jasper shook his head. "You're like Jekyll and Hyde."

"A gentleman in the streets and a freak in the bed," Irina gasped through her laughter.

"I didn't mean to—" Eli started to say.

"Oh yes, you did." Irina climbed over Eli, so he was in the middle, and cuddled against him.

"Are you trying to make me the little spoon?" he asked, bemused.

Jasper scooted over, so they were all curled together, arms and legs tangled.

"Eli," Jasper said seriously. "That was amazing. Don't ever hide that raw sex warrior from us."

"I don't want to hurt either of you…"

Irina patted his chest. "Don't worry, I'm the dangerous one, remember?"

Jasper dissolved into gales of laughter. Eli adjusted his glasses, which for some reason made Irina start to laugh too.

"You're both lunatics," he said. "But you're my lunatics."

"Damn right," Jasper said.

They were silent for a moment.

"So, when are we going to go downstairs?" Irina asked.

"Down, girl," Jasper said. "Give us a chance to recover."

"You get thirty minutes." Irina snuggled closer to Eli. "Then I expect some seriously dirty things to happen."

They were all downstairs twenty-eight minutes later.

Chapter Sixteen

She couldn't sleep. After the truly incredible sex of the past two days, Irina should have been exhausted, body and mind. But she couldn't sleep, even though her arms and legs felt heavy with tiredness.

She was…worried. Anxious. It hadn't even been a week since she'd walked through the doors of the Boston Public Library, sneaking into the rare book room and accessing the secret elevator.

A lot had happened in that week. She'd finally met her trinity. She'd participated in her first art heist. She'd subsequently screwed up her first art heist and had to stage a rescue operation with no planning and a team of two.

Her brain was humming along, thoughts popping to the surface only to be shoved aside by the next thought clamoring for her undivided attention. She'd ended up on one side of the bed, with Jasper in the middle, which made it easy for her to slide out from under the covers. Naked, she crept out of the bedroom, feeling her way down the stairs.

It wasn't completely dark down here. They'd left two of the lights on—the ones hanging over the stage area—pendant lights with variegated glass shades in tones of gold and amber.

She picked her way across the floor, which was scattered with pillows and, much to her delight, a discarded shirt. Eli's polo was huge on her and smelled like him. Rubbing the collar against her cheek, she opened the curtains. It was still dark out, but the sky was more blue than black. Dawn was coming.

Irina tugged a few pillows over, fluffing them into place just under the window. Settling herself amid the cushions, with her back against the wall beneath the window, facing the room, she watched the light. The gold lamplight did battle with the light streaming in through the window. The gold light was winning, but as she sat there, breathing in and out, still and quiet in the pre-dawn, the silvery-white light that promised day grew brighter, beating back the lamplight.

The end of their "task" was in sight. Tomorrow she'd check her email. Hopefully they'd have the all-clear from the Grand Master. They could return to Boston, be officially married, and then start their life together.

But what did that mean?

What would she do?

Irina pulled her arms into the torso of the shirt, hugging her waist. They'd turned Eli's whole life upside down, but Jasper had a plan for fixing that. He'd shared the plan with Irina, but they'd agreed not to tell Eli, in case it didn't work.

Best case scenario, Eli was able to return to his job in Denver. Jasper's job wasn't at risk, so he was fine.

That left her.

Huddled on the floor in that darkest hour before dawn, Irina admitted to herself how woefully unworthy she felt being married to these two handsome, brilliant men. Eli, the dedicated scholar, whose mild-mannered-professor exterior hid a core of raw passion. Jasper, the dashing, dangerous man who lived life to its fullest, and seemed willing and capable of taking on the world with a smile on his face.

Then there was her.

She should have amounted to more. Should have become something, someone *spectacular*. Instead, she'd peaked in college, and since then she'd slowly fizzled out. She didn't have a career she cared about; she had a job that had been handed to her through her Trinity Masters' connection. She was okay at it, but not great. She was pretty, but not beautiful.

Irina swallowed against the pressure in her throat. She was shaking, though whether that was from the cold or a physical manifestation of her feelings, she couldn't tell. She wanted to go for run. Needed to get away.

Don't be stupid, Irina.

She looked at the door, warring with herself. Running was the easiest way to control these rather pathetic feelings that periodically crept up on her, but if she went running, she'd have to leave the hotel.

A heavy plastic bag caught her eye.

Irina gasped in relief. Scrambling to her feet, she ran for the shopping bags. They'd sent her into a craft store to get gloves, and on impulse she'd purchased painting supplies along with the digital camera. She wasn't sure why she'd done it. She never painted in front of people. Didn't even tell people that was her hobby. But something had told her to do it. Her subconscious must have known this moment was coming.

If running was the easiest way for her to deal with unwanted feelings, painting was the best. Running was a Band-Aid. Painting was a healing.

She tipped the bag onto the floor, then tossed aside the pillows they'd used to half hide the stolen art. The second bag was under one of the pillows. She upended that one too.

Sitting cross-legged on the floor, she tore plastic off canvases. She hadn't gotten an artist's palette, so she used a bit of cardboard from the packaging, squeezing out indulgently large glops of oil paint. Oil paint was a silly choice, but she was glad for it now. Using one canvas as a tray, she gathered up brushes, paint, and her makeshift palette, and took everything to the tiled bathroom area.

She stuffed a washcloth over the drain, then turned on one of the shower heads just enough to create a pool of water on the floor and tossed the brushes into it, to soften the new bristles. She quickly prepped a canvas, with none of the care a real artist would take. Propping the canvas on the shower knobs gave her a makeshift easel. With the palette balanced on one hand, she dipped her brush into the paint.

A vivid stripe of blue appeared as she put brush to canvas. Irina closed her eyes in relief. This was what she needed, the outlet for all the emotions rolling inside her. Emotions that great sex could mute, but not vanquish.

Dawn's light grew, silver turning to white, then warming to gold as the sun rose. Irina poured herself onto the canvas, unaware of anything but the brush in her hand, the rapidly emptying tubes of paint at her feet, and the canvases.

Eli propped his head on his hand and watched Jasper sleep. He looked younger when he was asleep than he did when he was awake. He also looked innocent.

He'd come to regret the way he'd treated Jasper when they'd first met. For the most part, Jasper seemed to be less art thief and more morally ambiguous-for-the-greater-good scholar. There were a few times he'd mentioned stealing things like jewelry, and Eli wanted to figure out if those had been jokes just to rile him up, or if there was more to his thieving.

But even if Jasper had stolen jewelry, Eli respected him. Maybe even loved him.

Eli leaned over and kissed him. It was the first time he'd done that without Irina in the room. He'd expected it to feel weird, but it didn't. It felt nice. More than nice.

"Mmm, good morning," Jasper whispered. He sat up at the same time that he pushed on Eli's shoulder.

Their heads knocked together.

"Ow," Eli said.

"That didn't work out the way I thought it would."

"What did you think would happen?"

"I was going to roll you over and kiss you. If you were Irina's size, that would have worked."

Eli chuckled. "Not used to not being the biggest one?"

"I guess I'm not." Jasper levered himself up, this time more carefully, and kissed Eli's forehead. "Where is our wife, by the way?"

"I thought I heard her moving around downstairs."

"I'm hungry."

"Me too. Let's find her and go get breakfast."

They took turns in the bathroom. While Jasper was in there, Eli threw open the curtains, blinking at the bright sunlight. He wasn't sure what time they'd fallen asleep, but now it had to be at least nine a.m. Once they were both dressed, they made their way downstairs.

Eli hit the bottom stair and froze.

Jasper put a hand on his shoulder, bracing himself to lean around and see why Eli had stopped.

Three breathtaking paintings were propped along the wall in the open bathroom. Luminous color seemed to jump from the canvas, as if there was actually light inside the images, which was a truly astounding trick, considering the dark nature of the subjects.

One was a purely abstract piece that combined strong color play with an overlay of jagged shapes. Colors seemed to battle across the canvas in disjointed, angular installments, silver and gray at war with yellow and gold.

The next was an absurdist-style painting that didn't seem to be complete. A cutout of a happy couple, smiling huge, fake smiles, and with empty black holes for eyes, was acting as a barrier between a dull gray cityscape and a ball that at first looked like it might be the sun, but on closer inspection was actually a carefully entwined Celtic knot of variegated shades of yellow and gold. A trinity.

The last was a portrait. It was done in the modern style, the features angular and exaggerated, the neck and face elongated. The woman in the portrait had lank hair and lowered eyes. Despite the disproportionate features, sadness was clearly expressed. The figure itself was done in dull, flat tans and browns, but behind it the rest of the canvas exploded with color. The area behind her on the left was all reds and golds, while on the right it was vibrant cyan, turquoise, and azure.

Jasper gave him a little push and Eli let out the breath he'd been holding. He walked toward the bathroom area, Jasper on his heels. Eli crouched down to get a better look at the paintings. Up close they were even more amazing.

Eli would never get tired of the feeling he got when he first saw beautiful art. He'd never found a name for it, but it was as if a bright thread dropped into his heart, a thread that connected him to all of humanity, future, present, and past. For a split second, just a fraction of a thought, he experienced something divine.

"Jasper, I'm not a contemporary art expert, but these are…"

Jasper was crouched, hands over his mouth. He dropped them. "These are revelatory. Raw. Seminal."

"Did you know she could do this?"

Jasper shook his head, but didn't take his gaze off the portrait. "I see influences from all the major modern schools, yet there's a unique perspective here." Jasper's jaw clenched. "She's not who she says she is."

"What do you mean?" Eli blinked, trying to catch up to Jasper's line of reasoning.

"Maybe she's a forger," Jasper murmured.

A distressed noise made Eli turn. Irina was curled up in a ball on the floor. He'd assumed she'd gone to breakfast, but she was there, small and fragile-looking even as she uncurled and sat up. She was wearing his shirt, and the shirt, her face, and her arms were all streaked with paint.

She rose to her feet, face twisted in a worried expression. "I fell asleep."

Jasper pivoted in his crouch and then sprang to his feet. "Why did you lie to us?"

Irina fell back a step in shock. "Lie? I didn't lie."

Eli rose too, switching his gaze between them. "Jasper, calm down."

"I am calm."

"No, you're not," Irina pointed out levelly.

Jasper seemed incensed. "Clearly you're lying. I want to know why. I want to know what you're hiding."

Eli looked at Irina. Jasper couldn't be implying…

Jasper stabbed a finger at her. "Do you really work for Bennett Securities?"

Irina sputtered, then finally said, "You know I do. You went with me to pick up supplies."

Jasper's hand slashed through the air. "Easily faked." He looked over his shoulder at the paintings and his jaw muscle flexed. "Or maybe you technically work for them. Maybe your boss has you working there and you two were just waiting, biding your time."

"Jasper, stop." Eli tried to make it a command, but it came out as a plea.

Irina didn't respond. Her shoulders hunched and head dropped.

"Who are you really?" Jasper demanded. "And why are you lying to us?"

Irina covered her face, and Eli felt the bottom drop out of his world.

Chapter Seventeen

"It's time to go."

Bryan Cobb looked up from his desk, at the figure in the doorway.

He turned his attention back to his work. The papers were spread out in neat rows. His heavy fountain pen was poised to sign the letter printed on heavy linen letterhead. Rather than risk dripping ink, he screwed the cap onto his pen and set it in the narrow margin between two sheets of paper.

He had a computer, but he was a paper man. The computer was relegated to a smaller desk tucked into the corner of his large office. When computers were new, and he was trying to keep up with things like that, he'd had a temp come in one day a week and translate all his work from hard-copy pages onto the computer.

Now computers weren't new, and they weren't secure. Mr. Cobb's clients—client—wanted security above all. He'd gone back to doing things the way he had before, with paper and pen, using the computer only when he had to. He'd even bought a special computer and printer that didn't have an internet connection, and used it as little more than a typewriter.

Toward the end of his workdays, he'd sometimes admit to himself that there were some good features, like the big monitor. His oldest granddaughter had come in and helped him set it up so the type was nice and big. His eyesight wasn't what it used to be, and a typewriter, which he sometimes grumbled about being so much simpler, would have been harder on his eyes.

Mr. Cobb looked out the window on his left. He'd had this same office for nearly forty years. The skyline outside that window had changed, but the building where he worked had been built to last, by an architect who knew their craft. Things like that were important to Mr. Cobb.

"Did you hear me?"

The man in the doorway didn't raise his voice, but Mr. Cobb flinched. When he'd first hung out his shingle, he'd cobbled together a living by having a multitude of small fish clients. Most people with money weren't interested in a jack-of-all-trades like him. They wanted a broker for their stocks, a property manager for their real estate investments, and a whole accounting firm to handle their taxes.

He'd been in business three years, and close to giving up, when he'd gotten a new client. A man who called himself Mr. Storm, though Mr. Cobb never saw a single sheet of paper with that name on it. To be frank, Mr. Storm was a bit of a silly name. In the rare times that Mr. Cobb let himself be distracted by flights of fancy, he wondered if Mr. Storm, whom he'd only ever met in person twice, had made up the name as he'd walked into Mr. Cobb's office.

But Mr. Storm represented a group, a consortium, who had assets that needed management. It had taken several years—years that, looking back, he realized were a test—before Mr. Cobb handled all of the consortium's assets. They had a few pieces of real estate, some investments, but most of their assets were art. Art they didn't want catalogued or made public. Art which Mr. Cobb had painstakingly had insured. It had taken quite a bit of work on his side, and travel to locations he later couldn't pinpoint, to get all the art photographed and catalogued, then insured by a firm that valued discretion the same way his clients did.

It was during that time that he realized the people he worked for were evil.

Mr. Cobb was a good man. Or he had been.

By the time he realized what he was doing, why these people wanted these secrets kept, it had been too late for him to back out. They were by then his only client. He was married, and at the time had two small children. He'd returned from a cataloguing trip—a trip during which he'd flown into Portland, gotten into a car with no windows in the back, and been driven five hours away. The car had pulled into a storage facility; Mr. Cobb had gotten out and done his work. Then he'd gotten back in the car and was returned to the airport. He never spoke to anyone. Never knew where he'd gone.

But he'd recognized one of the paintings he'd photographed that day. His wife, bless her, was one of those people who loved learning. When she was out, Mr. Cobb and the kids would binge on bad TV while eating popcorn. When she was home, they watched educational programing. And just a month before that fateful trip, they'd watched a program about the art the Nazis stole, and all the famous paintings that were still missing. One was a Van Gogh. Mr. Cobb may not have been a huge patron of the arts, but he knew that name, and truly appreciated how beautiful Van Gogh's paintings were.

And there, in a climate-controlled storage unit, he'd seen a painting of a man in a blue suit and a straw hat walking with his easel and canvases, the sky turquoise and the fields golden. He'd even remembered the name of the painting, because it was simple and straightforward—*The Painter on His Way to Work.*

Since that fateful trip, Mr. Cobb had known this day would come. Known that he'd made a deal with the devil and that if he chose to stay, knowing what he knew, he'd pay the price. Mr. Cobb had chosen the easy way and lived a good life because of it.

Many times throughout the years, as he'd executed his employer's orders, he'd wondered if this would be the thing that brought the house of cards down on him. He'd had that same feeling a few days ago when he'd contacted a charity in Denver about the loan of some of his client's art.

The original arrangements for his client to have some of their collection shown at a charity gala had been made nearly a year ago. Mr. Cobb had taken care of the transport and insurance. He'd worked with the event management company and arranged for all contingencies.

Then, the day before the event, he'd gotten an alert from Mr. Black. Another name Mr. Cobb doubted was real. But Mr. Black was like Mr. Cobb. He was employed by the consortium, and all he did was computer work. Digital security and consulting was what Mr. Cobb called the payments to Mr. Black.

Mr. Black called to say that someone dangerous had RSVP'd to the event. An art historian, who, for some reason, was on a special roster of names Mr. Black kept. Mr. Cobb could only assume they were enemies of the consortium.

Mr. Cobb had gotten the message too late to stop everything from being taken out of storage, but he'd had the "sensitive" pieces held back. Then he ordered the most elaborate and impressive security detail he could get from the consortium's preferred security firm.

His precautions had been necessary—there'd been an attempted theft of the art. Mr. Cobb had received an initial report from the security company, alerting him to what had happened and that they were in pursuit.

That was several days ago. He hadn't gotten the final report from the company. He also didn't know which pieces had been taken.

In order to keep from drawing too much attention, Mr. Cobb had been forced to leave the bulk of the collection on display with the charity. It was only yesterday that all the art had been boxed up and returned to the storage facility. Mr. Cobb was waiting for the security report—and hopefully the return of all the stolen pieces—before going up to do an inventory check himself.

The art was insured, so even if any pieces were truly lost, his client wouldn't suffer any undue financial hardship. But it wasn't really about the money. It was about privacy and control. Mr. Cobb dreaded telling his clients what had happened. He'd waited several days, before his conscience, ethics, and the occasional sensational news story, bade him send a certified letter notifying Mr. Storm of the theft, and the steps being taken to return the missing pieces—whatever they were.

Since writing the letter, Mr. Cobb had been plagued by a bad feeling, like the devil was breathing down his neck.

And now the devil had come to collect. Or more precisely, he'd sent a very dangerous-looking man to collect.

Mr. Cobb stacked his papers, put his pen in the drawer.

"I heard you, young man. No need to be rude."

"Good."

"I've worked for you people for over forty years." It wasn't pleading, Mr. Cobb wouldn't stoop to that, but he wanted to make sure they took note of his loyalty.

"Not for me. But your loyalty is why I'm here." He stepped out of the shadows. "Your family was already taken care of."

Mr. Cobb surged to his feet, panic beating at his chest. "No. No. They don't know anything."

The man didn't reply, and his eyes were cold.

Mr. Cobb ran at him. A stupid move. He was an old man. The stranger avoided his desperate fingers, stepping to the side. He grabbed Mr. Cobb by the shoulder, plunging the syringe into his upper arm. Mr. Cobb's eyes started to close as he was lowered to the floor.

"I'm sorry, Mr. Cobb."

The stranger looked around the office, assessing. Ten minutes later, he left the building via the back stairs with Mr. Cobb draped over his shoulder.

The first window exploded as he closed the trunk with Mr. Cobb inside. A second window exploded a moment later as the heat of the fire shattered the glass.

***

"After all we've been through, you doubt me?" Irina was angry and sad all at the same time. She folded her arms protectively over her breasts. She felt unkempt and unprepared for this confrontation. Jasper's anger buffeted her, while Eli's cold silence made her shiver. Irina tried to gather her thoughts and emotions and get them under control. She wanted to laugh at Jasper's weird overreaction, wanted to stroke the worry lines from Eli's face.

But she was raw, exposed. As if her skin and bone had been peeled away. It had been a long time since she'd let herself get that way—allowed herself to let go to the point that she was so very vulnerable. And so she didn't say anything.

Jasper must have taken her silence as some sort of admission of guilt. "Stop pretending, you're—"

"Shut up, Jasper. Look at her."

There were footsteps, and Irina flinched. She took a half step back but there was nowhere to go. Her butt hit the wall and she froze.

"Irina." Eli's fingers were warm on her chilled skin as he took her hands. "Irina, it's okay. It's me. It's Eli. Shhh." He rubbed her fingers in long, smooth strokes. "Tell us about the paintings."

"They're just junk. I swear that's all they are. Sometimes I...sometimes I just need to paint. I'm not hiding anything from you. Not hiding anything important I mean." She winced at how stupid that sounded. Her stomach was knotted with embarrassment. Of all the people in the world to see her sad, stupid paintings, these two—the men she loved and who were so brilliant and knowledgeable about art— were the last ones on earth she'd want to see them. What must they think of her?

"How long have you been painting?" Eli's voice was kind. It was like he was asking a child about their scribbles.

Tears of embarrassment stung her eyes. She tried a dismissive laugh, but it came out as a choked sound that was closer to sob than debonair laugh. "I don't want to talk about it. Please, just let me throw them away. I meant to do it before you got up."

"Throw them away? *Throw them away?*"

"Jasper!" Eli barked. "Stop yelling. You're scaring her."

"Irina." Jasper ran up to them, crowding against Eli and Irina. He touched her face. "Irina, baby, will you look at me?"

Eli's presence beside her was intensely comforting and Irina started to feel more like herself—calm and confident. A spark of concern overrode her embarrassment. Jasper sounded slightly...crazed.

She raised her eyes, looking at her husbands. Eli's brows were drawn together in concern, but his expression was soft with worry. He stroked her wrists with his thumbs. Jasper's hair was standing on end as if he'd pulled on it with his fists.

The mess of emotions and anxieties that had driven her out of bed to create the sad little paintings was fading, to be replaced by rueful amusement.

Irina's lips twitched and Eli's face relaxed. "Jasper, you look like a mad scientist." She slid out of Eli's grasp, but not before she stretched up to plant a kiss on the underside of his chin. "Give me a minute to get rid of this stuff and clean up."

Slipping away from them, she hustled over to the paintings, grabbing the self-portrait, which was still wet. Her thumb slid across the canvas as she picked it up. There was a large trash can in the dining room, so she'd take them there.

"Stop!" Jasper yelled.

Irina jumped in shock, dropping the painting.

Eli and Jasper both rushed forward, right past her, kneeling on either side of the painting.

"It's okay, it's okay," Jasper chanted. "It landed face up."

Irina, with a mental apology to the hotel owners, grabbed a towel and wiped her thumb. She was so covered in paint, a little more hardly mattered, but she had to try to start getting clean. She really should have bought some mineral spirits.

"The paint here is smeared," Eli moaned.

"That's fine, that's fine," Jasper soothed. "We'll have a write up that explains the smear, posted beside it in the gallery. 'Artist attempts to destroy own work, painting saved by gallant and dashing heroes.'"

Irina crouched down, joining their little huddle. "Uh, guys, it's just some crappy thing I did. You don't have to pretend to care. Also, Jasper, have you been drinking?" She smiled at them. "I'm joking about the drinking. And thank you for taking that so seriously." She jabbed a finger at the painting and they both yelped in alarm. Irina shook her head. "It's sweet, but not necessary. I'll toss these and then get cleaned up."

Eli and Jasper looked at each other. As one, they rose. Jasper grabbed her hand and hauled her toward the seating area. He forced her to sit on the padded ottoman. Eli kneeled and, much to her shock, snatched up one of the restraints attached to the legs of the ottoman and quickly bound her wrist.

"Oh, I see." She tugged, the chain connecting the leather buckle cuff to the table clanking merrily. Her body started to heat, her nipples beading at the implied promise of pleasure. She leaned toward Eli, ready to kiss him, but he stood.

Jasper finished buckling her other wrist. He too stood.

Irina's blood cooled as she looked between them. "Jasper? Eli?" She swallowed. "Are you going to give me any hints about what we're playing?"

Jasper was half-turned, looking at the paintings, but as she spoke, his attention shifted to her. He touched Eli's arm, motioning toward two large pillows.

As one, they sat.

"Irina, why didn't you tell us you were an artist?" Eli asked.

"I'm not. I just paint sometimes."

"How long have you been painting?" Jasper asked.

She shrugged, uncomfortable with the questions but realizing that they were hardly unfair, given what they'd woken up to. "Since I was in high school. I told you my parents were divorced, right? The custody exchange was near the art department. Once, sometimes twice a week, I would end up waiting there. I got to know the art students, the teachers. After a while, they would bring me paper and charcoal or pencils. When the weather was nice the whole class would be outside, so I got to watch the lessons."

"Did the professor encourage you to study art?"

Irina was surprised by Jasper's weirdly on-point question. "Yes, he did. He felt bad for me once I told him why I was there."

"How often do you paint?" Eli asked.

"About once a week. I sometimes just need an outlet. If exercise isn't enough, I paint."

Jasper blew out a long breath. "I'm almost afraid to ask this, but what do you do with the paintings when you're done?"

"Throw them away."

Jasper made a strangled noise. Eli reached over and forced his head between his knees. "Breathe, Jasper."

Irina jerked, the chains clanking. "What's going on? Why are you two being so…weird?"

"Irina, you're an incredibly talented artist."

"Eli, you don't need to—"

Jasper sat up. His expression was so fierce that Irina stopped talking.

"You're *so* good," he said, "that for a minute, I actually thought you were a double agent, that you were one of the purists. That we'd been set up. For someone otherwise so self-aware, it's a bit baffling that you don't recognize how good you are."

Irina stared at him. She'd been so upset earlier, she hadn't really processed his words. All she'd recognized was his anger. She looked down at the restraints.

"You know I'm not one of the purists, right?"

"Yes," Eli said firmly, though he looked a little guilty.

"You thought I was one too?"

Eli looked sheepish.

"Eli!"

"It was honestly easier to believe that you were one of the bad guys than believe you have no idea what you are," Jasper declared.

Irina raised a brow. "And what am I?"

"An artist of unparalleled talent."

"Jasper, be serious—"

"He *is* being serious. So am I." Eli leaned forward, elbows on his knees. "I may not be an expert when it comes to what's going on in the art world in this century, but I know when I see a piece of art that means something, that could change the world. I see that in *your* art."

Irina's whole body stilled, as if time had stopped. Everything around her fell away, leaving her quiet and still in this moment.

"My mother is one of the most notable American artists currently living." Jasper spoke quietly. "Trust me when I say that *you* are an artist. That is what you were meant to be. A talent like yours needs to be seen, to be shared."

Tears gathered on her lower lids, then slid down her face. Irina went to wipe them away, only to be pulled up short by the restraints.

"Undo these stupid things," she sniffled.

Eli reached for her, but Jasper stopped him. "Don't. I don't trust her."

Irina reared back as if slapped. "Jasper, I'm not a purist. I swear I'm not. I wasn't even hiding that," she gestured to the paintings, "from you. Well, I was, but it was because it wasn't important. Because I was embarrassed."

"Did you, or did you not, destroy art?"

Eli grunted. "Good point."

"I didn't destroy anything!"

"What were you going to do with those?"

"Uh…"

"Irina."

"I was going to throw them away in the dining room."

Jasper's gaze narrowed. "When was the last time you painted something, before this?"

"When we were in Boston. When you both stormed off to have a hissy fit. I went for a run and stopped at a little artist studio I know."

"And what did you do with that painting?"

"It was terrible, it was just a—"

"What. Did. You. Do. With. It?"

"I left it there and told them to throw it away. Happy?" Irina was both irritated at the questioning and amused at their reactions.

They were wrong—she wasn't anything special—but her heart swelled with love for them. Clearly yesterday's marathon sex session had rattled their brains.

Jasper's mouth opened and closed like a fish's. Eli looked pained.

Irina couldn't help it. She laughed.

They both leaned back, looking scandalized.

"I'm sorry, I'm sorry. It's just…I love you. Both of you. I don't think I've said that yet. I've thought it, but I haven't said it. I love you, even if you have terrible taste in art." Irina smiled at them, and her eyes filled with tears once more, but these were happy tears.

Eli slid onto his knees and kissed her. Resting his forehead against hers, he said, "I love you too. I can't imagine my life without you."

Irina's heart swelled.

Eli looked at Jasper.

He crossed his arms. "Of course I love both of you, but I want to strangle her right now."

Irina laughed at Jasper's scowl, and Eli sighed.

"Jasper," she said, "it's really sweet of you to say you like my paintings, but you don't have to. I promise not to hide it from you, but just because I paint doesn't mean I'm some great artist. I'm okay with that." She looked down, watching her toes curl and uncurl. There was paint splattered on the tops of her bare feet. "When I woke up I was just feeling a bit...inadequate."

"Why?" Eli asked.

"I just...my job isn't exactly my great passion. It's a job. I'm good at it, I know that, but I'm not passionate about it. Not the way the two of you are about art. I was lying in bed and I realized that our trinity is really about the two of you—your skills, your knowledge. That's why the Grand Master put us together. I'm just the hired muscle, and now that we're almost done with our task, I guess I was just feeling insecure. My parents were disappointed when I graduated and took this job. Security work is not exactly what people imagine when you say you went to Harvard."

Now that she'd started talking, Irina couldn't seem to stop. And she didn't want to. It felt good, actually saying all these things she'd been feeling. "If I weren't in the Trinity Masters, I'd be...I'd be a bit of a failure, frankly. Dean Adams helped me figure out my major in school, got me my job with Bennett Securities." She took a deep breath. "I probably don't have a job anymore. Exposing the owner of my company as a traitor probably isn't good for job security."

Eli looked stricken. "I'm sorry. I was so focused on my job and my situation, I didn't even think about you."

She shook her head. "It's hardly the same thing. That's your career. I'll get another job."

"No, you won't," Jasper declared. "You're going to paint. I'll support you. I'll support both of you."

Irina couldn't grab Jasper, so she leaned back on one elbow, stretched out her leg and kicked him in the shin.

He grunted and grabbed his leg.

"You deserved that," Eli commented mildly.

"I'm not going to be your kept woman." Irina failed to keep the snarl out of her voice. "I should have known that showing even a hint of submissiveness would turn you two into raging misogynists."

"Why am *I* in trouble?" Eli demanded. "I didn't say it."

"I'm not a misogynist. I offered to support him too." Jasper rubbed his shin with one hand and pointed at Eli with the other. "And you *are* going to paint. Because you need to."

Moving gingerly, as if he were approaching a wild horse, Jasper knelt in front of Irina. "I want you to close your eyes. Do you trust me?" She nodded. "Then close your eyes."

Irina eyed him suspiciously, but she did trust him, so she did as he asked.

"Imagine a big room. There are concrete floors, and tall, tall ceilings. One wall is all windows. Nothing but natural light. There's nothing in the room except an easel. An easel and table. On the table are hundreds of tubes of paint. In every color. And brushes, every kind of brush they make."

Irina could see it—the dream studio. Nothing but space and light and a blank canvas waiting to be filled.

"That is what I want for you. I want to give you that room. I want, for myself, to see what you'd create in that room."

That stillness she had felt only a moment ago returned. This time she didn't turn away from the feeling, she embraced it. Her life had changed in this past week. It should have—she'd finally been joined in a trinity. But what Jasper and Eli were offering—encouraging—was for her to make another huge change.

They wanted her to listen to that tiny voice, a voice she'd been silencing her whole life. A voice that had something to say, something that could only be expressed through paint.

"If you're just saying this to...to make me feel better, or because you love me and are being supportive...don't. It would break me to find out later you were lying."

"Irina." Jasper grabbed her chin, forced her to look at him. "Irina, you know how talented you are. Someone has told you that before. But you didn't listen."

A thousand memories—art teachers, other people she met in studios, the few friends who'd seen pieces she'd left drying in her apartment, all people who'd exclaimed and admired her work—surged up. She'd brushed it all aside. "No, I didn't."

"Then listen to me. Listen to Eli."

Eli bent to kiss her hand. "He's right. The Grand Master may have put us together so you could be the muscle, as you say, but this is what our trinity is really about."

"I'm scared to hope. Scared to believe you." Irina's voice was thin.

"Don't be." Jasper finally relented and leaned in and kissed her. "I love you. I love both of you, and have since we were in that warehouse."

Eli wrapped an arm around each of them. Irina let out a small sob and buried her head into the safety of their chests. Hands stroked her hair, her back. When her tears stopped, Irina felt both lighter and giddy—as if she'd had a few glasses of champagne. Drunk on hope and love.

"This would be a lot better if I could hug both of you." Her voice was husky from the tears, but she was smiling.

Eli reached for the restraints, but once more Jasper blocked him. "Leave her there. It's safer."

"I'm not going to throw anything away. I'll fix the self-portrait."

"I mean it's safer for you. I have a very strong urge to turn you over my knee and spank you for your wanton destruction of art. Plus not telling us about it."

"Oh no, you did not just threaten me." Irina narrowed her eyes. "Don't forget I can still kick your ass. Eli, get these things off me."

Eli was looking between them with a decidedly lascivious expression. "I'd like to see that," he said thickly.

"See what?" Irina was alarmed by Eli's look. "See me kick his ass?" she asked hopefully.

"Him spanking you."

Irina's libido sat up and took note. She scowled to cover her reaction. "Well, tough luck."

"Let's take a vote." Jasper grinned. "Who thinks Irina needs a spanking?"

Eli and Jasper both raised their hands. Irina sputtered.

"Me thinks the lady doth protest too much," Eli murmured.

"Agreed. Come on, Eli." Jasper headed back toward the paintings.

"Why don't you spank her now?" Eli slid his hand up her thigh. Irina considered resisting, but that would be a lie. She wanted his hands on her. She let her legs fall open.

Jasper grabbed Eli by the collar and yanked him away from Irina. "Focus, man, focus."

Eli shook his head. "Right. But later?"

Jasper looked over his shoulder at Irina and his eyes were hot with promise. "Later."

Irina pulled on the restraints, but they held tight. She'd just have to wait. And anticipate.

Chapter Eighteen

"Price, we've got a problem." Gunner was yelling to be heard over the sound of sirens.

"What's going on?"

"Someone got here first."

Price Bennett leaned his fists on the conference table and bowed his head over his phone, which was on speaker.

"How bad is it?" he asked his husband.

"The whole building is on fire. I'm waiting to find out if they recovered a body, and I made a few calls while I was waiting. It might actually get worse."

"Of course it does," Price said.

"Bryan Cobb chartered a private plane. It left about an hour ago. There were fifteen passengers."

Price's head snapped up. "Fifteen?"

"Yes, and based on the names, it's the entire Cobb family—kids, grandkids, even his kids' in-laws."

"You're saying everyone who might have known Cobb got on a private jet bound for, oh, let me guess, Cuba?"

"The Maldives, actually. Man's got taste."

"Can TSA confirm identities?"

"Ah, well, you see, there was a computer glitch in the private terminal. TSA hand-checked all the passports and weren't able to take photos."

"Of course there was. You going to check the houses?"

"Yes."

"Let me know what you find. Love you."

"Love you too."

Price tapped his phone to end the call, then looked at the Grand Master. She was young, and Price was used to thinking of her as immature, but when he looked at her now there was no doubt in his mind that she was an Adams. That she would rule the Trinity Masters with the same cool control her brother and father before her had shown.

It had been a tense few days for him. It had started with the crisis in Denver, when one of his HRD teams was attacked after losing five packages they'd been there to protect. He'd been trying to piece together what had happened—including why an HRD team had been sent into Colorado in the first place. Then there was the issue of one of his D.C. operatives who had inexplicably checked out equipment from the Boston field office, and who matched the description of one of the attackers in Denver. That's when he'd been summoned to Boston.

Being called before the Grand Master and accused of treason was never a position he'd thought to find himself in. He'd served as counselor to Harrison Adams. He'd been the one to uphold their rules, resulting in Harrison stepping down. But none of that had mattered. The Grand Master had some damning evidence against him. However, that same evidence turned out to be the information he needed to make sense of the seemingly disparate events in Denver.

Now Price was playing catch up, trying to both get answers and assure Juliette of his loyalty.

He thought he'd finally gotten to the bottom of it when he was able to trace the order for the HRD team to a Mr. Cobb, who was the business manager for a VIP client. Bennett Securities was too big for him to know every client personally, but most VIP clients were members of the Trinity Masters. However, there'd been almost no information about this particular client in his system. No information except that he or she had been a client of his since the beginning—which was a very bad sign. Members of the Trinity Masters had helped him start his career by investing in him at the beginning.

And now Mr. Cobb, his best lead, was gone.

"What do you think, Mr. Bennett?" the Grand Master asked.

"It's possible that Mr. Cobb is a major player. After the problems in Denver, he grabbed his family and escaped, burning down the building to cover his tracks."

"Or?"

"Or Mr. Cobb and his entire family were killed as a cover-up, and the private plane is a ruse to keep the cops from looking too hard."

Juliette Adams turned to look at the painting of the Capitol behind her desk. "Fifteen people died for our secrets tonight."

Price clenched his fists. Mr. Cobb's grandchildren had ranged in ages from four to fourteen.

"We'll find them." Devon Asher laid his hand on his wife's shoulder.

"How many more people will die before we do?"

"We have another problem." Seb had walked into the room halfway into the conversation. "Price, it would have been nice if you'd let us know what you were doing. I was looking into the Denver situation too."

Price straightened. "You were investigating my business?"

"He was. On my orders." Juliette's gaze was cool and unapologetic.

"I found your Mr. Cobb too. But *I* found him yesterday." Seb crossed his arms. "And I told Irina and her trinity where he was, so they could look into it."

Juliette cursed, jumped from her chair and ran to her computer. "They weren't going to check their email until today. If we're lucky, we can stop them."

"Luck isn't something we've had a lot of," Devon muttered.

Price glared at Sebastian, who returned the glare. "I had it handled," he told the younger man.

"That wasn't your decision to make," Juliette snapped.

Price clenched his jaw. Sebastian and Devon both took a step toward him. He exhaled. "I'm sorry, Grand Master."

Price stalked out of the headquarters. He was no longer suspect number one in the kidnapping of one of the Trinity Masters' members—though technically his company, his HRD team, was the one to kidnap Eli Wexler. He needed to evaluate his organization from the bottom up.

If the purists had been using Bennett Securities as their henchmen, without Price realizing it, there would be hell to pay.

They huddled around the library's computer screen. It took a while for them to find the email from the Grand Master, since the actual sender address was "I <3 Boston." But after sorting through all Irina's emails, they decided the weird email from "I <3 Boston" had to be from the Grand Master.

The email subject line was blank, and there was no text, but there was an image embedded in the body of the email. It had been sent late Monday.

Irina opened the email from Monday.

Eli peered at the image. "Is that a clue?"

"What kind of clue is a picture of three baby goats frolicking in a field?" Jasper asked. He was looking over Eli's shoulder.

Irina made an aggravated noise. "This is an encrypted email. The image is just the vehicle for the encrypted text."

"How do we decrypt it?"

"I need to open this on my tablet. My *work* tablet."

"Shit," Eli said with feeling. He might not be the most tech savvy person, but even he knew that Irina using her work computer, which could probably be traced, was a bad idea.

Irina pursed her lips, then nodded definitively. "Here's what we're going to do. We'll find a coffee shop with free Wi-Fi. I'll turn on the tablet long enough to download the email and decrypt it, then we'll immediately leave. We'll set a timer. Five minutes tops then we jump in the car and move. If we don't get it done in five minutes, we find another place, stop, and try again."

Eli hummed in agreement. Jasper headed for the door—he was nervous about having the car out of his sight, and apparently wasn't going to spend one extra second away from it. Eli had felt the same when they'd first gotten hold of the Rodin, but now...well, now there were more important things.

Eli held out his hand to Irina. She placed her fingers in his.

"Why thank you, kind sir."

"You're welcome, pretty lady." He tried to do a drawl, but it was pretty bad.

Irina laughed, leaning into his side. She seemed lighter, happier than before. Admittedly, Eli hadn't had the opportunity to spend a lot of time with her when they weren't stressed out and running for their lives, but his instincts were telling him that this was more than just "relaxed" Irina. This was Irina happy and looking forward to the future.

He was still shocked that she'd been painting in secret and throwing away the results since she was a teenager. While they were packing, checking out, and loading the car, Jasper had grilled Irina about every place she'd abandoned or thrown away a painting. He had plans to track each of them down.

It had been bittersweet to say goodbye to the hotel, but it was time to move on. They'd found yet another library, this one in a small town in southern Kansas, and had figured once they got the "all-clear" email they'd head up to Kansas City to catch a flight home. The encrypted email had thrown that off a bit, but they had time.

Jasper was leaning against the car in a seemingly casual pose, as if he hadn't been stressing out about letting the car out of his sight the entire time they were in the building. As they emerged from the library, he unlocked the doors.

"Coffee shop?" he asked Irina once they were all in.

She was in the back, with the touch-dry oil paintings stacked on the seat beside her. "Yep."

With no smartphones to help them, they had to drive around for a bit, but finally found a national chain coffee shop with free Wi-Fi strong enough to reach them in the parking lot. Irina dug her tablet out of her suitcase, then closed the trunk and jumped back into the car. Eli twisted in his seat to watch her work.

Her fingers hovered over the screen. "Jasper, five minutes."

"Go," he said.

Irina started tapping. In moments her email program was open, and Eli watched, heart in his throat, as her emails slowly downloaded, populating the screen. The "I <3 Boston" email appeared and Irina pounced on it. It took what felt like twenty minutes for the picture to download. Once the frolicking goats appeared, Irina's fingers started to fly. The screen split so half was the image, half was a black box, with scrolling white, green, and red code.

"Time?" Irina asked.

"You have two minutes." Jasper was facing forward, eyes glued to the little clock display on the dash.

"It's going to be close."

More typing, and Eli's head started to prickle with sweat. He had no idea what she was doing, and knew he couldn't help, but he was fighting the urge to ask what he could do.

"One minute," Jasper warned.

"Got it. Drive."

Eli had a brief glimpse of the goats dissolving into a short message before Jasper threw the car into reverse. Eli fell against the window as Irina jammed her finger on the tablet's power button, turning it off.

Once they were on the freeway, Eli asked, "What did it say?"

Irina closed her eyes and recited. "Bennett under investigation, but order came from Bryan Cobb, business manager for Bennett client. No information available on client. Cobb address 1245 11th Street, Dallas."

"Dallas?" Jasper jerked the wheel to the right and they went careening onto an off-ramp. Eli braced a hand on the dash and prayed.

In less than two minutes, Jasper had them back on the freeway, this time headed south.

"Wait, are we going to Dallas?" Eli asked.

"Yep."

"If the bad guy is in Dallas, shouldn't we go anywhere *but* Dallas?" He knew even as he asked that it was a forlorn hope that his spouses would run *away* from the danger instead of *toward* it.

"I'd like to have a conversation with Mr. Cobb," Irina said.

"Conversation. Right." Eli sighed. "If he's a business manager, it can't be that bad, right?"

"This might also mean that Price Bennett isn't actually a member of the purists." Irina sounded relieved.

"If it's not him then we have no idea who the owner of this art is," Jasper said. "And that means we're still in danger."

"I know how to find the owners," Eli said.

"You do?" Irina yelped.

"You said the owner. The owner of these pieces is either European museums, or the descendants of the people they were taken from."

"Oh, I thought you meant the current owner," Irina said.

Eli growled. "The people who had these things and hid them away, clearly knowing exactly what they had, are not the rightful owners. They don't deserve that title. They're thieves."

"Aww, the way you said thief hurts my feelings," Jasper teased.

Eli narrowed his eyes. "Have you ever actually stolen something? Or are you just messing with me?"

"You mean besides the Gardner paintings?"

Eli put a finger on his left eye to stop it from twitching. "Yes, besides those."

"Art? Not really. With art, I've done more liberation and relocation than proper theft. Now jewelry..."

Eli groaned and covered his face with his hands.

Chapter Nineteen

Jasper was well traveled. The only continent he hadn't visited was Antarctica. He enjoyed traveling, and was no stranger to road trips. The driving trip from Baghdad to London had been especially heinous.

But after seven hours driving through north Texas, he was more than ready to be done with traveling.

They'd started out early-afternoon, and rolled into Dallas just past nine, after getting stuck in the tail end of rush hour traffic. Jasper finally spotted a big box store and pulled off.

"We need a phone," he said as he parked.

Eli, who'd nodded off, probably from sheer boredom, looked up and nodded.

"I'll go." Irina jumped out of the car. Her groan as she stretched was audible.

"I need to use the restroom." Eli climbed out too.

Jasper waited with the car while they went in, then when they were back, he took his turn using the facilities. He also ran through the store, which surprisingly had exactly what he was looking for. He bought all five of the soft-sided art portfolio cases they had in stock, plus two large duffel bags.

By the time he made his way back to the car, Irina had the phone working, the pieces of the packaging spread out on the trunk. She'd bought a pay-as-you-go phone, but it wasn't one of the cheap ones. It was a smartphone.

"Praise the Lord, we're connected to the big wild world once again." Jasper resisted the urge to snatch the phone from her and check the news headlines. Instead he propped his ass against the driver's door and bent, stretching his hamstrings.

"I've got a map to Bryan Cobb." Irina turned the phone to show Eli the screen.

Jasper straightened, raising his arms over his head. He caught both Eli and Irina looking as his shirt rode up.

He smiled. "Down, boys and girls. And before we go anywhere, we're going to email the Grand Master and tell her where we are and what we're doing. Someone needs to know."

They piled back into the car, the bags Jasper had just purchased riding in the backseat with Irina. He drove under the freeway to the shopping area on the other side, where another convenient free Wi-Fi location was waiting. This time they had to go inside to get strong enough service for Irina's tablet to work. Jasper stationed himself near the door, where he had a clear view of the car. Eli looked longingly at the line for coffee.

"We'll only be here five minutes," Jasper told him.

Eli sighed. "I know, but a man can dream."

"It's almost over," Irina assured him.

Jasper waited until Eli wasn't looking then caught her gaze and raised a brow. She grimaced slightly. If the Grand Master expected them to confront Bryan

Cobb then this might not be over. And it might be dangerous.

"I'm ready," she said.

Jasper started the timer.

Two minutes and thirty eight seconds later, Irina cursed. "Fuck."

"What?" Eli demanded.

Irina leapt to her feet. Jasper took the keys from his pocket, grabbed Eli's hand, and hauled him out the door.

As he threw the car into reverse, Irina said, "Jasper, give me the phone."

He tossed it back to her, watching her face in the rearview mirror.

"Where am I going?" he asked.

"I...I don't know. I'm so sorry." She looked stricken.

Jasper's stomach clenched. "Irina, what's wrong?"

She met his eyes in the mirror. "There was a second email from the Grand Master. It came just after we read the first one. We just missed it."

Jasper's whole body went cold. "Another email."

Eli was surprisingly calm. "What did the Grand Master's second message say?"

Irina closed her eyes, clearly reciting. "Bryan Cobb gone. Presumed killed. Do not go to Dallas. Call for further instructions."

Jasper was about to pull out of the parking lot and head onto the freeway. He jerked the wheel, bumping them into a parking spot near the exit. Throwing the car into park, he twisted in his seat so they could all see each other.

"Is there a number?" Eli asked.

"Yes." Irina held up the phone. She'd already typed the number in. Her thumb hovered over the send button.

"Why are you hesitating?" Eli asked.

"Because it could be a trap," Jasper answered for her. "Worst case scenario, we dump the tablet and the phone and run for the second time."

Irina looked worried, but she nodded in agreement with Jasper's statement, and hit send.

"Get out of there."

The Grand Master's voice rang with urgency. Eli's stomach dropped and he looked over his shoulder. If this were a movie, right now was when the bad guys would come roaring up in black SUVs and surround them.

"You think they're still in Dallas?" Irina had the Grand Master on speaker, the phone on the armrest between the front seats.

"I don't know, but Dallas is the last place I want the three of you to be."

"I'm sorry, it's my fault—" Irina started to say.

"Ms. Gentry, I assure you, none of this is your fault."

"It's a Rodin," Eli said. Irina and Jasper both looked at him. "I know Irina didn't tell you when she first called. We have a Rodin in the trunk of a car we stole. A sculpture by Rodin, two more sculptures by Barlach. A Nolde painting, and a blueprint we can't yet identify."

The Grand Master didn't respond, and for a second Eli was worried he'd made her angry. "Has anyone seen you? Anyone who can identify you? Who might know who you are?"

They exchanged several "oh fuck" looks before Jasper responded.

"Yes. We were hiding out in a hotel that I guess a lot of members use. There were two other members there. They recognized our jewelry."

"Who was it?"

Irina picked up the story. "The man's name was Caden, and I think his last name was Anderson. The woman's name was Darling. We didn't get her last name."

The Grand Master went very quiet for a moment. "Let me deal with him. Get that art back to Boston. Don't drive. Fly. I want you here tomorrow morning. There's a charter fleet company just north of Dallas."

"I know the one," Jasper said. "Are we safe to fly? How much reach do these purists have?"

There was silence, then the Grand Master said, "I wish I could tell you it was safe, but it's not. Right now, I don't know *what's* safe. Bryan Cobb didn't just disappear. His children and grandchildren and his children's in-laws all supposedly boarded a private plane headed for the Maldives. There's no security video of them, because of a glitch in TSA's system at the time they were going through customs."

Eli felt sick. "Grandkids?"

"The purists killed fifteen people to stop us from asking Bryan Cobb any questions."

No one said anything for a full minute.

"I've asked more of you than I meant to." The Grand Master sounded tired. "Ms. Gentry, I leave it up to you to decide what your best option is. If you don't choose to fly, I ask only that you call me every four hours, so I know you're safe."

"Of course, Grand Master," Irina responded.

"Oh, and one more thing. Mr. Wexler will need a disguise."

Eli blinked. "I will?"

"You probably haven't seen the news, but there's a nationwide manhunt for you, Mr. Wexler. You're accused of stealing several pieces of priceless art."

Eli leaned forward and thunked his head against the dash. Repeatedly.

"We'll get him a disguise, Grand Master," Irina said. "And once we're in Boston, we may need help with some damage control."

"Of course. What is that noise?"

"Mr. Wexler is having a small breakdown." Jasper patted Eli's shoulder. "Another one, I mean. He's banging his head against the car. Don't worry, we'll take care of him."

Jasper's voice was overly cheerful, and his comment dispelled some of the tension in the car.

"I'll leave it to you, Mr. Ferrer." It was easy to hear the smile in the Grand Master's words. "Good luck. Be safe."

Three hours later, they boarded a Gulfstream GIV-SP jet. It was just after one a.m. Thursday morning. Despite that, the flight attendant and pilots were well groomed and looked rested, though they must have been hauled out of bed only an hour ago.

Eli felt for the first step with his foot. Wearing sunglasses in the middle of the night did not make seeing easy, but it was part of his disguise. Irina had run into the same store where they'd bought the phone and come out with an armful of clothing for him.

They'd changed in a dark corner of the parking lot, Irina and Jasper into business-type clothes. Jasper was wearing slacks, a button-down shirt, and a tie. He had Eli's glasses perched on his nose. Irina was wearing a black skirt and jacket with a white blouse, and her hair was up in a demure bun.

Eli was dressed as either a musician or an athlete— Irina said it didn't matter which. He wore a stark white hoodie, thick headphones made of glossy red plastic, sunglasses, and jeans.

Eli found it vaguely offensive that he was getting typecast as either a rapper or football player, but Irina had said right now she wanted to get them out of Dallas safely, and a six-foot-two black man who looked like, and traveled like, an art history professor would be a hell of a lot easier to spot than a rich athlete/musician traveling with his assistant and chauffeur.

They'd taken a taxi from the parking lot to an affluent Dallas suburb. On the way, Jasper had called the charter jet company, who'd sent a car. If the driver of the town car found it odd that they were waiting in the driveway of a massive estate—which Jasper had picked essentially at random as the address where they should be picked up—he didn't say so.

So far everything had gone according to the plan. A plan Irina and Jasper seemed to be making up as they went along. Eli didn't know how much longer he could handle this. He wasn't built for this level of sustained tension.

He made it up the steps and into the jet without tripping. If there were requests for ID, he didn't hear them. Irina was taking care of everything. Jasper carried five art portfolios, the kind with shoulder straps, and two duffel bags, to the plane with them. He looked like a Sherpa. One of the pilots helped bring up the duffel bags. Their suitcases must have been stored underneath.

Eli eyed the portfolios, which held the Nolde—still in its box, which meant the case wouldn't zip closed— the blueprint, and Irina's paintings. The sculptures were safe in their boxes in the duffel bags.

The safety briefing was quick and to the point. Then glasses of champagne were served and the flight attendant retreated to the front, leaving them alone in the four seats closest to the rear of the aircraft, each of which swiveled and was obscenely comfortable.

"This is the first time I've been on a plane and my knees haven't hit." Eli stretched out his legs. He could get used to this.

"Am I the only one who's nervous something hasn't gone wrong?" Irina asked.

The plane's engines roared to life and they started to taxi. Eli took off the sunglasses and looked out the window, expecting to see men with guns—either the cops or the bad guys—running after them. He didn't realize he was holding his breath until his chest started to hurt. He exhaled as the wheels lifted off the runway.

"We made it," he said.

Irina and Jasper returned his smile, each of them relaxing slightly.

"We're safe enough for the next four hours," Irina said. "And, better than that, we have Wi-Fi. In-flight Wi-Fi is nearly impossible to track in real time." She opened her bag and pulled out her tablet, a small laptop, and the burner phone. She turned on each piece, set up the Wi-Fi, and then doled them out. Jasper handed Eli his glasses.

Out of morbid curiosity, Eli googled himself.

Popular Denver Professor Makes Off with Priceless Art

Art Historian to Art Thief: Where Is Eli Wexler?

Colleagues Shocked by Local Professor's Crime Spree

Eli put the phone down, then picked up his glass of champagne and drained it. Irina and Jasper weren't drinking theirs, so he drained those too.

"Maybe giving him that wasn't such a good idea," Jasper said mildly.

"Yeah, maybe not." Irina snatched the phone. "Let's talk instead."

Eli grabbed at the phone, but Irina tossed it to Jasper, who held it out of reach.

"The art," she said, clearly trying to distract him. "You two never told me what you discovered about the art after you went to the library that day."

What must his parents think? And his grandmother? His friends and colleagues...

"Eli, why isn't someone looking for that Rodin? He's really famous. Shouldn't someone be looking for it?"

Eli snapped his attention to Irina. "Actually there isn't a definitive list of all of Rodin's work, despite him being one of the best known sculptors."

"Why not?" Irina propped her chin on her fist and kept her gaze on him. He knew she was trying to distract him, and it was working.

"He didn't keep a list, and he was incredibly prolific. His larger pieces, and anything done for the public, are mostly well documented, but smaller pieces, especially if they were done on private commission, wouldn't necessarily be recorded anywhere. He also painted, and there's no telling how many paintings and sketches are out there."

"That lunatic Gurlitt had a Rodin sketch."

Eli narrowed his eyes. "Jasper, what do you know about Cornelius Gurlitt?"

"Who is Cornelius Gurlitt?" Irina asked.

Eli stared at Jasper, who was looking pious. "Jasper..."

Jasper cleared his throat. "The Gurlitt family is famous in the art world. In two thousand eleven, German authorities were, let's say, tipped off about the most recent Cornelius Gurlitt's—there are several other Corneliuses in his family, which is why I'm specifying it's the most recent one I mean—possession of quite a few pieces of valuable art. They investigated him, supposedly for tax issues, and found a massive cache of Nazi art."

"Was he a Nazi?"

"His father was," Eli said. "Hildebrand Gurlitt was one of the art dealers the Nazis used to sell off degenerate art."

"Wait, if this family is known to have helped the Nazis, why didn't someone investigate them before?"

"Just harass a random German citizen because their ancestor worked for the Nazis? Not possible. The only way anything ever happens is if a piece of art is located, and there's a descendant of the original owner alive and willing to fight for it. Plus, there's no law in Germany requiring that stolen art be returned. And for degenerate art like our Nolde, the law the allied forces signed off on after the war legitimized the Nazi confiscation, and any subsequent sales. Getting art back to where it needs to be is nearly impossible."

"Unless you have, ahem, help." Jasper swiveled his chair side to side, smiling slightly.

Eli peered at him. "What did you do?"

"I may have, theoretically, in my misspent youth, broken into Gurlitt's apartment—he was a total recluse, you know—to see what he had squirreled away in there." Jasper's smile faded. "There were hundreds of paintings. Most unframed. Stuck behind stacks of canned goods. It was a nightmare."

"Tell me you took something."

"Oh, now you advocate theft? I'm shocked, Professor Wexler."

"Well, according to the news, I'm a major art thief." Eli tried to make it a joke, but Jasper's smile disappeared and Irina looked worried.

There was a moment of silence, then Irina straightened in her seat, frowning. "If it's hard for someone to claim the art, and the only good records are the ERR albums, why kill to keep this a secret? We've been assuming they're protecting their reputation. But wouldn't there be easier ways to do that?"

Eli frowned at Irina. He was so embedded in the world of art and art history that it made sense to him that this information was worth killing for, but Irina was right.

"Fifteen people, including kids, are dead." Irina's words were sobering.

Eli shook his head. "No piece of art is worth the life of a child."

"Why wouldn't they just lie and say they saved it from the Nazis or something?"

Eli pursed his lips. "With the Rodin you couldn't, because it's listed in the ERR albums, so it has clear provenance. The others...they would have been labeled degenerate art and either sold or theoretically burned."

Jasper frowned. "It would be easy enough to fake a paper trail saying your family bought the pieces after they were smuggled into the U.S. Or you could claim someone in the family purchased them in order to save them from the fire, and that after the war, they were forgotten about. Maybe stashed in an attic. Stranger things have happened."

Jasper shook his head. "She's right. The degenerate art could easily be legitimized. It's only the Rodin that's the problem. And worst case scenario, you have to return it to the heir of the pre-war owner, assuming they can be found and bother to sue you for it."

"How much would that Rodin be worth if it was sold?" Irina asked.

"It's a bronze, not marble, and small, so maybe fifteen million, maybe twenty."

Irina pursed her lips. "That's a lot of money."

"True," Jasper conceded.

Eli fiddled with his glasses. "This made sense before fifteen people died. That's out of proportion for the kind of money we're talking about."

"And actually it might be worth even less," Jasper said, "because they'd have to auction it without ownership records."

"Could they do that?"

"Auction houses aren't known for their scruples. They could, but they'd probably get less for it."

Eli rubbed his temples. "I thought we had it all figured out, but the more we talk about it, the less sense it makes."

"We don't know how many other pieces they have. Maybe they have tons of the items listed in the ERR albums." Jasper's shoulders slumped slightly.

"And we don't know if 'they' are two people, five people, or twenty people," Irina added.

"None of that explains the blueprint," Eli added.

"True." Jasper yawned. "That's the odd man out of our little collection."

It was either very late, or very early, depending on the perspective. As the silence lengthened, Eli laid his head back and closed his eyes. He fell into that twilight state of half awake, half asleep. His mind flitted between worry over his decimated reputation, guilt for what his family must be going through, and happiness because he was in love. Mixed into all that was art—Nazi art, Irina's paintings, the history of art and what it meant, what it represented.

Eli sat bolt upright. "Gold."

Irina and Jasper both yelped as he startled them awake.

"Gold what?" Irina asked.

"You said 'why kill to keep the art a secret?'" Eli bounced his fist on his thigh. "I think I know why. What if it's not really about the art, but it's about making sure that the art doesn't lead to other questions? Questions about what other loot you may have."

Jasper's eyes widened. "Gold."

"You mean Nazi gold?" Irina shook her head. "I thought that was a myth."

"The lost train cars full of gold are probably a myth, but the Nazis stole a huge amount of gold from both people and governments." Jasper tapped his fingers against his lips. "What if members of the purists helped them launder the gold?"

Irina hunched over her keyboard. "Most of the gold went through the Swiss National Bank or the Vatican Bank."

"I doubt that an American, even if they were a Nazi sympathizer, would have connections with either of those."

There was something just on the edge of Eli's consciousness, a thought that wouldn't quite form.

"I need to look something up."

Jasper passed him back the phone and Eli opened the browser, ignoring the search results about himself. It took a few minutes of clicking around, jumping from link to link about Nazi art and loot, before he found what he was looking for.

"In nineteen forty-five, a U.S. submarine accidentally sank a ship that had been a Japanese cruise ship. It was turned into a hospital ship, used by the Red Cross, and should have been safe."

"That's sad, but what does that—"

Eli cut off Jasper's question. "Supposedly the ship was carrying over five billion dollars in gold, platinum, and diamonds. The Chinese located the wreckage not that long ago and didn't find any treasure, so everyone figured that the stories were wrong. That the eyewitnesses on the docks were wrong."

Jasper frowned. "There's nothing connecting our Rodin to the sinking of a Japanese ship."

"You're right. I'm just using this as an example to make a point. Maybe it's not this particular ship, but something like this? What if you made a profit from the war—a profit that was all blood money? You played both sides, ended up with some Nazi gold, diamonds, and you also ended up with some art. You use the gold and diamonds to build your family's wealth. If these people were members of the Trinity Masters, they probably already had some money, so now they just had more money. No one is going to look too hard, unless you give them reason to."

"You think they'd still kill to protect the secret, after all this time?" Jasper asked.

Eli sat back, thinking. It didn't quite fit—the greatest generation was dying, reparations had been made. Why keep this secret so many years later?

"You would if you're a member of the Trinity Masters," Irina said suddenly. Her eyes were round. "Think about it. The Trinity Masters bleed red, white, and blue. If your family disobeyed the Grand Master and sided with the Nazis, worked against the allied forces, profited from the war…any one of those things is enough to have the Grand Master come down on you. There's no Trinity Masters' court, no jury. If the Grand Master found out…that would be the end. End of you, end of your family."

Eli felt the pieces click together. Though the details weren't all there, he felt like they'd finally figured out the big picture.

"We still don't know who 'they' are," Jasper said.

Irina cleared her throat. "And we're not going to. We did what the Grand Master asked. More than what she asked. We identified a piece from the ERR album, and we're bringing it to her. We've got four other pieces of art. I'm not going to risk either of you by trying to hunt down the owner or owners of that stuff." She gestured to the cases. "Once we get everything into the library, we're done. We have…we have a life to start."

"And a reputation to fix." Jasper pointed at Eli. "And a new artist to nurture." He flipped to pointing at Irina, who blushed.

The intercom dinged, and the flight attendant announced that she'd be coming in to check on them one last time before they started their descent. Eli pulled up his hood and put on his headphones, keeping his neck bent as she brought them warm towels, cold bottles of sparkling water, and French-press coffee.

The plane touched down as the sky turned dawn-gray. Though the lack of sleep made his eyes gritty, Eli wasn't tired. He was excited—not because they'd figured out what was really going on, but because this was it. The end of this insane "task."

In an hour, they'd have handed over the paintings and sculptures—though Eli had plans to ask to study them, and hopefully write about them later—and then he and his trinity would leave this mess in the hands of people better equipped to handle it. And they could focus on what was really important—each other.

There were still so many things they didn't know— could any of them cook? Hopefully someone could cook. Eli could BBQ like a master, but in an actual kitchen he was a disaster. Where were they going to live? Did they want to have kids? Were they open to adopting or maybe fostering?

Irina trotted over. "There's a private car service coming for us. The charter company will deliver our suitcases to the hotel. That's all we're taking." Irina pointed to the portfolios and duffel bags Eli and Jasper had divided between them.

Jasper nodded, looking tense.

"What's wrong?" Eli asked him.

"This is too easy. It's gone too smoothly. There's always a snag, always a complication."

Irina rubbed Jasper's arm. "We've had plenty of complications. Eli got kidnapped, remember? Don't borrow trouble."

Jasper nodded as if he agreed, but the tension didn't leave him. As a black sedan pulled up beside the small plane, Eli wondered if Jasper wasn't right. If this was the calm before the storm.

Chapter Twenty

The car service dropped them off on Dartmouth Street, right in front of the library as the clock clicked over to 6 a.m. Across the street, Copley Square was nearly deserted. There were a few stoic joggers taking advantage of the paths, and groundskeepers picked up trash off the grass and skimmed leaves off the surface of the fountain.

Irina climbed out of the car first, looking around. She'd used the burner phone to call the Grand Master as they got closer. She'd answered right away, despite the early hour, and promised to have someone meet them on the steps to bring them in through one of the side doors.

Irina tensed as a man jogged around the corner of the library building. He raised his hand, and she recognized Devon Asher. She waved in return, but stayed leaning against the door, preventing Eli and Jasper from getting out.

Devon slowed to a walk as he got closer. Out of the corner of her eye, she saw another jogger headed their way. Rather than jogging around the square, he was taking advantage of the empty sidewalk in front of the library.

She turned slightly, keeping the jogger in her peripheral vision even as Devon got closer. Behind her, one of the groundskeepers started up a leaf blower, the high-pitched whine drowning out the other sounds of a city waking up. Irina's right hand was behind her back, her gun pressed between her lower back and the car window. She leaned forward just a bit, and shifted her index fingers from alongside the trigger, to on the trigger. She had no reason not to trust Devon.

But after the week she'd had, she didn't trust anyone.

Devon was twenty feet away when he stopped, swayed, and dropped to his knees. He grabbed at his chest and gasped, "Run!" then pitched forward.

Irina raised her gun as she turned, aiming at the other jogger, the only person in range. He dove to the side, behind one of the huge stone balustrades that flanked the library steps.

Irina flung open the passenger door, ignoring the startled protest of the driver when he saw her gun, and yelled at him to drive.

He leapt into action, leaving rubber behind as he hit the gas. They turned left on St. James, skirting the edge of the square. There was a *thump* and the car fishtailed wildly. Irina was thrown against the window, the gun falling from her hand as the car jumped the curb, slamming into one of the stations that guarded the edge of the square's grassy area.

The airbags deployed from the head-on collision, and Irina lost a few seconds as the airbag threw her back. She coughed and shoved the bag out of her way.

"Out!" she shouted. "Stay down." She shook the driver's shoulder. "Get out. Hide."

He seemed dazed. Irina couldn't wait for him. She slid out, staying low. She lost precious seconds fishing for her gun under the seat, and nearly wept with relief when she felt it.

Eli and Jasper were crawling out too. Jasper's paranoia meant they'd ridden in the backseat with the bags of art on their laps. That paranoia paid off as they slung straps over their shoulders. Irina crab-walked along the edge of the car, peering over the trunk. The jogger was less than fifty yards away, running up the sidewalk, one hand jammed in his pocket. The groundskeepers were just now noticing the accident. The leaf blower that had covered the sounds of gunfire had stopped.

She risked one glance at the rear tire—it was shredded. He'd shot out the tire.

Irina looked around. They were up on the sidewalk on the north side of Copley Square. Here, grass gave way to brick underfoot. They were only steps away from the ornate Trinity Church, which seemed to sparkle in the sunlight that was just hitting the top spires.

The door to the church was standing open.

"There," she hissed. "Into the church. Go. I'll cover you."

"Irina, we won't—" Eli started.

"We do what she says," Jasper cut in.

Eli, who'd been the rescued not a rescuer in their last mission, looked like he wanted to argue, but Jasper tugged him forward. They were defenseless, their arms occupied keeping the portfolio bags from tangling between their legs, and the duffels were heavy on their backs.

Abandoning stealth, Irina jumped onto the trunk. She needed to buy Eli and Jasper time to get to the church, and the driver time to snap out of it and get out of the car. The groundskeepers came running up, and Irina crossed her right arm across her stomach, tucking the gun under the flap of her jacket.

"Lady, are you okay?" one asked.

She couldn't see the jogger. Where was he? There were plenty of places to hide in the square—stanchions and shrubs and the walls of the fountain.

"I'm fine. Can you help the driver?"

"Why don't you get off the car, lady?"

"Help the driver," she snapped, eyes scanning the square.

There, a flash of darkness. The jogger had swung wide, to the opposite side of the square, and was now headed straight for the church, coming in at an angle. He had to have seen Jasper and Eli run in.

Irina leapt off the car and ran full speed for the church. There were yells as the groundskeepers realized she had a gun.

The jogger pounded up the steps and disappeared inside. Irina ran faster, desperately glad she was wearing flats.

She skidded to a stop, letting her eyes adjust. There were sounds of a struggle—grunts and thuds. The change in light between outside and in was enough to have her blinking.

As soon as she could see, she slid fully into the church, heart thudding with fear. In the seconds it had taken her to adjust, the church had gone silent. *Please let them be okay.*

She scanned the interior of the church, but there was no sign of Eli or Jasper. Or the jogger. Irina stayed where she was, trying to breathe quietly.

Her patience paid off. A slight flicker of movement at the front of the church caught her eye. Irina leaned to the side just in time to see a dark figure, with two portfolio bags over his shoulder, disappear into the floor.

She froze, unsure of what she'd just seen. Irina took two steps down the aisle, gun at the ready with a two-handed grip, but pointed at the floor. A tapping noise had her spinning to her right.

The tapping came again, in a pattern. *Tap, tap-tap, tap, tap.*

Irina realized what the pattern was. *Shave and a haircut.*

She tapped the butt of the gun twice on the closest pew, completing the seven-note riff. *Tap, tap. Two bits.*

Jasper and Eli popped up from behind a high-backed bench that had been up against the outer wall. The full length of the pews separated her from them.

"He got two of the paintings," Jasper said immediately. His lip was bleeding. "He must have heard you coming because he gave up on the others."

Eli started opening the bags, checking to see which three they still had. Irina didn't wait for the report.

"Here's the phone." She took it from her jacket pocket and slid it along a pew toward them. "I'm going after him."

"No, Irina." Eli stopped looking through the bags. "It's too dangerous."

"I have to. I saw where he went. I don't have much time."

"You're the one who said it wasn't our job to figure out who these people were!"

"I can't just let him get away. What if this is the only chance anyone ever gets? The lead might be cold by the time anyone else gets here." Irina hopped up on the pew, walked along the seat to Eli, who was closest. She kissed the top of his head. "I love you, both of you."

Jasper hadn't moved; from the look on his face, it was clear he knew she was going to go after the guy.

She kept her gaze on him as she said, "Take the phone. Call the Grand Master. It's probably too late, but see if you can help Devon."

"Be safe, love," Jasper said.

Irina ran back along the pew, jumped down into the aisle. Eli turned to argue with Jasper, but he was picking up the phone, dialing. Irina shut them out and went to the spot in the floor where the jogger had gone down. It had been less than two minutes since he'd disappeared. But that was a hell of a head start, but Irina wasn't trying to catch him, she was going to trace where he'd gone, and the Grand Master could mobilize others to pick up the trail from there.

The floor in this part of the church was made of two-by-two stones. She ran her hands along the area where she'd seen him go down, and was rewarded with a draft coming up between two stones.

She was kneeling, feeling along the edges of the stone, when Jasper jogged up.

"Jasper, take Eli and get out of here," she said.

"He's talking to the Grand Master. I'm going with you."

"No, you're not. You and Eli need to get the art out of here. I'm not going to confront him—I'm not an idiot. This is strictly follow and report back."

Jasper didn't look convinced.

"There's no way I'm going to catch him, and I hadn't planned on it anyway. That's why I'm wasting time talking to you." She stared pointedly and Jasper snorted out a laugh.

"Fine, Eli and I will head for the library."

That made Irina pause. "Maybe I should go with you. There might be another ambush waiting inside."

"I'm trusting you to go after this guy. You trust me to get Eli and I to safety."

Irina nodded sharply, then whipped her attention back to the floor. There had to be a way to open this.

"But before I go..." Even without looking at Jasper's face, Irina could hear the smile in his voice. "They don't call me Indiana Jones for nothing." He fished a battered plastic loyalty card out of his wallet, ran it along the seams between the stones. His eyes were closed, a slight smile on his face. He stopped, went back, did something she couldn't see. The square just in front of Irina's knees popped up.

"How did you..."

Jasper winked, jumped to his feet, and ran back to where Eli was waiting, whistling the Indiana Jones theme tune as he went.

That was just what she needed, a little boost of confidence, a note of whimsy. Irina lifted the stone, which was on a piano hinge. There was nothing but darkness below.

Sticking her gun into the back of her waistband, Irina felt around in the dark, finding a ladder by touch. She swung her legs in, turning to plant her feet on a rung. Closing her eyes, she said a quick prayer, then started down. When she was three feet down, the stone above her snapped shut, locking her into total darkness.

It took more courage than Irina knew she had to keep going. She closed her eyes, moving by touch. When her right foot touched a flat surface that was cold even through her shoes, she didn't know whether to be relieved or terrified. She opened her eyes, expecting complete darkness, but there was the very faintest hint of light. Just enough for her to make out the vague shape of the ladder.

Pulling the gun from her waistband, she pivoted. The light was coming from somewhere to her right. From the feel of the air, she guessed that she was in a corridor that ran right to left, as if the ladder had dropped her into the middle of a long hallway. There was nothing but darkness to her left, so she turned right.

Irina kept the gun in her right hand, and trailed her left hand along the corridor wall. It was stone, and it was slimy. Gritting her teeth against the urge to yank her hand away from the nasty texture, she kept going. After twenty steps, the light had grown enough for her to see that she was coming up to a turn.

Irina crouched, gun once more held in two hands. She counted to three, then whipped around the corner, finger on the trigger.

This hallway was as deserted as the last, except for a glow stick, which lay forgotten or dropped fifteen feet in front of her. It was a large, heavy-duty tube that emitted a strong green light. It might be a trap, or the gunman had dropped it as he ran.

She waited for a count of twenty, then crept forward in a crouch. She scooped up the glow stick, suppressing a sob of relief at having a source of light. The problem now was that he'd see her coming. The light would give her away.

She considered leaving the glow stick, but in the end she couldn't do it. She was alone underground. She needed the light, for both courage and to see by.

Irina held on to the light until she reached a junction. The hall she'd been traversing dumped her out into a small round room. A room with five openings coming off of it.

You've got to be kidding me.

Irina scraped the butt of her gun against the stones at the mouth of the hallways she'd just come out of, leaving herself a bread crumb. Maybe she should turn back. Come back with a team of people and a thousand flashlights.

Eli and Jasper would love this.

That thought made her smile. She wasn't sure why she thought they'd love this creepy tunnel and mysterious network of hallways, but she did. She walked the perimeter of the round room, examining the first few feet of floor in each of the hallways. She didn't expect to find anything, but there was a small puddle of water in the third corridor, a puddle that had recently been disturbed, as evidence by the darker areas of stone around it where the water had splashed up.

Damn it.

Holding the glow stick and gun together in a two-handed grip, Irina started down the corridor. She walked for what felt like hours, occasionally passing an unexplained archway in the stone that created an alcove, or a heavy wooden door with no visible handle. She knew time passed slowly in combat situations, but even allowing for that, she'd been walking for far too long. There was no way she was still under the church. With nothing to guide her, she had no idea where she was.

Another one-way turn and the corridor dead-ended. Irina suppressed a curse, and was about to go back, when another of those odd archways caught her eye.

She stepped closer, illuminating the two-foot-deep alcove. This one wasn't empty. There was a ladder going up, disappearing into a small hole in the ceiling that had been concealed by the arch.

Irina didn't even stop to think about it. Up was good. Up meant the surface and light. Gun tucked into her skirt, she snugged the glow stick into the neck of her shirt and started to climb. It wasn't a long climb, and instead of emerging through a manhole into the middle of one of Boston's busy streets, which is what she'd imagined, she found herself in yet another corridor.

This one was made of wood rather than stone, and was drier. It was also smaller, and Irina had to walk in a crouch to stop from hitting her head on the low crossbeams.

Twenty feet, then thirty. This didn't seem to be going anywhere, and the hair on the back of Irina's neck was standing on end. She was about to turn back when the floor under her cracked.

Irina looked down in time to see the wood below her was black with rot, before it gave way.

She screamed as she fell, only to be brought up short when her feet hit something. She was waist-deep below the floor, her upper body still in the corridor. Pain zinged through her right ankle and she scrambled to hold on to the wood around her, but it kept crumbling away, into the ever-widening hole.

She was standing on something frigidly cold and slanted. She'd lost her shoes when she fell, and dug her toes into what felt like stone, but it was hard to get purchase. Every time she thought she'd braced herself, her feet would slide or more of the wood would crumble away, forcing her to shift her upper body, and causing her to lose her footing.

Irina's nails dug into the wood braces on the walls as her feet lost their tenuous grip on the slanted surface and she slipped, falling all the way through the corridor's floor. She landed with a *thunk*, her cheek cracking against the stone, and started to slide. Her gun and the glow stick were somewhere above her, and she was alone in the dark, sliding farther and farther down, away from the weak light.

Pain and fear shredded the professional calm she'd been using as a shield. Now she was just alone in the dark, falling, falling.

Irina screamed, and kept screaming until she hit hard stone. Finally her screams fell silent.

Eli felt sick with worry. He paced the width of the hall. The grand hall of the library above them was world famous. A smaller version of it was replicated here. Columns supported the double-high arched ceiling, and sound bounced off the walls, echoing from one end to the other, where double doors guarded the entrance to the inner chambers.

Devon Asher sat on the floor, back against a column, breathing deeply. He'd been hit not by a bullet, but by a tranquilizer dart. The rest of the Grand Master's counselors were there too—Sebastian, Juliette, and Franco.

The bags—the three portfolios they still had and the two duffels—lay forgotten on the floor. The elevator door opened—it was the only way into the headquarters. Jasper jogged out. Eli froze, but Jasper shook his head.

"No sign of her, and I can't get back into the church. There are cops everywhere."

"I'll start on damage control," Seb said. There was almost no cell phone service so he took Jasper's place in the elevator, taking it up to the rare book room.

Juliette knelt with Devon and Franco. "They attacked us right on our doorstep," she said softly.

"Where is the Grand Master?" Eli demanded. "She needs to get the National Guard or the Army or someone to go get Irina."

Juliette rose to her feet.

Jasper tapped Eli's shoulder. "Uh, Eli, *she's* the Grand Master."

"No, she's not." Eli frowned. "She was there at the same time as the Grand Master."

"The second time we saw the Grand Master it was actually a decoy wearing her robe," Jasper explained coolly.

Juliette Adams sighed, her face resolving into a lovely but cold mask. "I see there's no fooling you, Mr. Ferrer."

"Well, *I'm* an idiot," Eli muttered.

Jasper squeezed his shoulder. "I suspected, but now it's fairly obvious. And it's obvious you're worried about your husband." Jasper nodded to Devon. "Well, we're worried about our wife."

Franco jumped to his feet. "I'll get the map."

"Map?" Eli asked.

"There's a network of tunnels that connect this," Juliette gestured around them to the headquarters, "to the subbasements of Trinity Church. Until recently, the purists had the map, and we had no idea the tunnels were there. We thought we'd located all the access points and closed them up, but there must be others that aren't on the map."

Devon raised his head. He still looked a bit drugged. "It's a maze. We'll go after her, but we need manpower, equipment..." Devon trailed off.

"Then we'll go after her ourselves—" Jasper started.

Eli slapped Jasper's shoulder. "Shhh." He closed his eyes, listening. "Did anyone hear that?"

Everyone looked at Eli, who was starting to doubt what he'd heard. It had sounded like a scream. Just as the silence stretched too long, it came again. A scream that lasted for nearly half a minute.

"Irina," Jasper breathed, fear etching lines into his face.

Juliette whipped around, hair flying. "Where is it coming from?"

Devon staggered to his feet. "I need a gun."

Franco came back, holding a large sheet of paper. "I've got the map."

Eli glanced over at the line drawing Franco held, and it clicked.

Map. It's a map. A map of here.

Eli ran for the portfolios. "Please, please," he muttered.

"Eli, leave it!" Jasper said, irritation in his voice. "We need to spread out, search."

"It's not a blueprint," Eli snapped. "It's a map."

They'd lost two of the portfolios to the man with the gun. He'd grabbed one from Jasper, yanking him back by his strap so hard, Jasper fell. Eli had moved in to help, but by bending down he'd made it easier for the guy—who'd been wearing what looked like a fencing mask under his hoodie—to yank a bag away from Eli too.

"It was never about the Rodin," Eli cursed, ripping open the zipper on the first bag. The box with the Nolde. He tossed it to the side. "It was about the map."

Jasper sucked in a breath as he realized what Eli had figured out. He ripped the paper from Franco and dropped down beside Eli. He slammed the flat of his hand against the floor. The sound rang like a crack. "If we lost it…"

The second bag had one of Irina's paintings. Eli shoved it aside also.

"Please, please," he whispered. The zipper stuck, so Eli grabbed the edges of the portfolio and ripped.

The edge of a gold frame winked at him. Gold—not the brassy, glossy look of gold paint, but the rich glow of real gold. If you had to smuggle both art and gold, why not use the gold to make a frame? Eli paused for less than a second to digest that thought, then pulled the map out, scattering shards of glass. At some point the glass had shattered and was now just a spiderweb. Eli shook the glass out and laid the heavy frame flat on the floor. Franco knelt beside them, taking the map he'd brought for Jasper and laying it beside the frame.

"There's twice as many passages on this one." Franco sounded both excited and horrified.

"They're secret tunnels?" Jasper asked.

Franco nodded.

"Are there any that open up near here?"

Franco studied the map. "I...I can't tell. There's too much going on."

Juliette walked to the middle of the hall, cleared her throat, then yelled, "Irina!"

The acoustics of the hall made the single word bounce and echo. They waited, waited.

Then there was a reply. A thin, reedy cry.

"Spread out," the Grand Master barked.

Sebastian returned in time to help them with the search. The acoustics that made a single word carry also made it impossible to pinpoint the source of a sound. Eli walked along the edge of the hall, in the corridor created by the columns on one side and the actual wall on the other. Someone called Irina's name, and in the silence that followed, Eli heard her cry, more distinctly than before.

"Over here!" he yelled.

The six of them spread out near Eli's position, running their hands over the wall and floor. It was Jasper who found the door. The trigger was a small, decorative stone on the floor carved with the triquetra. Jasper cleared the seams around the stone by blowing on it, then pushed down. With a puff of dust, a door-sized section of wall opened up. The door swung in, revealing another wall, less than a foot away.

"What the hell?" Jasper asked.

Eli stuck his head into the darkness. "Irina!"

"Eli? Eli?!" Her voice was distinct and clear. She was somewhere in the thin envelope of space.

"We're here, baby! We're coming," he yelled. Eli felt light-headed with relief that they'd found her.

The only reply was a sob.

Franco appeared with heavy flashlights. It took a few minutes of investigation before they figured out what was going on. The arched roof of the hallway helped hold up the weight of the public building above them, but in order to construct the arch, the original builders had created a chamber within a chamber. The arched hallway was constructed inside a larger rectangular box, and the door was essentially a construction access point. At ground level, the wall of the outer shell and the wall of the hall itself nearly met, but ten feet up, where the arch caused the roof of the hall to curve in, the space opened up.

"Move, let me see." Juliette elbowed the men out of the way. She whipped a small headlamp out of Franco's hand and put it on.

"Juliette, don't—" Devon was too late. Juliette braced herself in the narrow space between the outside of the arch and the other wall and climbed in with the ease of a scrambler. She was the only one small enough to do it.

"Toss me in some light," she called back.

Devon ran his fingers through his hair and looked aggravated. Franco looked worried.

Sebastian handed in a flashlight. "Don't die," he told her cheerfully.

Less than a minute later there was a cry from Irina, followed by the sound of voices.

"Irina!" Jasper called. He and Eli were crowded in the opening.

"Got her," the Grand Master called back.

A few minutes later, legs appeared. Eli reached up and took hold of Irina. They must have crawled along at a higher point, then come straight down to the door opening. Irina was dirty and dusty. There was blood smeared on her face, hands, and feet. She was shaking.

Eli retreated a few feet, dropping to his knees. "We've got you, we've got you," he chanted.

Jasper wrapped his arms around both of them. They stayed that way, huddled together, until Irina stopped shaking.

Chapter Twenty-One

"And the Trinity Masters are going to be Irina's patron of the arts."

"Jasper…" Irina said tiredly. She was huddled in a chair wearing a pair of Juliette's leggings and a "Boston Strong" T-shirt.

"Anything else?" Juliette asked mildly.

Eli and Jasper looked at each other. They matched, in that they both looked exhausted. Their eyes were sunken, jaws scratchy with the need to shave. Neither looked as bad as Irina, who, even with the blood washed off, looked like she'd been beaten with a stick.

Juliette made sure she took note of every bump and bruise. She needed to know what they'd been through. Needed to understand the ramifications of her own actions. She'd given them what should have been a no-danger task. It had ended with fifteen people dead, Eli Wexler's life in ruins, and severe damage to the trust between her and someone who had been one of her brother's closest advisers.

It was midafternoon now. She'd kept these three in headquarters, not wanting to risk them being spotted and identified by any witnesses from this morning. Sebastian was working damage control with the cops.

After some food and rest, Eli and Jasper had confronted her with their list of demands. Jasper required her help and support to fix Eli's reputation—Jasper had an elaborate, daring plan that involved spinning a tale of adventure, intrigue, and art theft that would paint Eli as the gallant hero. It was so crazy it might work, but it would take the power of the Trinity Masters to keep people from asking too many questions. Juliette was happy to help.

Additionally, Eli wanted first crack at studying the art they'd brought back. Irina would no longer work for Bennett Securities. And finally, the Trinity Masters had to find Irina a patron to support her as she pursued her art full time.

"No, Grand Master," Jasper said. "That's it."

Juliette looked at the painting that they'd propped up on a chair. Not the Nolde painting, which was beautiful, but the painting Irina had done. Apparently there had been others, besides this rather heartbreaking self-portrait, but this morning's attacker had mistakenly grabbed two of Irina's paintings, instead of the map.

"It is good to remember that this is part of what we are meant to do. We're meant to nurture scholars and artists." She didn't add that it was especially good to be reminded of that at a time like this.

After this past week, there could be no doubt: they were at war.

Franco got Eli, Jasper, and Irina settled in one of the smaller meeting rooms—one that had been hidden until the discovery of the original version of the tunnels' map. The trinity was arguing about something—something Caden had said to Jasper. Whatever it was, the discussion included Jasper grinning devilishly, Irina looking both irritated and intrigued, and Eli shaking his head.

Sebastian appeared, reporting that since there had been no damage besides that done by the car crash, and there were no victims, the cops were already moving on to more pressing issues.

Franco and Devon joined Sebastian at the conference table, while Juliette stayed at her desk. Her computer chimed and she opened the message, praying it wasn't bad news of some kind. There was no "from" address, which wasn't unusual. The people who had this particular email address were mostly those in the inner circle of the Trinity Masters. People who would know to take precautions.

Once it had been decrypted, she found herself looking at an image of a group of people on the beach. Frowning, she ran *that* image through the decryption software, but nothing happened. That meant either there was something wrong with the decryption or the image itself was the message. She carried her laptop over to the table.

"I just got this."

She turned the screen so everyone could see. They looked as befuddled as she felt.

"Maybe the encryption is new and your software can't read it?" Franco suggested.

Sebastian narrowed his eyes, pointing. "Wait. Is that Bryan Cobb?"

Juliette peered at the image. An older man with a straw hat, loud Bermuda shorts, and smears of sunscreen on his arms was building a sandcastle with a little boy.

It *looked* like Bryan Cobb. Juliette had spent a lot of time staring at photos of the man, alternately angry with him, and sorry for him and his family. Mr. Cobb had a strong, recognizable face and profile, as did the man in this photo. That same profile was shared by many of the people in the photo.

"He's alive?" Franco asked.

Sebastian grabbed the computer, muttering as he tried to trace the sender.

Devon scrubbed his hands over his face. "What the hell is going on?"

"I don't know." And Juliette really hated not knowing. "I'm going to send someone to the Maldives to check. If Bryan Cobb is still alive, that means…"

There was silence. No one knew exactly what that meant, except that maybe fifteen people hadn't died because Juliette sent a trinity to look for some art.

Franco hauled a box onto the table and started unloading it. He had a personal stake in taking down the purists, since they'd tried to keep his family from continuing their membership. He'd decided to pull any and all records he could find around WWII, figuring he might find a record of someone expressing sympathies with the Nazi party, especially in the early years of the war. Franco had also been talking to Devon's mother, who always seemed to know everything—if she weren't an Asher of the New York Ashers, she would be called a busybody, but rich women weren't nosy, they were well informed. She'd been the one to first tell them about the purists, but assumed, as everyone else had, that after WWII, they'd disbanded or changed their politics.

Franco pulled out a battered box full of pictures and newspaper clippings that had been on a bookshelf here in the office, squished behind some books. It was mostly full of newspaper clippings about the war.

Juliette had no idea who'd put together the sad little collection—it could have been her father, her grandfather, or one of their counselors. She didn't know if it had been hidden or if it had been forgotten at the back of the shelf, but Franco was working his way through each piece of paper with a patience Juliette admired even if she couldn't emulate it.

He laid the articles in neat rows. The headlines screamed German Army Attacks Poland. U.S. Declares War. Pacific Battle Widens. USS Bluebird Sinks Spanish Ship. Restitution Begins. Hidden Art Found in Salt Mine.

Franco had carefully recorded what Eli, Irina, and Jasper had said—their theory that the art was being kept hidden because it could link the purists to something bigger. They'd talked it through, and concluded that this morning's attack was about retrieving the map, but Mr. Cobb's orders to deploy an HRD team must have been about keeping the Rodin a secret. Layers on top of layers. Every time they found an answer or solved a mystery, ten more sprung up in its place.

"We need someone to parse the new map, and we need someone to secure this place. We're too vulnerable right now," Seb said. "And we have to investigate Caden."

"Agreed on securing this place." Devon grabbed a copy of the roster—there was only a single handwritten copy of their membership list, plus the individual member folders. "I know we have a couple people from the Army Corp of Engineers."

"Find an architect too." Sebastian scooted over to look at the list. "And someone close to the Andersons."

"Seb, we don't need to investigate Caden Anderson," Juliette said. They'd already had this argument once. It had ended, as most of their arguments did, with exaggerated threats of death and violence. That had actually helped dispel some of Juliette's earlier tension.

"We do," Sebastian insisted. "That's a coincidence I don't like. The Andersons are an old family. They might be purists."

"They're West Coast liberals. I seriously doubt they're secret Nazi sympathizers."

"Juliette, I need you to trust me on this."

"Well, you are an expert on being a sneaky asshole," Juliette said sweetly.

Devon, standing beside Sebastian, hunched his shoulders a little bit, as if he were making himself smaller so *he* wouldn't get in trouble for the lies he'd told Juliette in the past.

"You're right, I am. And I don't trust the coincidence of Caden being at the same hotel as them."

"It's that weird fetish hotel in Oklahoma. Plenty of our members have gone there."

"And who is this Darling? We don't have anyone with the first name Darling."

"This needs to be investigated, but not now."

Sebastian looked up, and his eyes were serious. "Jules. Please. Let me play this hunch."

She stopped to consider Sebastian's words. "Seb, we're talking about setting up a trinity. Putting people together for the rest of their lives. Is it important enough for that?"

"Yes, Jules, it is."

She nodded once.

Sebastian flashed her a grin, then turned back to the list. The minutes ticked by. Franco, Sebastian, and Devon were all working, but she couldn't settle on anything. Sebastian stepped out to get on his phone, then came back. Franco rose and went to check the shelves. Juliette sat, unable to get a handle on her emotions. She had this itchy, nervous feeling she couldn't shake.

Devon and Sebastian conferred quietly for a few minutes before they finally set down the list.

"Grand Master, we have a proposal for the next trinity," Devon said formally.

"Christian." Sebastian pulled Christian Stewart Rogers' membership file from the pile and pushed it across the table. "He'll make sure we get what we need."

Juliette sucked in a breath. "You're willing to put Christian, your own brother, into a trinity right now? Gamble his whole future?"

"Christian can handle it," Sebastian said, a bit of familial pride in his voice. "And we need him. We can tell him more about what's really going on than we can tell the others."

Juliette shook her head. "I don't want to send him in as some sort of double agent."

"Uh, that's exactly what you did to *me*."

"Well, that's because you're a jerk."

Devon raised his voice to be heard over their bickering. "Charlotte Mead. She's the best option for dealing with that map, and helping us secure this place." Devon slid a second file across the table.

Sebastian picked up the final file. "Irina said that Caden was in the fetish hotel with a submissive, right? Well, I called Grant. He suggested that if we wanted to get close to the Trinity Masters' members who are also into BDSM, we should talk to Vincent Clayton. He's not in a trinity yet." Sebastian slid the third and final file across the table.

Juliette flipped open the files, reading through the information they had about the members. She wasn't just reading to see if together these three could handle the task she needed to give them. She was reading to see if she thought they could fall in love. Could form a lasting trinity.

Irina, Jasper, and Eli were the second trinity she'd called to the altar—the first had been Sebastian's, and that one hadn't been meant to last. She'd done it mostly to fuck with Seb and to help him get close to Grant, whose family history included known purists.

This most recent trinity was the first one she'd really called to the altar. It had been based on need, on a task, but she'd tried to think about the personal aspect of it. It had worked; they were clearly on their way to being in love, even after only a week. But was that the result of her good decisions, or dumb luck?

But she was at war, and doubts were a luxury she didn't have time for.

Juliette closed the files, one by one. "I'll call them to the altar, immediately."

The clock was ticking.

Epilogue

He tossed a few pain pills into his mouth, washed them down with whiskey, and examined his newest art acquisitions. One was an abstract painting of warring colors. Beautiful and disconcerting. The second was a tongue-in-cheek representation of a trinity—the cardboard cutout of the happy couple a shield between a dull and mundane world and the glowing golden fire of a triquetra.

Lowering himself into the chair hurt. He'd either bruised or cracked a rib in the fight to wrestle the portfolios away from Eli and Jasper. He'd wanted to take back the map, but these were interesting consolation prizes, and all in all, the Grand Master having the map wasn't the worst thing that could have happened.

Until a few days ago, he'd been one of a select few who knew that there were two different maps showing all the tunnels and secret rooms that connected the Boston Public Library and Trinity Church—one drawn by each of the architects responsible for the tunnels.

His partner in crime had the other original map. She stored it in a waterproof sleeve in a hidden compartment in her bathroom. She'd done her best to keep the other purists—God, he hated that name—in the dark about the existence of all but a few tunnels by altering any copies she was forced to make.

The second map should have been safe in art storage. If it were up to him, the art would never have left storage, but that hadn't been his decision. He might be arrogant, but not so arrogant as the man who'd volunteered a volatile art collection for some fundraiser.

It was sheer dumb luck that the map had been stolen along with the Rodin. And even more random luck—or maybe the hand of fate—that they'd spotted the map in the possession of three other members of the Trinity Masters.

He winced as he remembered her fury when she realized that there was another, even more detailed map, and that he'd known about it and hadn't told her.

How sad it was that, though he loved her more than life itself, and trusted her more than any other person, he hadn't told her about it.

When you were raised to keep secrets, the truth felt dangerous.

On the plus side, they'd had some extremely enjoyable angry sex after she'd seen the second map. He had the scratches on his back to prove it.

His phone beeped, and he winced as he leaned over to pick it up.

Got Cobb family settled. Coming home. Anyone suspect?

That was followed immediately by, *When will I see you again?*

He smiled the stupid, sappy smile of a man in love. He wished he was the kind of man who could respond with one of those kissy faces, or X's and O's. Or the kind of man who could show her how he really felt—to kiss the ground each place her foot trod, curl up with her on a Sunday afternoon and spend the day lazing away while making easy, gentle love.

It was only in the privacy of his own thoughts that he indulged such ridiculous fantasies. He simply wasn't that kind of man. He couldn't afford to be. Too much depended on his ability to remain in control. To keep secrets.

Before he could respond to the text, his phone rang. The screen showed the smiling face of the only *other* person he loved.

"Hello, beautiful," he said as he answered.

"Hello, han-handsome." Her words were labored, but she got them out.

"How are you feeling?"

"Not t-too bad. Where are you?"

"Someplace hot," he lied.

"It's cold here," she reported. "And raining."

"It's always raining."

"Rain makes rainbows," she told him.

The phone groaned in his hand, and he forced himself to relax his fingers. Hearing her voice, and the soft, happy optimism that enlivened it, terrified him. She had no idea how much danger she was in.

She had no idea the lengths he'd gone to, the lengths he planned to go to, to protect her.

There were still so many pieces that needed to fall into place before he could put his plan in motion. He lived for the day that happened, the day he could scoop up both of the women he loved and escape.

If they left now, they'd be hunted down and killed in a matter of days. There was nothing the purists—his "family"—wouldn't do to protect their secrets. He'd seen that firsthand.

There wasn't a day that went by that he didn't mourn his brother.

In order to be safe, he needed secrets. Secrets would be his weapons. And there was one particular secret he wanted, one that he'd been slowly piecing together all his life.

He just had to hope that the combined skills and attention of the Trinity Masters didn't beat him to it, didn't discover the secret and thereby rob him of his best weapon.

Without the ERR album, the Rodin was beautiful but not significant. But together, the sculpture and book, both of which the Grand Master possessed, were a frayed thread. A thread that if Juliette Adams pulled on long enough, or hard enough, would unravel and reveal truths that should never see the light of day.

There were plenty of mysteries hidden in those tunnels. Enough to keep every member of the Trinity Masters busy for a lifetime. The trick was to make sure no one looked into anything that would bring them too close to the purists' secrets. If they did, he'd do what he had to do to protect the purists.

Not because he believed in their cause. No, his loyalty was a ruse and a defense—and he was no more or less loyal to the Trinity Masters themselves than to the purists. All he wanted to do was to escape with the people he loved. He'd play all the sides, every side, to make that happen.

"Brother. Are you-ou-ou listening?" His sister finished her sentence with a coughing fit.

"Sorry, Tabby-cat," he said. "I'm listening."

He sipped Scotch with his eyes closed, focusing all his attention on his sister. When they finished their call a few minutes later, he finally returned to his lover's text.

Next Thursday. The cabin in Utah.

Her reply came almost immediately.

Yes, Master.

His jaw clenched. He'd ordered her, instead of asking. Goddamn it, no matter how many times he told himself not to, he did it. He would give anything, *anything*, to be normal with her. To love her the way she deserved to be loved.

He flung his glass across the room, watching with pleasure as the crystal shattered.

When they were free, he'd make it up to her. He'd learn how to love her without being her master. Together they'd shower his sister with the kind of love she deserved. The kind of love she didn't get at the expensive but cold institution his parents had stuck her in. She was the reason they hadn't already run.

Wishing he were different, and hoping it was enough, he texted back, *I love you.*

Join the world of the Trinity Masters…

Elemental Pleasure

Trinity Masters, book 1

A dangerous Marine. A tech genius. And a brilliant scientist.

When Carly Kenan joined the secretive Trinity Masters in college, she received *entrée* to an exclusive club that gave her access to wealth and power. But there's a price all members must pay—they accept an arranged marriage, between not two, but three people.

Ordered to return to the Trinity Masters' headquarters in Boston, Carly meets Marine Lance Glassco, a mathematician for DARPA, and Preston Kim, a dangerously intelligent chemist.
Though on the surface they have nothing in common, it's clear the Grand Master thinks that together the three of them can do something amazing. And that's why he's declared that Carly, Lance and Preston must marry.

Though the physical attraction is instantaneous and incendiary, Carly is unprepared for the emotional intensity of the *ménage* relationship. Pushed beyond her limits, Carly runs from Lance and Preston. What she doesn't understand is that she now belongs to them, body and soul…and they belong to her.

When Lance uncovers a dangerous crime at Preston's company, Carly is caught in the crossfire and the struggling lovers are forced to move beyond desire…to trust. For the Trinity Masters, there is passion and power in three.

Primal Passion

Trinity Masters, book 2

An FBI agent. A billionaire CEO. And a virgin scientist.

Deni Parker doesn't have time for anything but her cutting-edge scientific work, and that's how she likes it. She doesn't have time for relationships. When she's called to the altar—years ahead of what she expected—by the very intimidating, and far too handsome, Price Bennett, Deni's more than a little unprepared.

Price didn't join the Trinity Masters to play messenger. As CEO of a major security firm and heir to one of the largest fortunes in the world, he's annoyed when the Grand Master orders him to transport the disorganized scientist to the ceremony to meet her partners. It's only when they arrive that Price realizes he isn't a messenger—he's been matched with Deni.

Gunner Wells has been in love with Deni for years, but he's resisted giving in to his attraction. When he arrives at the Trinity Masters headquarters to be bound in marriage, he's delighted to discover Deni is not only a member of the secret society, but one of his partners…along with billionaire playboy, Price.

Their strong personalities clash—in the bedroom and out of it—but Price and Gunner have to put aside their overprotectiveness, and Deni must put aside her pride, when someone tries to stop her research—with deadly methods.

Scorching Desire

Trinity Masters, book 3

A reformed spy. A respectable lawyer. And a renowned playboy.

When Damon Corso is blackmailed it's not just his career that's in jeopardy, but the existence of the Trinity Masters–America's oldest and most powerful secret society. He and fellow member Marco Polin, a world famous playboy musician, enjoy sharing women, a secret that until now they've kept quiet.

Tasha Kasharin, the reformed spy sent to help them, knows this is more than simple blackmail. Marco and Damon's lives are in danger. She ignores her increasingly vivid fantasies about being part of a trinity with them until their investigation is interrupted by the Grand Master, who calls them to the altar and binds them in a *ménage* marriage.

The men must trust their futures to the unexpectedly innocent woman who's now their wife, while dealing with the change in their own relationship, and the complicated feelings that come with it. Blackmail escalates to violence, and they'll have to trust and accept one another if they're going to survive.

Forbidden Legacy

Trinity Masters, book 4

An enigmatic leader. A talented doctor. And the man who can bring them together.

Harrison Adams has served as leader of the Trinity Masters for a decade. He's always placed the group above his own needs—even when it comes to the one woman who calls to him. When a dangerous threat to the secret society surfaces, Harrison sets a plan in motion that could save the organization, but it comes with a price.

Alexis turned down an invitation to join the Trinity Masters, afraid to relinquish control over her life, her future...her heart. That rejection means night after night of unrequited lust as she and Harrison are forced to ignore their desires. Her heart aching, she throws herself into her job and her difficult working relationship with her boss, Michael. He's attractive and maddening, but Alexis has zero plans to give in to the crazy chemistry between them.

Harrison asks Alexis to experiment in a ménage relationship with him and she agrees unable to take another moment of longing for him. Perhaps with a third around she'll be able to keep her heart intact. She is completely unaware their third will be Michael. She couldn't have known how giving herself to them would inflame her desires. Or how much she would enjoy submitting to them.

But when an evil man looking for revenge sets his sights on Harrison, time is the one thing none of them have. And it soon becomes apparent Harrison's forbidden legacy could destroy them all…

Hidden Devotion

Trinity Masters, book 5

A reluctant leader. A CIA agent. And a lost legacy.

Juliette Adams's spent her life running, from both her status as the daughter of the Grand Master and her arranged marriage. Until the day everything changed and she became Grand Master—a position she was never meant to hold.

Devon Asher has more than a few secrets, the least of which is that he's desperately in love with Juliette, which shouldn't be a problem since they were betrothed when they were children. Now that she's Grand Master his secrets aren't safe.

Franco Garcia Santiago always assumed the tales of a Trinity Masters were fantastical stories his grandfather made up, until Juliette shows up at his door. Together they uncover the secrets of the Trinity Masters, unaware of the danger they're putting themselves in.

Juliette must decide if she'll turn her back on her destiny or embrace the role of Grand Master, and if she'll use her power to discontinue the trinity marriages she grew up despising, or follow her heart, which tells her happiness lies with both Devon and Franco.

Elegant Seduction

Trinity Masters, book 6

A spoiled heiress. A corporate mediator. And a man with a secret.
Sebastian has dedicated his life to upholding the ideals of the Trinity Masters. However, when his best friend, Juliette, is named Grand Master, he knows secrets he's harbored will be revealed. While he expects Juliette to be angry, he does not expect her to call him to the altar, to bind him to a stranger, Grant, and to Elle, the woman who's haunted his dreams for years.

Then Juliette reveals a secret of her own. There's evil at play in the secret society and she needs him to root it out. Sebastian has no choice but to go undercover to spy on his own trinity. As the danger surrounding the trio grows, Sebastian is forced to choose between loyalty and love.

Because reluctantly bound to Elle and Grant or not, Sebastian can't deny the pair have earned their place in his heart.

Delicate Ties

Trinity Masters, book 8

A Broadway star. An adventurous architect. And the powerful Dom determined to claim them both.

Christian Rogers Stewart is no stranger to the stage, nor is he a stranger to the ways of the Trinity Masters. A legacy, he's grown up among brilliant, powerful people and he's more than ready to contribute to the society's noble cause when initiated as a member. However, he is blindsided when he's called to the altar by the Grand Master. First by lust for his arranged partners Charlotte and Vincent. And then by the revelation that the Trinity Masters are under attack, from within, by an insidious faction called the purists.

At their binding ceremony, Christian, Charlotte and Vincent are given two tasks: study the web of tunnels hidden beneath headquarters and investigate a suspected member of the purists, a fellow Dom in Vincent's clubs. By day Charlotte struggles to make sense of a coded blueprint of the tunnels. By night they investigate the wealthy, powerful Dom, with Vincent guiding his new lovers into the dark and sensual world of BDSM.

Both tasks lead the new trinity to earth-shaking discoveries. Not just about the purists, but about themselves and their own erotic desires.

ABOUT THE AUTHORS

Writing a book was number one on Mari Carr's bucket list. Now her computer is jammed full of stories — novels, novellas, short stories and dead-ends. A *New York Times* and *USA TODAY* bestseller, Mari finds time for writing by squeezing it into the hours between 3 a.m. and daybreak when her family is asleep.

You can visit Mari's website at www.maricarr.com. She is also on Facebook and Twitter.

Lila Dubois is a top selling author of paranormal, fantasy and contemporary erotic romance. Having spent extensive time in France, Egypt, Turkey, England and Ireland Lila speaks five languages, none of them (including English) fluently. She now lives in Los Angeles with a cute Irishman.

You can visit Lila's website at www.liladubois.net. She loves to hear from fans! Send an email to author@liladubois.net or join her newsletter for contests, deleted scenes, articles, and release notifications.

Look for these titles by Mari Carr

Big Easy:
Blank Canvas
Crash Point
Full Position
Rough Draft
Triple Beat
Winner Takes All
Going Too Fast

Boys of Fall:
Free Agent
Red Zone
Wild Card

Compass:
Northern Exposure
Southern Comfort
Eastern Ambitions
Western Ties
Winter's Thaw
Hope Springs
Summer Fling
Falling Softly

Farpoint Creek:
Outback Princess
Outback Cowboy
Outback Master
Outback Lovers

June Girls:
No Recourse
No Regrets

Just Because:
Because of You
Because You Love Me
Because It's True

Lowell High:
Bound by the Past
Covert Affairs
Mad about Meg

Bundles
Cowboy Heat
What Women Want
Scoundrels

Second Chances:
Fix You
Full Moon
Status Update
The Back-Up Plan
Never Been Kissed
Say Something

Sparks in Texas:
Sparks Fly
Waiting for You
Something Sparked
Off Limits
No Other Way
Whiskey Eyes

Trinity Masters:
Elemental Pleasure
Primal Passion
Scorching Desire
Forbidden Legacy
Hidden Devotion
Elegant Seduction
Secret Scandal
Delicate Ties

Wild Irish:
Come Monday
Ruby Tuesday
Waiting for Wednesday
Sweet Thursday
Friday I'm in Love
Saturday Night Special
Any Given Sunday
Wild Irish Christmas
January Girl

Individual Titles:
Seducing the Boss
Tequila Truth
Erotic Research
Rough Cut
Happy Hour
Power Play
One Daring Night
Assume the Positions
Slam Dunk

Look for these titles by Lila Dubois

The Trinity Masters, Erotic Ménage Romance
Elemental Pleasure
Primal Passion
Scorching Desire
After Burn (free short story)
Forbidden Legacy
Hidden Devotion
Elegant Seduction
Secret Scandal

BDSM Checklist, BDSM Erotic Romance
A is for...
B is for...
C is for...
D is for...
E is for...

Standalone BDSM Erotic Romance
Betrayed by Love
Red Ribbon

New Adult BDSM Romance
Dangerous Lust

Undone Lovers, BDSM Erotic Romance
Undone Rebel
Undone Dom
Undone Diva

Glenncailty Castle, Contemporary Romance
The Harp and the Fiddle
The Irish Lover (short story)
The Fire and the Earth
The Shadow and the Night

Monsters in Hollywood, Paranormal Romance
Dial M for Monster
My Fair Monster
Gone with the Monster
Have Monster, Will Travel
A Monster and a Gentleman
The Last of the Monsters

The Wraith Accords, Paranormal Romance
Carnal Magic

Zinahs, Fantasy Romance
Forbidden
Savage
Bound

Standalone Paranormal Romance
Calling the Wild
Kitsune
Savage Satisfaction
Sealed with a Kiss

Made in the USA
Coppell, TX
04 March 2020

16474269R00178